Limerick County Library

D0585833

The Mystery Writer

The Mystery Writer

JESSICA MANN

WITHDRAWN FROM STOCK

LIMERICK
COUNTY LIBRARY
00505451

First published in Great Britain in 2006 by
Allison & Busby Limited
13 Charlotte Mews
London W1T 4EJ
www.allisonandbusby.com

Copyright © 2006 by JESSICA MANN

The moral right of the author has been asserted.

This book is sold subject to the conditions that it shall not,
by way of trade or otherwise, be lent, resold, hired out or
otherwise circulated without the publisher's prior
written consent in any form of binding or cover other than
that in which it is published and without a similar condition
being imposed upon the subsequent
purchaser.

A catalogue record for this book is available from
the British Library.

10 9 8 7 6 5 4 3 2 1

ISBN 0 7490 8214 3

Printed and bound in Wales by
Creative Print and Design, Ebbw Vale

JESSICA MANN has published eighteen novels, two non-fiction books, many articles and reviews and has appeared on TV and radio programmes including *Question Time*, *Any Questions*, *Round Britain Quiz* etc. She has been on the board of South West Arts, English PEN, the Crime Writers' Association, and Honorary Secretary of the Detection Club. She and her husband, the archaeologist Professor Charles Thomas, live in Cornwall.

Other titles by Jessica Mann

Fiction:
A Charitable End
Mrs Knox's Profession
The Only Security
The Sticking Place
Captive Audience
The Eighth Deadly Sin
The Sting Of Death
Funeral Sites
No Man's Island
Grave Goods
A Kind of Healthy Grave
Death Beyond The Nile
Faith Hope and Homicide
Telling Only Lies
A Private Inquiry
Hanging Fire
The Survivor's Revenge
Under A Dark Sun
The Voice From The Grave

Non-fiction:
Deadlier Than The Male
Out Of Harm's Way

Author's Note

I started writing *The Mystery Writer* while I was still working on *Out of Harm's Way**, a non-fiction book telling the story of the overseas evacuation of children from Britain during the Second World War. I was one of those evacuees myself but remember nothing at all about my early childhood in Canada and America, so the information is derived from other people's memories and from documentary research. The natural tendency of a novelist is to make things up but in writing *Out of Harm's Way* I resisted that temptation and stuck firmly to the facts.

Some of those facts are the basis of this story. Turning them into fiction left me free to invent and embellish, bringing together history and imagination, actual places and altered ones, real people and others who never existed, though the only real name I have used is my own. *The Mystery Writer* contains some truths and some untruths. In literature, as in life, it is not always obvious which is which.

I am grateful to Miriam Gross, Joanna Hines and Imogen Olsen for their help with this book, and thank especially my daughter Lavinia Thomas for her interest and advice.

Jessica Mann
St Clement, Cornwall, 13 September 2005

* published by Headline in March 2005

Chapter One

~

1940

AFTER SUPPER ON the fourth day of the voyage Ted sneaked out and made his way up to the paying passengers' part of the ship, where evacuees were forbidden to trespass. He kept his eyes peeled and slid from shadow to shadow in the wide, empty corridors, balancing easily as the ship rolled and swooped in the rough sea. Showers of hail sounded a light percussion against the glass portholes, backed by the deeper thump of hull against waves. Through the crack in the swing doors Ted saw that some passengers were still dancing to the music of a four-piece band, swooping chest-to-chest across a circle of shiny wood. I wouldn't half mind a go on that drum, he thought, and decided to come back later when they were all in bed.

He moved on to look into the other lounge. It was full of posh people as per usual, with their drinks in triangular glasses and cigarettes in holders. Funny, to be out in the middle of the ocean and sitting round so calmly, playing cards or nattering on and on, blah blah. Nearly all of them were old except for one with a clinging flowered dress and golden waves of hair like Lana Turner and a chap reading a heavy book who only looked about fifteen although he had a proper evening suit on. Where was his life vest? It wasn't fair. The evacuees were made to hang on to their uncomfortable cork waistcoats at all times.

Ted checked the waiter wasn't looking, having caught a clip round the ear from him the day before, sneaked a little iced cake from a silver platter and ducked back into the passage before cramming it into his mouth whole. He had reached the blackout doors on the first-class deck when he caught sight of another boy in the corridor, bent as far as his life-jacket allowed, retching and spewing into a bucket of sand. Ted was wondering if he could get outside when – that noise! Something's happened. What was...where...? It was so sudden, so loud, the unstable floor felt so peculiar, you couldn't understand what was going on. There'd been an enormous thudding bang. An explosion. The sound burst out, so loud it hurt, but at the same time, oddly muffled. That's just what it would sound like if you got inside that big drum and somebody hit it with a stick, Ted told himself, as though from far away, just watching, nothing to do with him.

And then the screeching alarm bells started sounding off and Ted shook himself, like a dog out of a river, and took in that he was hearing people screaming and a man shouting, 'Keep calm. U-boats. Keep calm.'

'We're sinking!'

'Torpedo! There'll be another one!'

'She's going under!'

'We're all going to die!' a female shrieked.

Another voice called, 'Don't panic.'

Ted knew exactly what he was supposed to do, after four days of never-ending boat drills and rehearsals. A sailor rushed towards him shouting, 'Get to your muster station.' Ted stood watching, still inexplicably calm and detached. Then the man, straining against the wind, managed to push open the door on to the deck and more seamen ran out past him and started to tug furiously at the lifeboat ropes. Now passengers were crowding towards the deck bearing Ted and the other fellow along with them. The boy struggled, clinging on to a brass rail.

'Come on,' Ted snapped.

'I can't.'

'Git out of it – you hear!'

'I can't.'

'Out.' He clamped his hand on to a puny wrist and dragged him out.

'We'll drown.'

'You been told where to go just like us lot. Come on.'

Outside in the wet, windy, unstable darkness nothing worked as planned. Men and women fought to get into the lifeboats. Panicked crewmen pushed passengers aside to take their places.

'This way!' Ted shouted. The two boys squirmed underneath a boat and climbed in on the seaward side, pushing and pulling until both of them fell inside. Ted's sling had come undone but there was too much else going on to notice the throbbing pain. Someone started lowering the boat towards the water below, irregular jerks and sways, pointing up then down.

'Hold tight!'

Then the boat stopped its descent, dangling above the waves.

'It's jammed,' someone shouted.

'We're falling!'

'Hold tight.'

'Darling, where are you?'

'Help – help me!'

The boat began to tilt, the people inside clinging to anything they could grab. When at last it touched the stormy Atlantic the sailors tried to row away from the ship, but the lifeboat was so overloaded and the inexorable waves were so high that it was quickly waterlogged. People who had nothing to catch on to were washed out, but almost at once those who had clung on found the boat's angle increasing until men, women and children were tipped screaming into the sea.

Ted felt himself sinking, going down and down. He was still holding on to the other boy. Side by side, lungs bursting, they found themselves popping out of the water. Ted could hardly swim but the cork jacket kept him afloat, and his desperate arm movements propelled him towards something in the water. It was a narrow pair of wooden planks. Bottom boards out of the lifeboat. He grabbed hold, spluttered and coughed, took in another mouthful of sea, but at least he was on the surface. He rested his head on the wood.

'Look!' The boy was still there. Ted twisted his head and saw the huge ship, fully lit up, with tiny silhouettes against the brightness, people still on the steeply sloping deck. He saw some slide and others leap off into the water.

The sea was full of debris, some so peculiar and weird you couldn't take it in: the little potted palm trees that had been in the dining room floating past in their stands, somebody's teeth, a feathered hat. Soon the ship's stern was right underwater and the bow rearing upwards out of the sea. Then came an explosion which was loud and muffled and sharp all at once. The sea churned violently as the ship slid downwards, stern first, with all her lights still ablaze. From one moment to the next she was gone and the sea was dark.

The gasps and groans and screams died away. The only sounds were the sigh of the wind and waves, a few whistles faintly wailing, and choked cries for help. Clouds covered the moon and stars. Some people had torches, they flashed like dots on the water, but weren't bright enough to show anything. There'd got to be other lifeboats and rafts somewhere near. They couldn't be alone.

A flare went up and in its brief light Ted saw floating debris, and a row of other hands beside his all clinging on to the makeshift raft. Suddenly it reared upwards. Someone was trying to lie himself flat on the boards. Screams came from the others.

'Don't, stop, you'll kill us all,' a woman gasped.

Another voice cried, 'Damn your eyes – keep off!'

Ted felt the other silly bugger sliding against him and snapped, 'Hold tight, you!'

'I can't...'

'Don't let go!'

'Are you there?'

'Here. I can – that's my hand.' Salt water splashed into Ted's mouth. The plank was flat on the water again. Another, more distant flare. Fewer hands holding the wood now. There was a lung-choking stench of oil.

We can't hold on much longer, Ted thought and gasped out, 'Need...string. Cord. Tie on...'

'Strap. Here. Pouch.'

'Give it here.'

'Promised not to – mustn't take it off.'

'Here – get it – over this.'

It was almost impossible to manage in the choppy water and black dark. As he struggled Ted felt the plank's buoyancy changing and realised that the other clutching hands were sliding away. Five people were left still clutching on, then four, and then another gone... Davy Jones' locker, a seaman had called it. Lost at sea.

It took hours, or seemed to, but at last it was done. Each boy had an arm through the narrow leather strap and it was hitched to a slimy plank.

A choked voice said, 'Royal Navy – they promised...'

Ted forced out, 'Destroyers – with the convoy.'

'To the rescue.'

'Coming.'

'Sure to be.'

The cries and shouts receded into the distance. Fish. Big fish in the water. Ice too. Tired. Hurts, dull aches, sharp pain, the salt water torture on cut skin. Moaning, without even knowing the sounds were their own.

'I'm Jonathan. What's your —'

'Shut up.'

'Keep awake,' Jonathan croaked.

'Can't.'

'Go under. Got to try...talk.'

He was right. If Ted stopped thinking about it the waves would fill his mouth and nose and he'd be dead, even if he stayed attached to the plank. He gulped the words out.

'Where you going?'

'Cousins…' Coughs. 'California.'

Splutter, gag, spit.

'Pictures! Movies!' Ted gasped out.

'A painter…art.'

Farming. Saskatoon.

Stay conscious. Keep talking. The past, the present, the war, the future – something neither would have, unless they held their heads above water. Stay awake. Keep it up. Someone will come. Survive.

Ted had guessed he'd be meeting Master Jonathan, sometime, somewhere, ever since that afternoon. Three months before, the middle of June and hot. He'd been on the beach mucking around in Sheep's Pool till the tide came in and covered it, but you couldn't keep out of the way all day. He only came in to nab a bite to eat but his stepmother caught him and said the old woman wanted him to go up after school and do some work on the south lawn.

'Why should I?'

'The Missus said, that's why.'

'Shan't.'

'Want her to turn us out now your dad's gone, do you?' she yelled.

'Think I'm going to do his dirty work instead?'

He ducked before she could reach his ear with the flat of her hand. 'Do what you're told, you cheeky little bastard.'

'The only bastard round here's that there in your belly,' he told her, snatched a heel of stale bread and got out of the house.

'And stay up there whatever the old witch says, keep out of here till dark.' That meant her fancy man was coming round.

'My dad will kill you when he gets home,' he shouted over his shoulder. But Ted and Nancy both knew that wasn't going to be any time soon. Dad had been captured along with Colonel Hicks in Norway in May, and now they were prisoners of war somewhere in Germany.

Mrs Hicks was standing beside the bean rows, holding a garden fork the same way she'd held a croquet mallet. The garden had been turned over to food production and the house prepared as a clinic for wounded servicemen, though none had come yet and nor had medical staff. Nancy said it was a trick and the old woman would do anything to stop getting evacuees billeted on her.

'She said you wanted me.'

'She's the cat's mother, Ted. You should say, my stepmother.'

'Yes, ma'am.'

'Ted, have you washed your hands? Next time don't come up so grubby.'

'No, ma'am.' he said. She meant sweating. He wiped his arm over his wet forehead. All very well for her to talk, see her getting clean if she didn't have her fancy bathroom.

'I was just remembering our poor old garden, just think of all the time and trouble we took to grow things so close to the sea, and our perfect lawn too. Ah well...'

'Yes, ma'am,' he said, thinking, All very well for her as never had to slave away behind the mower, just wait, one of these days it'll be me that's the gentleman of leisure bossing people about, not a hand's turn again, I'll show them.

'Though it will be a long time before anyone plays croquet here again, with my son in Germany and my grandson going to America —'

'America!' Ted's voice didn't come out as astonished as it ought to but Mrs Hicks looked startled, as though she'd forgotten she wasn't just talking to herself. 'His stepmother thinks it's better for him to be out of harm's way.'

'On account of the invasion.'

'That's defeatist talk, Ted, you should know better.' Ted could tell she only said that for show because she'd automatically looked up at the sky to scan for parachutes. Everyone knew the Germans were coming, the only question was how soon. 'My daughter-in-law needs to concentrate on dealing with Mr Hitler, she's so very busy with her Red Cross work. But I don't know if my grandson really wants to go. Do you remember Master Jonathan, Ted?'

'Sort of.'

'You must have seen him that summer when he was here.'

'Poorly, weren't he?'

'Mumps, poor child... Do you think other boys will say he's running away, Ted?'

'I dunno, ma'am, but I'd go like a shot,' Ted said. He was so jealous it gave him a bellyache. He'd seen America on the flicks, there were cowboys and Red Indians and deserts and mountains and dirty great cars. Why's he getting all that? I'm as good as him any day, and he'll be over there and me stuck here for the duration, digging vegetables. Until the enemy come. They might choose this bit of Cornwall to land in, you only had to look at a map. And why else would all those rolls of barbed wire and the new tank traps and skull-and-crossbones danger signs be on the beach? Goonzoyle could easily be the front line.

'Would you really want to go, Ted?'

'You betcha sweet life.'

'I beg your pardon?'

'I mean, yes, ma'am.'

'Would you indeed? Let me see, you're thirteen now, aren't you?'

'Yes, ma'am.'

'Wait here a moment, will you.'

She went up the three steps to the terrace, and in through the glass doors that opened from the morning room. Ted didn't follow. As far as the Missus knew he'd never been inside the house. In fact, Connie had sneaked him in ages ago, tiptoeing through the pantry to show off the dining-room table laid for dinner, all shiny with silver and crystal, and then she'd given him a peek at the Missus's boudoir. He'd sniffed at the sweet smell from a great bath of dried flowers, and fingered a tiny dagger on the desk. Connie slapped his hand away. 'This room's a bugger to dust,' she whispered. There were hundreds of ornaments crammed on to every surface and the walls were covered with pictures and photos.

After that he'd found his way in often. It was easy. The doors weren't locked during the day and most of the servants had been called up or gone off to do war work. Ted would touch things with envious interest, fingering the soft materials, bouncing on the billowing cushions, tasting stuff in jars. Then he'd see if the silver cigarette boxes were full and help himself to some. Once last year, after war broke out and the servants had mostly gone, he'd even taken one of the vackies from London in for a quick peek, but she got scared and ran away. She went back to her family after a few weeks so he wouldn't be seeing her again.

Actually Ted quite liked going up to the house, which didn't mean he was going to spend his life at the Family's beck and call like his dad. He thought, Not me. Nor'd I go and join up again after twenty years just because the Colonel had gone back to the regiment. But then, his dad was daft. Got to be, to have married Nancy. Ted wasn't daft. He knew how to take care of number one, which was why he tried to keep an eye on the Family. He knew the Missus was having money troubles, he'd seen the way there were fewer silver things in the glass cupboards in the pantry, and patches on the wallpaper where pictures had disappeared. He noticed when things changed. And when he was the one that did the changing he knew how to manage it without leaving traces. When he needed pencils he took them one at a time over weeks like he did the paper. He'd got quite a decent stash now. Sucks to Nancy. She said things like that weren't for the likes of him.

Ted had started to keep an eye out for statements from the

bank in Buriton. Sometimes the Missus left them open on the desk for anyone to see, with red-inked figures written into the columns. He'd seen a rough copy of the letter she was writing to the Colonel, which was how Ted knew she'd sold three fields to Farmer Hosking and was planning to let him have all the rest. 'Your poor dear father took no thought to the morrow...' one sentence began.

So Ted had already scanned the looping handwriting of a long letter signed 'Marcia'. That was Mrs Colonel. 'Dearest Belle Mere', it began, which Ted didn't understand, but the main part was interesting.

'It has been a terribly difficult decision, but the Sturrocks' invitation is so pressing and they expect to keep him for the duration. I am afraid you will think it vulgar of me to mention money, but John S writes that all his businesses are doing very well, even the art dealership he set up to help with taxes, so I am not to worry about paying them back until after the war. The responsibility is quite a trial for me, with poor dear Philip out of reach, for although of course I have always tried to think of Jonathan as my own child it does make a difference being a stepmother and I cannot be sure what his mother would have done, if she was here now. But then of course I wouldn't be. It is all too complicated and difficult and some of my friends say it's wrong, but a good many people one knows are sending their families and I really think it will be best for Jonathan to be out of harm's way. Don't forget, he has always lived overseas, and knows how to adapt himself quickly to new places, with Philip posted so many times. I've always done my very best to make him accept me but he's not been easy so I really think he'll be better off overseas, and of course from my own point of view, the sooner he's safely in California the sooner I can concentrate on doing my bit. He seems keen to go, so I do hope he escapes his school's measles epidemic. I have had no further word from Philip yet...'

From where he stood on the once-smooth croquet lawn, Ted could see Mrs H looking for something in the books and papers she always had lying about on a round table. They were held down against draughts by a little box made of blue metal, with a picture on it of ladies dancing. Then she came out holding a folded newspaper. 'Here we are, Ted, this is about a scheme for children to be evacuated overseas.'

'To America?'

'No, to the British Empire.' She said those two words with reverence. 'All the Dominions, Canada, Australia – all the countries of the Empire have offered to take young British refugees and the government's announced a scheme for sending them.'

'Not for the likes of me,' he muttered.

'Speak up when you're talking to me, Ted.'

'Yes'm.'

'In fact the scheme's intended for people exactly like you, children whose families can't make private arrangements as Mrs Hicks has done for Mr Jonathan.'

'Too old, ain't I?'

'Certainly not. Children between five and sixteen are eligible – there's no reason why your stepmother shouldn't apply for you to go.'

Ted wrote Nancy's name in the space for a signature, stole a tanner from her apron pocket to buy an envelope and stamp, and posted it off to some posh London address. He wasn't very hopeful, and even less so after listening in to the news. They didn't have a wireless in the cottage, or for that matter electricity to run one on, and Nancy was perfectly uninterested in the war news. Ted might have built a crystal set if he'd had the gear. Instead he'd sneak up to the house in the evenings and crouch outside the morning room to listen in.

The very same day he posted his application Alvar Liddell read out on the nine o'clock news, no less, that the people Ted wrote

LIMERICK
COUNTY LIBRARY
00505759

to had already received thousands of applications to send children away, and the police had been called in to control the crush of parents trying to apply in person.

The next day a government geezer told listeners they were stupid to talk about sending hundreds of thousands of children overseas when there weren't enough liners to put them in or Royal Navy ships to escort them. So it was a real surprise, a couple of weeks later, when the reply came. Nancy could just about read her own name, but luckily Ted met the postman and took the official envelope off him before she saw it. Ted went to open it in private. He wormed through the undergrowth to his den. It was his secret, the place he hid in when he skived off school. Ted didn't believe in going to sit in a row with boys who couldn't even read and thought they were funny when they made jokes about a chap's sister. He didn't go in for friends much either. Why would anyone want those morons around? So nobody had ever seen his hidey-hole, except for the vackie girl from London. She'd promised not to tell, 'Cross my throat and wish to die.'

Nobody else remembered there was a disused mine so close to the house. When Ted had come upon the capping that was supposed to block off the shaft he moved stones to build his private little shelter. This was where he kept useful things out of Nancy's greedy sight, such as his grandfather's bayonet from the last war and a switch knife the gamekeeper had lost, a primus stove, though it was missing a burner and he hadn't any fuel, a paintbox they'd chucked out at the house, a spare box for his gas mask, a half-empty bottle of pop and a tin of pilchards he'd nicked from the shop.

Confidential was written above Dear Sir (or Madam). 'You are notified that your child has been selected for evacuation overseas...'

Ted whooped, but caught the sound by clapping his hand over his mouth. Strictly secret, we ask you not to discuss the matter even with your neighbours, the typed words warned.

Nancy'd have to be told though. He chose his moment but she screeched anyway, hit out, connecting with his nose, which bled, and said she wouldn't let him. Then another letter came with the list of stuff he'd need. 'Suggested outfit for each child undertaking the journey', it said, but Ted could tell it was more than a suggestion, all the others would have at least one of everything required: gas mask, overcoat, suit, pullover, school cap, two shirts (coloured), two pairs stockings, two under vests, two pairs pants, two pairs pyjamas, one pair boots, one pair plimsolls, not to mention all the other stuff like handkerchiefs, comb, toothbrush, face flannel and towel.

How could he ever get hold of all that? 'Well, that's it, then, I'll not be going,' Ted muttered.

'You're not going anyroad, I said, didn't I?' Nancy told him. 'A right little scaredy-cat you are, trying to run off and leaving us to they Nasties.'

Mrs Hicks saved the day. She wrote to his uncle, sending two copies so they'd go by different ships in case one was sunk. Then she made the rector give Ted clothes from the poor box in the parish rooms, as well as a cardboard suitcase, and she produced a wallet for vital documents to keep on his person at all times. Nancy was outraged. 'What makes you so special, may I ask? Just 'cos your ma weren't no better than she should be. And you can take all that stuff back. You're staying put.'

The day the last letter came, the one that said when he was to get on the train, Nancy was carrying on at full throttle when in came Mrs Hicks, without knocking as per usual. Nancy began trying to heave herself out of the chair.

'No, no, don't get up, you need to put your feet up.'

Nancy didn't dare be rude to her face. 'Yes'm.'

'Now then, Nancy, we must have a little talk. I do understand it's upsetting for you to think of Ted going on that dangerous voyage, in fact I'm quite anxious myself about Mr Jonathan. You know he'll be setting off soon now he's got over the measles.'

'He's not going, Ted isn't.'

'Come now, his journey's all arranged and his uncle's expecting him.'

'S'not right.'

'You mustn't be anxious. The government's promised they'll be safe, Ted will travel in the care of a kind escort and his ship will be convoyed with an escort of Royal Navy ships, no less. I know how we'll miss him here at home and at school too.'

The old woman, slightly deaf, missed or pretended to miss Nancy's mutters and continued, 'Now Ted, I've brought you a travelling companion.' She passed him a brand new copy of the Bible inscribed with his name and the message, 'May this be a stout staff to support you along your way. Blanche Hicks.'

The next day Ted walked the three miles to the station and caught the train. His sister Connie, who had been helped by Mrs Hicks to a job as a nursery-maid in a shipowner's country house, was given the afternoon off – a very unusual concession – and caught a bus to Plymouth where she found her brother hanging out of the train window with his hand wrapped in a dirty rag, smuts in his hair and a bruise on his cheek, which he called 'Nancy's leaving present.'

'Still at it, is she?'

'She tried to take the strap to me but I'm too big for her now,' he told his sister.

'I felt badly leaving you alone with her.'

'She'll have scarpered by the time our dad's back. She said he needn't think he could leave her alone in this dump and he's not worth waiting for.'

'But she's having a baby!' Connie protested.

'Not our dad's, sure enough – the little bastard'll be no kin of our'n.'

The train had been filling up with sailors, and now they heard slamming doors and the guard's whistle.

'Teddy, come and sit down.'

'Who's that?' Connie asked.

'She's called the escort.'

'Where you going anyway?'

'Dunno. It's a secret.'

'Well, good luck. Come back safe.'

'So long, Con.' He tugged on the wide leather strap to pull the window up. He had to get the hole in the strap in exactly the right place for a stud on the door to go through and hold it up. Then it was nearly dark again, with the glass painted black. The compartment was lit by one faint bulb. The air was thick with cigarette smoke. When he touched things his hand came away black. He'd never travelled by train before or been further than a few miles from home in his life. The wooden bench seat, meant to hold five, had eight people crammed intimately together and the corridor outside was jam-packed. Nearly everyone was in uniform. The sandwich he was given had something unfamiliar and disgusting in it, the two girls who joined them at Taunton wouldn't stop crying. They had been going for hours when the train came to a stop. Then the noise began.

'What's the matter, young 'un, never been in a raid before?'

There hadn't been any in the far south-west, not yet anyway. After the initial shock Ted got used to the noise quickly, which was just as well because the mystery destination of the seemingly endless journey turned out to be Liverpool, where Ted and hundreds of other evacuees were billeted in an old orphanage. Air raids happened every night and all night. And the little ones cried for their mothers.

By day there were games, sing-songs and more or less tactful demonstrations of how to use indoor plumbing or eating irons since not all the evacuees had ever encountered them. Then they had to have medicals after which some rejects were sent back home. A boy who knew said they wouldn't take children with something wrong, 'and no niggers or yids or morons either, my father told me the Dominions won't have them.' A posh boy called Gwyn failed the second medical and was sent home along with the twins from south London who everybody could see were half-wits, a very tall boy with a touch of the tar brush and a girl who'd come from a hostel for refugees. Gwyn said he didn't mind, he'd not wanted to go in the first place and it was yellow for a chap to rat on the old country at its hour of need. But he gave Ted his panama hat to show foreigners he was a British gentleman. 'Good luck,' he said. 'You'll need it.'

A white-faced redhead called Daffodil Watkins said, 'Wait for us, Gwyn, we're coming with you, me and Millie.' She'd already told everyone that her dad wouldn't have let his daughters come if he'd been told their destination was Liverpool, specially if he'd known they would be kept waiting there for days. 'We'd have been better off back home, there haven't been any air raids there. Poor little Millie's ever so scared.'

'They won't let you leave.'

'They will if I say I've just remembered someone in my class got polio. Then we'll be in quarantine and they'll have to send us home.'

At that moment the sirens' wail started up again and little Millie and other children began their well-known yelling. Daffodil went even paler, if possible, as she picked up her sister and rocked to and fro with her face buried in the child's hair. This was the noisiest one yet, Ted thought, roll on embarkation. Five days at the Fazackerley children's home were enough, sleeping on straw pads on the ground under army issue blankets or, more likely, crammed into the air raid shelter.

One of the chaps had been told by his cousin in the docks who'd got it from a mate in the Merchant Navy that a whole fleet had been hired for the evacuees. Mr Gilligan, who was one of the escorts, heard them talking and got in a bate. He said Mr Hitler would be interested to know what they knew, thank you very much, and didn't they know that walls had ears. Old

Gilligan was shouting at the top of his voice to make himself heard above the explosions and crashes outside the shelter. Ted was going to tell him where to get off, making a fuss about something like that right in the middle of the fifth air raid of the night, but then one of the girls got hysterical and the escort had to go across and help try to calm her down.

On the sixth day they were loaded on to a blacked-out bus and driven to the docks, where they waited in a crowded shed for hours. A government geezer made a long speech about them being their country's Little Ambassadors, and said they had to be well behaved and do Old England credit. Someone else promised they would all be back home by Christmas. It was only at this point that the evacuees learnt that they were bound for Halifax in Nova Scotia. The last thing they did on British soil was hand in their gas masks. It felt very peculiar without the box dangling at one's side. Their name labels were left firmly attached.

The enormous liner loomed above them. Her name on the side had been painted out but it was stamped on to all her equipment, from lifeboats to handtowels, so they quickly realised that the steep gangplank led into the unimagined world of SS *City of Benares*. There were sailors with dark brown skin, and gold fittings and carpets and baths with taps and water closets with chains and lights that turned on with a switch. The government-sponsored evacuees were supposed to keep out of the paying passengers' sight, but even on the bottom deck the bunks had white sheets and soft blankets. Ted lay low at first, watching other people. He copied the way they ate the unfamiliar meals and used the luxurious gadgets which some of them took for granted and a few even complained about. When they sailed the evacuees lined the rail, waving and singing 'There'll Always Be An England', but then nearly all of them went greenish and started vomiting. So did most of the escorts. One groaned that ten days at sea would kill him.

Ted was free to explore unsupervised, though more cautiously after the pallid group was warned that first-class passengers had complained to Captain Nicholls that unsupervised evacuees were running wild.

On the third morning, Ted had been chased away from the boat deck by a Lascar, as he had learnt the brown sailors were called. Passing the big room where people danced, empty at this time of day, he went in. It don't half stink, he thought. Tobacco, perfume, spilt alcohol and the permanent, sour background of sickness and engine oil. The blackout was still over the portholes. He coughed, which frightened someone who was apparently hiding. A boy made a dash for the far door, tripped, skidded and ended up in a heap on the floor, with a cut, bleeding forehead. His grey flannel short-trousered suit was stained, his tie was twisted under the collar, his knees were scabby and he was wearing the requisite cork life jacket, with under it a flat oilskin and canvas package attached to him by narrow straps. Ted recognised Jonathan Hicks and thought, He's not lording it over me any more, that's for certain sure.

The swing doors opened and a hand gripped hold of Ted's ear. 'What d'you think you're doing up here?' a deep voice demanded. 'You're in trouble, my lad! As for you, young 'un, what are you up to?'

'Please sir, I was looking for my fountain pen.'

'Are you first class?' The child nodded. 'Where's your escort?'

'Nanny's too seasick to move. And actually, please sir, I...' The pale face was now faintly green.

'Right, you don't look too good. Run along to the sick bay.' The officer escorted Ted to the lowest deck to be locked in a cabin for the rest of the day. The date was 16th September 1940.

On the evening of the 17th, the Ellermann line's flagship, the City of Benares, was sailing at a slow 7 knots at the head of a nineteen-ship convoy whose Royal Navy escort ships had parted company earlier that day. The headwind had freshened to force 6 and there were showers of hail, but visibility was good enough for the commander of the German U-boat Number 48 to follow her progress though his periscope and, at 10.05 p.m., to launch a 500-pound torpedo which sank the *City of Benares*.

It was fourteen hours later, noon on the following day, when HMS *Hurricane* arrived to conduct a desperate search of the area where the liner went down. As the sailors came upon the pathetic debris they cursed and wept. They found a lifeboat containing twenty-one dead children and three ghastly rafts to which corpses were still lashed, but among the dead there were survivors: they found 175 adults of the 305 who had been on board, and nineteen children were still alive to be plucked from the water and transported back to England. HMS *Hurricane* landed these survivors at Greenock on 20th September. That morning's newspapers, all over the world, led with the story. Headlines blazed three words: MURDERED AT SEA.

At Goonzoyle a telegram was delivered by a boy on a bike who handed it over to Mrs Hicks but didn't wait. The last housemaid had left to join the ATS so it was not until the following day that the old lady was found in a heap on the floor, still clutching the scrap of paper. Dr Tredinnick arranged for her to be moved into a nursing home over on the south coast but she wasn't expected to recover.

The local papers announced and bewailed the shipwreck, all the more prominently because two of the lost boys were Cornish. A schoolmistress said Ted Johns had been something of a loner. But they found more to say about Jonathan Hicks. Various Hicks relations and local notables gave their reaction to Jonathan's fate and the tragic news awaiting his imprisoned father. Ted's stepmother had already moved out of the isolated cottage. 'Just walked out without a word of warning, left poor Mrs Hicks in the lurch, I really don't know what things are coming to,' the vicar's wife had explained. Local gossip, delicately imparted in hints, suggested that Nancy seized on Ted's departure as an excuse to join the father of her baby.

Mrs Hicks died two days later. Colonel Philip's wife came down straight away on the sleeper train and went by taxi to the deserted Goonzoyle. Marcia Hicks looked for her mother-in-law's diamonds, found nothing except cheap glass beads, marcasite and enamel, and in the same box a folded note from a jeweller in Truro. Blanche had sold the lot. Some of the better furniture had disappeared too, and the reason became obvious when Marcia glanced at the contents of the in-tray on the desk. Final demands, polite reminders, unpaid bills – the poor old thing was stony broke, Marcia muttered, having had no idea. She pushed aside the question of Philip's expectations, and rang the removers to arrange for the remaining contents of the house to be put into store. She attended her mother-in-law's funeral at noon, remained dry-eyed as the rector spoke of the bereaved grandmother dying from grief, and caught the afternoon train back to London. Within a few days she had arranged for Goonzoyle to be taken over for use as a training school for some hush-hush trade. In late October an advance party arrived to get things ready. They explored the house, relieved that it looked manageable in comparison with some of the country houses they had considered. One of the staff went across to the cottage, where she found and thought she'd better open the 'On His Majesty's Service' envelope still lying on the floor where the postman had pushed it under the door.

'I am very distressed to inform you that, in spite of all the precautions taken, the ship carrying your child/children to Canada was torpedoed on Tuesday night, 17th September. I am afraid your child/children is/are not amongst those reported as rescued and I am informed that there is no chance of there being any further list of survivors...'

As a matter of fact, there were a few more survivors. HMS *Anthony* found twelve adults and six children who had been adrift in a lifeboat for a week; and two days after the disaster the crew of a New England whaler had spotted two waterlogged bodies supported by a drifting plank. Two boys were hauled out. One, though still tied on to his companion and the raft, had been face down in the water. He was dead. The other was in a bad way, his limbs and fingers and tongue all hugely swollen, his skin sodden, in agony from the salt in his cuts and wounds, his whole body black and blue from neck to feet and his system dehydrated and hypothermic. He could not speak so had to be identified from the papers in his oilskin pouch. The sailors cared for him as best they could, reached Boston four days later and delivered the boy, wrapped in bandages, blankets and seamen's clothes, still mute, to hospital. When he was well enough to travel, he was taken to his unknown cousins, the Sturrocks, in California.

The Robert Hicks who went to New Almaden in the 1880s had built a fortune on quicksilver mining at the lower end of San Francisco Bay. Mining slumped and revived again over the years. The family expanded into fruit and horse farms. By 1940, Robert's granddaughter and her husband John Sturrock lived in a luxury which must have surprised their little refugee. None of the evacuee children, so accustomed to the austerities of life in England, had previously encountered the American comforts of endless hot water, central heating and refrigeration, ice cream and Coca-Cola.

The boy was mute but the doctors said speech would return, just give it time. What mattered, and English newspapers reported, was the happy news that Jonathan Hicks, aged eleven, had survived.

Chapter Two

1951

WHEN THE OWNER of a new art gallery in St Ives offered a spring show to the exciting young abstract painter who signed his work 'Jix' she had no idea that the artist had a local connection. It was not something Jon took much notice of either. He had no close family left. Marcia Hicks, Jon's stepmother, having become a leading light in the Red Cross, was killed when the basement where she'd taken refuge during a doodlebug raid received a direct hit. Her husband Philip was brought back a year later, after five years in a prisoner-of-war camp. He had had a bad time, probably suffering minor strokes that were not diagnosed or treated and then another, more serious, stroke on the journey home. On disembarkation he was taken directly into a home for disabled officers but remained unable to speak or communicate, showing no reaction to names and photos. The family lawyer wrote to warn Jonathan about his father, and in a separate letter told the Sturrocks that the Colonel was unlikely to recover or recognise his son again. So Jonathan decided he might as well stay on in California and put himself through college.

The Colonel's death three years later coincided punctually with the nursing home's receipt of the final payment from his emptied private bank account. It was a relief to anyone who knew him and perhaps – though how could anyone tell? – a merciful release for Philip Hicks. He never saw his son again, but as one cousin wrote to Jonathan, there really wouldn't have been much point. Jonathan had been painting more than studying, just managed not to flunk and had his work included in an exhibition immediately after graduation. The show might have done better if it had not coincided with the start of America's next war, in

July 1950. One critic, remarking on his fierce abstracts, oblongs and squares of shocking colour, suggested that they presaged the bloodshed coming in Korea. Another listed the influences (Braque, Klein, Picasso) apparent in the young artist's oeuvre and added a rhetorical question as punch-line: 'or, rather than "work" should I say, mimicry?'

That September Jonathan went to New York and joined the Tanager Gallery's artists' cooperative, stood at the bar of the Cedar Street Tavern in Greenwich Village arguing about art, and was invited to put some work in a shared show. The story went that his paintings sold at the private view and the following day he was drafted. The call-up papers and review clippings came together in the mail. So, he explained later, 'I got my British passport and shipped right out on the Normandie.'

The passport said he was six foot one and a half inches; eyes: grey; hair: brown; distinguishing marks: scar on jaw and left hand missing two joints on little finger, outward and visible legacies of two days and three nights in the Atlantic.

Jon arrived in England looking shockingly well nourished in comparison with people whose food had been rationed for a decade. In his baggage was a big envelope he hadn't looked at since his foster mother handed it over the last time he saw her, just before she upped sticks and resettled in Florida. It contained old letters, telegrams announcing deaths, all Jon's report cards and the address of the London law firm which would be in charge of his inheritance till he was twenty-five. That was the age specified in the family trust set up by his great-grandfather. By then, the old man had said, his wretched son might have acquired some discretion. Mr Hardman quoted the words with a kind of sly amusement. 'What did Grandfather do to rile his dad?' Jon asked, but all the solicitor could suggest was 'youthful indiscretions'. He went on to reassure Jon: 'He became a pillar of the community in later life.'

'So there'll be some dough for me.'

'Dough.' Mr Hardman repeated the word like a man tasting a new kind of food.

'Cash. Moolah. Money.'

'Of course there is the trust fund which was set up at your birth. Otherwise – well, you know what tax is like under this government, I dare say, and the capital was sadly diminished, what with your late grandmother staying on in that big house – far too big for her even before the war, rattling round without the staff to keep it up. And then she actually sold land, and what's more, at the bottom of the market. Never asked my advice, of course – I would have tried to dissuade her but she went to a local firm. And then your late father needed round-the-clock nursing, very expensive. His service pension was nowhere near enough. To put it brutally his death was quite timely, in financial terms.'

'All used up, huh?'

'Were you expecting to be a gentleman of leisure?'

'I thought as the heir I'd have enough to live on, sure.'

'With our taxes that's hardly possible any more.'

'That's a bummer.'

'I beg your pardon? Well, well, as dear Mr Churchill put it, we are two nations divided by a single language. If I may, a word of warning...'

Mr Hardman's brief lecture on bad language was followed by itemisation of a few puny investments and some household goods. He read the list aloud in a lugubrious manner. The good antiques had gone before the war. People were buying old furniture rather than the utility-marked junk which was all you could get new, so Jon might make something from selling off the remaining items, but tax was punitive these days, under this government.

Jon stood up and moved restlessly round the dark, old-fashioned room, threading a path between leather chairs and pink-taped folders.

'OK, turns out I'm broke after all, right?'

'D'you know, I simply can't get over your accent. Your poor father meant you to go to Eton, you know, your name was put down at birth. And then his regiment – well, there it is. The chattels can stay in store. You might go over to the house and take a look when you're down, though I can't imagine it being manageable as a private house these days.'

'How far is it from St Ives?'

'Not a long drive at all. Did you say you'd shipped your motor?'

'It's outside now.' Jon took a cigarette from a flat gold case, and as an afterthought offered it to the lawyer.

'Luckies – yes indeed. I acquired quite a taste for them during the war. Thank you.' Mr Hardman tapped the end on his blotter, snapped the desk lighter and breathed in pleasurably. Jon moved over to the window, which was grimy and had little tatters of blackout material still showing round the edges. His long, sleek Oldsmobile was parked in the Strand below, and Jon noticed that one passer-by in every half-dozen stopped to stare at it.

'I guess I might as well take a look.'

'You could combine it with the service in St Budy, Mr Hicks – Jonathan – may I?'

'Jon. Service?'

'Dear me, did the letter go astray? I'm sure Mrs Polhearne told me she'd written as soon as she heard.'

'I haven't been getting mail much recently.'

'Ah. Well, as it turns out you'll be able to attend. I'm only sorry I can't make the journey myself. But I know how much Mr and Mrs Polhearne are looking forward to your return home.'

'Journey to…?'

'The unveiling of the family memorial, Jonathan – Jon, a plaque in St Piran's Church, in St Budy.'

'Church?'

Mr Hardman's dry voice carried unexpected authority. 'Just this once. Everyone's been waiting until you came home.'

'Who is this Mrs Polhearne anyway?'

'She's married to Mr Gerald Polhearne, of Polhearne, a very old family indeed, one of the county's leading... Let me see now, is she your second cousin once removed? She was a Miss Hicks, so her grandfather would have been your —'

'Am I supposed to remember her?'

'I doubt if you met. You had mumps when you stayed at Goonzoyle so nobody was allowed anywhere near.'

'It's all a blank. I forget things that happened before —'

'Of course. That dreadful ordeal. I don't wonder you've forgotten. Perhaps it will come back to you when you see Cornwall again. You were there in 1938, Munich time, when your late parents were on leave from Bucharest.'

'Do you mean Romania?'

'Colonel Philip Hicks was military attaché.'

'Was that the only time?'

'I dare say you were there as an infant, but as far as I know you always went out to join your parents in the school holidays. I believe it was a disappointment to your grandmother.'

'I guess people are in for more disappointment when the prodigal heir comes home and has to cash the – what was it? Chats?'

'Chattels. Does that mean you propose to return to the United States?'

'Not so long as there's the draft.'

'Your father would have —'

'I'm not the colonel type.'

'So you plan – what?'

'I paint, these days.'

'Dear me, really? They say it's rather a raffish society. You may find that Mr and Mrs Polhearne take quite a dim view of your getting involved with – that's to say, artists do tend to be somewhat unconventional. Do you think it's really quite the thing?'

'Sure do,' he said.

Jonathan Hicks turned up at church late, and wearing an open-necked shirt with paint under his fingernails. If he'd been anyone else they mightn't have let him in at all. 'Someone should have warned him,' Rosina Polhearne's mother said quite clearly, and Rosina heard her father growl, 'Shut up, woman.'

At the end the vicar came down from the pulpit and showed Jonathan where to stand. Rosina's sister Lucia, who claimed to remember him from before the war, though Rosina didn't believe her because she was only seven when it started, got up from the front pew and moved to stand beside him. 'Pull the cord,' she told him. He awkwardly drew on the string and moved the tiny curtain. 'Say something!' Lucia hissed bossily, and Jon read aloud the names of his grandmother, father, mother and stepmother. 'In loving memory of Blanche, The Honourable Mrs Edward Hicks, 1887–1940, Colonel Philip Hicks DSO of Goonzoyle, 1905–1948, Lady Mary Hicks 1901–1935, Mrs Marcia Hicks, 1917–1944. Rest in Peace.' He spoke like a film star.

There wasn't applause, just the awkward rustling sound of people who wanted to clap but remembered they were in church and stopped themselves. Lucia was wearing a home-made two-piece suit with a stand-away collar, slightly skew-whiff. She tilted her head to look up at Jon's face. You could see that she knew how prettily the new straw hat was framing her face. Rosina noticed Lucia's eyelashes were fluttering energetically.

Jon's entrance had widened the eyes of lots of the females in the church. He looked quite exotic five years on from the war, though in those days people had got used to Yanks being so big and brawny. Rosina had been too young to notice but last

Sunday she'd heard Father and the vicar discussing Americans.

Father thought they were vulgar. He said Jon would have to be taught. 'Luckily Hardman tells me the feller's not too bumptious.'

'Mr Hardman said he seemed a quiet young man,' Mother said.

'He'd better keep quiet till he learns to talk like a gentleman. OK, sure, hi... What's more he actually calls shooting hunting – and Hardman says he's virtually illiterate. I ask you!'

Rosina had sat shifting uncomfortably on the hard seat as the meat congealed on her plate.

'Eat up your dinner, dear.'

I'll be sick, Rosina thought. Mother knows I can't swallow it. The smell of pork plus cigars was so disgusting. She'd begged for the pig to be spared, but the slaughterer came all the same. To think they'd scratched her back and talked to her, treating her like a pet. Father stood there quoting Mr Churchill. 'Dogs look up to you, cats look down on you and pigs treat you as an equal.' And then he murdered her. They are just cannibals in my family, that's all, brutes. Torturers.

'Rosina.'

'I'm not hungry.'

'It's most delicious,' the vicar said. 'Such a rare treat, I can't remember when I last saw so noble a joint of meat. And will you be smoking bacon?' His voice sounded yearning. Rosina used to love bacon herself though she didn't often get any. With the ration only one rasher a week per head, the girls' share was given to Father.

'Mr Hardman said Jonathan used up his whole week's sugar when he came to see him,' Mother said. 'I suppose nobody had warned the poor boy about rationing.'

So the grownups got talking about the GIs and their diet, and how big and strong they seemed compared with local men, and how lots of Cornish people hadn't got enough to eat and couldn't afford doctors or dentists when the mines closed down before the war. When the vicar said the National Health Service was a boon, indeed a godsend, Father humphed into his napkin so you could see he was stopping himself from saying what he usually did about the government. Lucia was in some kind of dream but Rosina thought the subject was interesting. When she was twenty-one she might vote Labour herself.

'Well, Rosina, what do you think?' the vicar asked. Father didn't glare, so she repeated something she had read in *Collins Magazine*, which still came every month although Rosina really felt she had grown out of it.

'Some people think the war might have been a blessing in disguise —'

'I beg your pardon?'

'— because it brought in the Welfare State,' she finished.

'Don't be cheeky,' Mother said.

'Rosina,' Father growled. He wouldn't actually do anything, not when everyone else was in the room, and the vicar there too, but Rosina stopped talking. Better not let him see her dropping little chunks of the meat to Rufus and Janus under the table. Then Father started saying Jon's life had been ruined by not going to a proper school and Mother signed to Rosina to help Mrs Tremellen clear, so she escaped before anyone could say, 'You sit at this table till that plate's clean.'

Rosina could only just remember the Yankee servicemen who'd been stationed in Cornwall before they sailed away to invade France but she'd have known Jon was American the minute he came into the church, even though he had been born in England, because he looked sleek and glossy like a well-fed horse. The people Rosina knew didn't wash much and they wore the same clothes day after day – they'd had to before clothes and soap came off coupons last year. She still automatically breathed through her mouth to block her sense of smell.

Jonathan looked like a different kind of being, even with paint on his trousers which were, Rosina realised, cowboy clothes: blue jeans. And he had such even, white teeth. One of the girls in the dorm at school always wore a dental plate at night to straighten hers. Rosina resolved to talk to Mother about having it done, though she'd have to be tactful and not make it sound like a criticism of Mother's own crooked, discoloured smile.

Lucia was saying something that seemed to amuse Jonathan. Her seams were crooked. Serve her right for flirting, Rosina thought, glaring at her sister. At least her cousin wasn't responding. He didn't say much, just stood there, but there was something that made you look at him.

Mother had invited selected local worthies to come out to the house for tea.

She said, 'Ride on ahead, dear, would you, and make sure they know we're on the way.'

'Oh Mother, must I?'

'Run along, Rosina, do as you're told.'

Why didn't anyone realise she was fourteen years old, too old to be treated like a child? Thank goodness she was going back to school tomorrow. It was so beastly at home, nobody understood what it was like.

Chin up, Rosina told herself, less than a year to go. She was counting the days till her birthday, crossing them off on a tiny calendar kept hidden in a prayer book, because when she was fifteen and could leave school she was going to get away. They were sending her to Paris to learn French and ladylike behaviour. The prospect was the only thing that kept her going.

The wind had got up while they were in church. Rosina's bike, left propped against the churchyard wall, had fallen over into some battered daffodils. The elm trees were tossing around noisily, untethered wreaths blown off their graves. Rosina set a vase upright beside the nearest headstone, pushed the bike through the lych gate and into the road. A car like the ones in films was parked behind Father's Rover, which looked short and squat in comparison. Oldsmobile, she read. It had the steering wheel on the left, a front bench seat wide enough for four people, and the roof folded back. A corner was flapping and Rosina refastened its strap through the eyehole, tutting at the way the wind was blowing cherry blossom on to the leather upholstery. There was a blue paint stain on the driving seat, a pair of sunglasses on the dashboard, a sketchbook and box of oil-crayons on the glove shelf and a motoring map in the foot well. It was folded open to show Cornwall, with a circle scrawled round St Ives, another round St Budy and an X to mark the site of Goonzoyle.

'Hi.'

Rosina jumped. 'Oh, hello Cousin Jon. Is this your sketchbook?'

'Sure is.' He rifled quickly through pages of formless colours. There wasn't anything Rosina could recognise. Actually she thought the pictures were awfully like the doodles she sometimes did in lessons and everyone in her form knew Rosina wasn't much of an artist. All the same, she said:

'They're nice.'

'Here, want one?' He tore out a page and held it out.

'Oh, I couldn't – don't you need to keep them for your next exhibition?'

'Take it.'

'What did you do to your finger?'

'Just an accident.'

'Did it hurt?'

'Some, yeah.'

'Thank you, Cousin Jon.' She put the paper in the wicker bike basket.

'You're welcome. Maybe it'll make you lots of dough.'

'Oh golly, d'you mean someone would pay money for it?'

'Sure.'

Rosina didn't like to ask how one set about selling a picture, but Father had confiscated her running-away money (hidden, though not well enough, in the nursery window seat) so she certainly could do with making some if only she knew how. She asked, 'Wouldn't it hurt your feelings?'

'Only if you sell it for the wrong reasons.'

'But how can I be sure what they are?'

'You'll feel it, like this.' As he spoke Jon bent and put his hand under Rosina's chin and lifted it up and then he put his lips on hers. Dry, they felt, and hot, and she held her breath, and then he did something really peculiar in her mouth, pushing in a rough, wet lump – oh, it's his tongue, ugh, ugh... She was trying to pull away and trying not to breathe, and terrified by his strength and angry that she couldn't fight him any more than she ever fought back; and then she began to realise she was feeling something else, tickles running through her like electric shocks, and she didn't want to get away after all. But then she heard voices, and they were coming out, and Jon let go, suddenly, and Rosina's legs felt as bendy as liquorice sticks. He said:

'You're sweet. Better go, your dad's coming out.'

Rosina leapt on the bike incautiously, winced, yelped and pedalled urgently away.

If Jon Hicks was impressed by Polhearne he did not say so. Nor did he appear to be aware of the attention concentrated on him. The gathering was of local worthies, rather than 'the county', which meant there was an atmosphere of deference, disguised or even denied, but death, taxes and a socialist government had not toppled the Polhearnes off their perch. During the war Polhearne had been used as the meeting place of most local volunteer groups so nearly everyone at the gathering had been through the front door before, but invitations to the big house were still regarded as an honour. The only guest who was ever allowed to penetrate beyond the drawing room was the doctor. She was a locum, working for the socialistic National Health Service and actually female! When she first arrived in St Budy some patients travelled as far as Buriton to find 'a proper doctor' – that is, a man. The locum only set foot across Polhearne's threshold because Mrs Tremellen had a fall. The doctor found herself trekking along dark corridors into a big kitchen with an eight-oven Aga and twenty-foot table, then on through a scullery with three big white sinks, and beyond it into a wash kitchen where soapy steam was bubbling out of a copper. At last she reached a snug little room with a turkey carpet, a row of bells and festoons of bobble-crochet antimacassars, where Mrs Tremellen was draped across two chairs, peeling potatoes. The test was passed, in that the 'guinea pig' patient was soon back on her feet.

After that the doctor was honoured with a summons to the mistress. She was in her bedroom, a huge, cold space, lying in an ancient four-poster bed. Its dusty crewel-patterned hangings made the doctor sneeze uncontrollably and cast a masking shadow over the patient, who modestly refused to remove her substantial and rigid corset.

The next visit found Mrs Polhearne in the morning room, a small chilly cube crammed with gilt-framed watercolours on flowery, faded wallpaper. There was a strong smell of old, wet dogs. They were whining and barking in competition with scratchy operatic arias blaring out from Mr Polhearne's estate office down the hall. The doctor diagnosed and treated Mrs Polhearne's thyroid disorder after years of old Dr Tredinnick insisting the only thing wrong with her was nerves. Mrs Polhearne announced that she felt like a new woman, after which many patients decided that a woman doctor might be acceptable after all. The tradition of deference to Polhearne and the Polhearnes had survived the war, as it had so many previous changes and battles. In a pamphlet about the parish history, the vicar called it 'evolution not revolution.'

The medieval hall had grown into a rambling manor. St Budy

developed from hamlet to village, and when metal mining began to flourish the fields disappeared under rows of workers' cottages until the once rural Polhearne estate was on the edge of a small industrial town. But the huge gardens were still magnificent. Some of the shrubs had been planted decades if not more than a century earlier, and camellias and magnolias had grown into tall, thick, gloriously blossoming trees. The grounds showed less trace of wartime shabbiness than the house itself. Pin marks remained on the drawing room's green damask walls; utility bookcases were still full of brown official files. Other decorations had been in place since before the Great War, the walls hung with oil paintings of pastoral scenes and a great many stuffed heads, trophies of animals killed by generations of sporting Polhearnes. There were plaster cornucopias crumbling away from the ceiling, walnut and mahogany tables with flimsy pedestals, brocade sofas, heavy dark velvet curtains and, on the high marble mantelpiece, ornaments made of silver and gilt. Not much cosiness here; but that wasn't the point. Demonstrating status was.

The local gossip said Mrs P had done well for herself, lucky to snaffle the most eligible local bachelor, and some of the people now in the room remembered hearing of a time when those jumped up Hickses hadn't been fit to speak to a Polhearne let alone marry one. They looked curiously at young Jon Hicks in his unsuitably casual clothes. He was the kind of man who made a strong impression on other people though he hardly spoke or even smiled. A composed figure, watched and watchful, aware that they were talking about him, and about his family and father, the late Colonel Philip Hicks. An old soldier said:

'He was a proper hero, God rest him.'

'Pity the Nazis didn't finish him off while they was about it.'

'I went to visit him,' a woman said. She had a fox fur round her neck, a tilted hat with a veil, and high, chunky heels, the fashionable get-up spoiled by lisle stockings hiding a maze of bulging veins. The doctor had pressed the arguments for surgery, but the patient believed in healing through prayer. 'I'm a sensitive, you see, in touch with the higher plane,' she explained. She'd also been sensitive to the paralysed Colonel Hicks. 'You understand that I feel emotions,' she was explaining. 'When I met his eyes, they were watery and staring, I tell you, he had a venomous aura. Acid yellow, like sulphur. The room was suffused with misery and – yes, I will say it – hatred. He hated me because I could walk away.'

'It was a merciful release,' the vicar said piously.

Mrs Polhearne drew close. She pulled her sleeves over a bandaged wrist and said, 'You must be talking about the poor Colonel,' she said. 'He's so much in one's mind today, and dear Marcia, and poor dear Mary too. His first wife, Jonathan's mother. D'you know, I have such a vivid memory of them, just after they were married, the perfect couple. Philip had a London posting so I went up to stop with them for a ball – whose was it? I forget. This was when I was still single. I can see myself going along Birdcage Walk with him in his blues, so handsome with that little moustache. He looked – what's the word? – gallant. It's all such a pity. Perhaps if he'd seen his son – though of course now he's mixed up with all those vulgar artists. Just a phase, no doubt, only Philip would have been quite appalled, but all the same I can't help wondering whether if only Jonathan had come back sooner —'

'My dear Mrs Polhearne.' The reverend spoke with authority. 'Banish that thought. It would have made no difference.'

'You're right, of course, I know poor Philip wouldn't even have recognised his own son. Goodness knows we didn't, he's turned out quite good-looking. His grandmother was always saying his hair would come in darker, and of course his foster parents had his teeth straightened and his ears pinned back and tonsils removed. American medicine is so advanced. But I don't see very much family likeness now.'

'Should'a set eyes on the Colonel's da', then,' said the Polhearnes' driver-handyman. He was an ex-soldier and one-time miner, uncomfortable in a stiff demob suit instead of his usual oil-stained khakis.

The vicar said, 'D'you know, Tremellen, you're quite right, I just remember Mr Edward Hicks, and young Mr Jonathan really is a chip off the old block.'

'Said so, din' I? Spittin' image of th'old ram, he is.'

The young doctor hid a snigger; the old doctor had told her that the Colonel's father, who once lived at Goonzoyle, had been responsible for an epidemic of involuntary and unconscious incest in the district.

Another group was clustered round Miss Margery. She was the proprietor of a kindergarten now, having taught empire builders' infants in Malaya before the war and returned afterwards suffering from a variety of conditions, chronic and acute, all caused or exacerbated by years in a Japanese prison camp. She was respected for coming through, pitied and deferred to, despite always sounding critical and crabby. She held forth about modern art after a visit to St Ives.

'The youngest infant in my school could do as well, or better even. I was shocked, yes, I was literally appalled. What they've got hanging there, asking money for too, ridiculous prices, mere daubs, the paint just splashed around with no attempt at perspective or scale, those so-called artists can't even draw! And they have the cheek to offer their scrawls for sale, you won't believe it but I'm perfectly serious, there was one by someone called Nicholson, I could have done better myself, and it cost twenty guineas! And there was another by a man with a German name – well, I ask you! And my cousin tells me the locals are being edged right out of the town, it's overrun by these vulgar Bohemians, artists they call themselves. St Ives isn't the place it was in the old days.'

'Did you see any of young Mr Hicks' pictures?' someone asked.

'I could hardly go inside, one shouldn't encourage them, not after looking in the window. I saw quite enough, believe me, he'd coloured his canvas blue, all over. Prussian blue. That was all. Nothing else. Now he's a nice enough young man, you can see that, but call that art! A two-year-old could do it.'

The doctor made a mental note to look at a dark patch on Miss Margery's neck and turned her attention to Lucia Polhearne who was exercising her feminine wiles on Jonathan. A beautiful girl, at first sight, though not very bright, with an expression that could be discontent, or even a kind of fear. What a responsibility to be the heiress to all this – enough to make anyone afraid. Despite her over-blatant giggles, chatter, eyelash-fluttering, Lucia didn't seem to be making much impression on the young man. Possibly inhibited by her younger sister's hostile stare? Her pale face showed – what? Fear, perhaps, or anger: something wrong there, the doctor thought.

Actually Rosina wasn't any more cross than usual. She felt a funny mixture of amazement and pride – I had my first kiss! I've actually been kissed! He must like me! She was also keeping her usual cautious lookout. Lucia always said she was a beastly little nosy parker but it was useful to know what was going on, and it was just as well to practise being observant because Rosina rather thought she might like to be a beautiful female spy. It would certainly be more exciting than learning shorthand typing like Lucia, and taking dictation all day.

You could see Lucia wasn't getting anywhere. He likes me best! Lucia's mouth drooped further, but she perked up when she saw Adrian Gore come in. He was an eligible bachelor, heir to a baronetcy. Adrian Bore, Rosina thought, but that wasn't her lookout. Jon was obviously poised to leave. Rosina sidled across the room, keeping below the attention level of her mother.

'Cousin Jon.'

'Hi and bye.'

'Can I come with you?' Rosina asked.

Lucia snapped back to attention. 'Rosina!'

Jon had made that uh-uh grunt and turned away so Rosina jabbed Lucia's arm with her elbow, quite hard, and snapped, 'Mind your own business.'

Lucia put her face close and whispered, 'You've got a crush on him!'

'Shut up!'

'Knew it – you're blushing. I'll tell on you.'

She wouldn't really. Rosina followed Jon's tall, narrow back.

Adrian Gore said, 'Good afternoon, Rosie.'

She never answered to Rosie, on principle. To Jon, she said, 'I just thought I could have a go in that super car.'

'Another time, maybe.'

'I'm going back to school tonight.'

'Sorry, kid,' he said.

He doesn't understand! 'But I'll be gone the whole term.'

'Take a raincheck, OK?'

He's pretending not to like me so's my family won't realise. 'I'd get in trouble for saying that,' Rosina said in her social voice.

'Saying what?'

'OK. Or kid, and raincheck too, actually. Any American slang.'

'Uh huh.'

He went to say goodbye to Mother, and she told him a fib about Father, who had escaped as usual. Everyone could tell that he was in his estate room because that hateful voice was uttering the madwoman's shrieks. Rosina's flesh crawled as she heard it. Father had named his daughters after the operatic heroines whose songs he listened to over and over again, and she disliked Lucia di Lammermoor only a little less than *The Marriage of Figaro*. But Mother was saying that Father had been called away. 'I sometimes think this district would simply collapse if he wasn't there propping everything up.' Rosina waited for the usual next line about Atlas bearing the weight of the world, but the vicar was on his way out and he said:

'Very true, my dear, my sentiments exactly. Welcome home again, Mr Hicks, and God bless you.'

'Rosina, have you got your hand luggage packed?'

Treating her like a baby! Was Jon the only person who could see she wasn't a child? 'Mrs Tremellen did it after Pickfords called for my trunk, so you needn't fuss.'

'That's enough. Rosina's taking the sleeper tonight.' She directed a grown-ups-ganging-up-on-the-children sort of smile at Jon. 'Back to school tomorrow.'

'Right,' Jon said.

Mother laid her hand on his arm. She's going to talk about him being an orphan, she'll be all soppy and maternal, Rosina thought. She slid out of the room through the door into the library, sneaked across the hall into the back passage, past the pantry and out of the bootroom door into the garage yard, to where she'd left her bike. It had been a birthday present. Mother had been apologetic because it was only second-hand and father harumphed as usual, saying it was all this Labour government's fault that there were still shortages five years later, you wouldn't think we'd actually won the war. Rosina didn't care. It was a good bike, sometimes she could go miles in a day though she wasn't supposed to go far on her own. But she'd be back before Mother noticed, she was only interested in her boring party and nudging Lucia towards her 'sir', much they cared if Rosina was there or not.

Rosina pedalled hard, trying not to notice how uncomfortable she felt, and sang loudly but off key, 'You'll take the high road and I'll take the low road and I'll be in Scotland afore ye.'

Chapter Three

~

THAT NIGHT, IN the small hours, the doctor was called out to a holiday camp near Trevena. It was pouring with rain, pitch dark, and she got lost. Not for the first time she thought how glad she'd be when this locum job was over.

Another dead end, this time in a very muddy farmyard. The engine stalled. Damn. She'd flood the damn thing if she wasn't careful. She waited, timing half a minute by humming a few bars of the *Messiah*. 'Comfort ye, comfort ye...' She pulled cautiously on the starter button. Thank goodness for that. Up to the road. Which way now? She always had trouble finding her way round Cornwall even in daylight. Map-reading had never been her strong point and things weren't made any easier by the missing signposts. Some had been re-erected since the war, but not nearly enough to get anyone to Trevena at the first attempt.

It was freezing in the little Austin 7, with no heater and windows that didn't properly close. And its roof leaked. Several three point turns later, and having taken a very long way round, she saw a swinging light ahead and stamped her foot on the brake just in time to avoid killing a man who'd been almost invisible in a black oilskin and sou'wester. He aimed the torch beam towards a sharp turning between two stone walls into a steep, unmade road with a torrent of water pouring down it. She wound the window down a couple of inches, her face instantly soaked by horizontal rain.

'Is this Trevena? The holiday camp?'

'Up the lane. They're waiting for you, doctor.'

The message hadn't said who they were or what accident or emergency she'd face – if she ever got there at all. The middle of the lane scraped against the bottom of the car, the wheels in ruts like tramlines, as she nursed it up the slippery slope in bottom gear. It seemed ages before it levelled out and light appeared through the stripes of rain: a man carrying an oil lantern.

'Where's my patient?'

'Come, it's over yonder.'

'Can't I get the car any closer?'

'Not unless you want to drive over the cliff.'

Until that moment the doctor had not taken in that she was hearing the thunder of waves close by. And shouting. People were calling – she couldn't make the words out. She licked her lips and tasted salt, knotted a scarf under her chin, buttoned up her trench coat and reached her bag from the back seat.

'I'll carry that for you.'

She tightened her grip on the handle. 'Thanks, but I can manage.' The brown leather doctor's bag was heavy and awkward but it gave her a feeling of authority. The man walked ahead, aiming his light beam between sand dunes until the narrow path came out on a flat area edged by the darkness of the cliff edge. Dim lights in small windows showed about a dozen caravans, placed close together. She could make out what people were shouting now. 'Sheila. Sheila.'

A lost child. The doctor's stomach knotted in apprehension. Oh God, those cliffs, the darkness, that wild sea.

'Where are you? Sheila!'

What had her parents been thinking of, to lose sight of her in a place like this?

'Doctor. In here.'

Two steps up into a hot, crowded little compartment lit only by a paraffin lamp which hung, hissing, from a hook on the ceiling.

A padded bunk down one side facing a kitchenette on the other, one gas ring and a tiny sink clogged with tea leaves. A table at the end was covered with mugs, cups, a tin of jam, a metal teapot, spilled tea and overflowing ashtrays. A battered pink doll presided forlornly on a high shelf, beside a watercolour, gaudy and abstract, in a cardboard mount. The stale air was thick with lamp fumes and tobacco. A man sat stiffly upright in the middle of the bunk with a uniformed policeman on either side. His hands were flat on the mattress pushing his shoulders to hunch up by his ears, his face protruding forwards, his chest heaving as he noisily and arduously sucked at the air. It didn't take a medic to diagnose an asthma attack.

'DC Bennett, doctor.'

'Who is my patient?'

'This is Mr Mark, ma'am. Mr Stephen Mark.'

'Would you take off the jacket and roll the sleeve up, please?' She pointed the syringe upwards and expelled the air. 'What's happening here? Is a child lost?'

'No, ma'am, it's Mrs Mark that's disappeared.'

A quick jab into the arm. 'I expect you've had this treatment before, Mr Mark, you should be feeling better very soon,' she said. 'Mrs Mark – is that why you're here, officer?'

'The lady was reported missing, ma'am, at four thirty this afternoon – I mean, yesterday.'

Stephen Mark was already showing the signs of relief, his rigid muscles beginning to relax, the breathing sounding less desperate. One could see now that he was perhaps in his early thirties, already balding and with two front teeth missing. He had a flat, long face with narrow-lidded, light-coloured eyes: Slavic descent, the doctor thought. He was not wearing pyjamas, but ex-uniform trousers with an open-necked shirt and canvas shoes. There was a bleeding scrape on his hand, and a bruise on his arm. He croaked out:

'Delia. Where's my daughter?' His accent was foreign. A Pole, perhaps, or a Czech.

'Mrs Oliver's got the little girl, sir.'

'Who?'

'In the chalet by the shop, sir.'

'She's only young, don't let —'

'She'll take good care of the little maid, Mrs Oliver will, there's six of her own.'

'You should rest now, Mr Mark.' The conventional words were pointless; how could he rest? But outside in the windy dark and the incessant roar of the surf, the shouts had stopped. A policeman said, 'Might as well give up till daylight. Sunrise six thirty-eight ack emma. We'll find her in the morning.'

Chapter Four

ROSINA'S PARENTS BOTH escorted her to the station. Mother got into a fuss, saying Rosina looked pale and was anything wrong? Rosina was afraid she might cry so didn't answer aloud, just shook her head. Then Father came out to the car puffing his pipe like a dragon and still swinging that stick dangerously from side to side. They put her in the back like prison warders and drove across the town.

Not long now, Rosina thought, digging her fingernails into her palm. They were still in a serious bate.

'You didn't ask permission.'

'You just walked out.'

'On our guests.'

'Without a word.'

'Not even saying goodbye.'

'Or thanking them for coming.'

'Where did you go anyway?'

Rosina drew in a lungful of air to stop her voice wobbling. 'Trevena.'

'Why? The truth now, Rosina.'

'I said goodbye to Delia.'

'To whom?'

'She came over on Saturday.'

'Oh yes, your new friend,' Mother said.

'That foreign child.'

'She's English, she was born in London.'

'The one you picked up on the beach.' Father's tone was condemnation enough, but he added, 'The one you took nosing round the place.'

'She did ask very politely, Gerald,' Mother said.

'Mother said I could.'

'I'd have thought they would have returned home by this time.' Mother sounded like she did if she saw something not very nice. Rosina, there's a spider on your collar. Rosina, use your handkerchief. She'd been ever so snooty, pretending not to take any notice when Delia said 'pardon' and held her knife like a pen, but Rosina saw the look she and Lucia exchanged. They thought Delia was common.

Father kept them waiting while he pulled up at the station and held a match flame to his pipe. Then he asked, menacingly in his specially low and level voice, 'And you were where in Trevena, precisely?'

'I... I was just at Goonzoyle.'

'What happened?'

'Nothing.'

'What were you doing there?'

'I wanted to see Nanny.'

'Rosina, have you been talking out of turn?' Father asked in a frightening monotone.

'No!'

'Don't use that tone of voice to me...'

'I didn't say anything.'

'Gerald, not here – look, there's – Good evening, Mr Gundry.'

'The train's on time, ma'am.'

The station master moved majestically onwards. Father had lowered the walking stick. He growled, 'You need to keep an eye on the girl.'

'Wipe your eyes, you can't get on the train like that,' Mother said.

I can, if only it would jolly well hurry up and come. 'Sorry, Father.'

'You followed that boy, you little —'

Mother interrupted, which was unusual. 'No, dear, don't, not with Mr Gundry… Rosina, your cousin Jonathan wasn't going to Goonzoyle, Mr Hardman thought he was too upset about it.'

'Marcia should never have sold the place,' Father growled.

At last the signal had gone down, Mr Gundry was closing the level-crossing gates. Mother said, 'Now, your aunt will meet you at Paddington, make sure you give her the saffron cake and cream.' Rosina did not kiss either of her parents goodbye. She climbed into the train and followed the attendant to the third-class compartment. Three berths were still empty, though a woman with a hairnet lay snoring on one. Without taking off her clothes, Rosina climbed on to a top bunk and, lying face down with her knees pulled under her aching tummy, covered herself completely with the tartan blanket. In the dark fug of acrid smoke and the horrid, intimate smell of her 'time of the month', with sounds masked by the train's familiar chug, it was safe, at last, to cry herself to sleep.

Chapter Five

~

ONCE IT WAS daylight the search recommenced. Most of the men who lived in Trevena joined in, and others had come out from St Budy. Several had dogs which sniffed busily at a cardigan belonging to Sheila Mark, though there was not much point if she'd gone in the water. The lifeboat had turned out too. But everyone knew that bodies along this coast were usually swept out to sea. The chances of finding anything were pretty slim.

Stephen Mark, pale, gaunt, hunched into an ex-army greatcoat, was out on the cliff top too. A police officer stood on his either side. Conversation had rapidly become questions and undisguised interrogation. What happened yesterday, where were you, when did you last see your wife? The answers were fluent but sometimes mispronounced.

'We went for a walk and then she said she wanted some time to herself.'

'Where was your little girl then?'

'She was on the beach with a child she'd chummed up with the other day. I forget, Rosamund...Rosie. Something like that.'

'On their own?'

'Delia's perfectly sensible, she's learnt to be self-reliant. Sheila's my second wife, I should have explained. Delia's mother died in the war. We came from Prague together when our country was invaded, you understand, by —'

'That's as may be, sir, but it's the second Mrs Mark we're interested in just now.'

'Sheila and Delia have always been wonderful friends, you'd never know that —'

'How old did you say your daughter is now, sir?'

'She's thirteen and grown-up for her age.'

'If you say so, sir.'

Stephen Mark's face looked raw, as though the wind were stripping its top layer away. He stared through pale, watering eyes at the scene they were facing, the foaming white waves breaking on to the dun-coloured sand below, the heaving steel-grey ocean, the exclamation point of the looming lighthouse.

'It was so calm the day we arrived, so beautiful. Blue, yellow, brilliant white. Sheila used to go on about the smells here, bracken, gorse, the sea...and now...now? I don't know, it's beyond me.'

'Just let's have it again, sir. You're saying your wife went off on her own leaving you behind?'

Stephen Mark sighed. 'I told you, we'd gone down to the village, we've tried to see inside the church a couple of times but they keep it locked, so we had another look round the churchyard, we thought of having a cider but it was still half an hour till opening time so we agreed to meet back at the caravan and I walked back. I last saw Sheila sitting on the wall outside the shop, I don't know which direction she went in, all I know is she never came back.'

'She didn't say anything about her intentions, sir?'

'No, but earlier she'd told me she wanted to see how much she could remember from when she was little.'

For a moment the official chill seemed to thaw, as the officer said, 'She's a local, then?'

'Unlike me, you mean. In fact, no, but my wife was sent here as an evacuee in 'thirty-nine, only for a little while till her family moved out of London and had her back, but she's always remembered it.'

'Was this where she stayed, here in Trevena?'

'It was over there, in St Ives.' He pointed at the shadowy town over on the far side of the bay. 'On the far side because you couldn't see the lighthouse from the house.'

'You've been there yourself?'

'We went over yesterday. I have no motor car so we had to catch the bus, there's one a week on Wednesdays, so it was the day before yesterday. Sheila showed us the house, but I didn't want to presume so she took Delia in to see the lady who'd put her up and I went down to the harbour and sat by the water till it was time for the bus. On the way back Sheila showed us the beach where she went cockling and the school she'd gone to, it wasn't in the same place because there were too many children, so many evacuees. Sheila had to catch a bus to the school, near here, just for that term, which is how she came to know Trevena.'

'And when she went off yesterday, on foot, surely you asked your wife where she was going?' the older, taller policeman asked.

'Not exactly, I didn't, she said she wanted some time to herself, I didn't want to pry – but what does it matter now? Isn't it time to find her? Instead we stand here wasting time.'

When the tide was far enough out, they began to spread out at the foot of the cliffs, slipping on unstable shingle, to search in the caves, torch beams flashing into wet, dark hollows, searching, though not for a sign of life. If Sheila had been caught there by the ravening sea, she couldn't have survived.

At the far end, under an overhang, a man crawled into a child-sized hollow and came out with a piece of sodden, acrid-smelling wool.

'Do you recognise this, sir?' They didn't let him touch it, but dangled the ruined fabric of a hand-knitted cardigan, dripping, before his eyes. 'Is this your wife's?'

'I don't think so. It might be. I'm afraid I'm not very observant about ladies' clothes. A green cardigan – she does wear things she's knitted, but I don't remember...I can't tell if it's hers. Delia might know, or we could see if it matches any of her other things.'

But they would not let him back into the caravan. The Chief Inspector had arrived from Buriton and decided to lock it until a person he referred to as 'Dabs' had dusted for prints. Sitting in the black bull-nosed Morris he asked all the same questions as his colleagues, yet again. And again in other phrases. His voice grew louder as heavier rain thundered on the metal roof.

'You and Mrs Mark had a row yesterday morning, is that right?'

'Who told you that?'

'Is it true?'

'That caravan's so flimsy – I can hardly deny it, since your eavesdropper told you of our discussion.'

'What was it about, sir?'

'The usual subject. Money. It is not easy when one is a bloody foreigner. I am naturalised, I changed my name, my child is a British subject born and bred, but still I am outsider. I cannot earn enough, money is tight. So we discuss it. Even argue about it. But I told your colleagues all this already. I don't understand why you keep asking me the same questions instead of letting me go and try to find her, it's almost as if you suspected me of doing away with her.'

Which was exactly what they did suspect. The search carried on for the rest of the day, and in the evening the missing woman's husband was arrested and charged with murder. But convictions are unlikely in cases where there is no dead body. Circumstantial evidence is not enough to prove murder. At the committal hearing a bench of local magistrates felt unable to send the accused for trial at assizes. Their regret at being forced to the decision was unconcealed, and the proceedings were widely reported in terms that carried an unequivocal subtext. Sheila Mark had disappeared without trace. Less explicit, on account of the libel laws, was the suggestion that her husband had got away with murder.

Released from custody, reunited with his daughter and back in

London, Stephen found that nobody would greet him or serve him in shops or sit in the same pew at church. Whispers followed him down the road.

Delia learnt to cook and clean. She played truant from school, partly because she was cold-shouldered by the other girls. But attending lessons didn't go with being a person who stood in food queues, was careful with ration books, learnt how to make a pound of scrag end stretch over three meals, took the laundry to the communal wash house and scrubbed the floor. Nor did it suit her to be treated like a child any more. Delia was the one who shared Father's pay packet out between the pots labelled 'Rent' and 'Milkman' and 'Coalman', the one who negotiated a lower rent because the water pipes kept freezing, and the one who censored Father's reading. She hid in her special place, with her picture postcards of the holiday, a newspaper announcement of the engagement of Rosina's sister, and after that a photograph of the wedding party, with Lucia Polhearne in satin and Jonathan Hicks in a morning coat, arm-in-arm in the doorway of the bride's famous home. Delia pored over the photo with a magnifying glass but could not recognise Rosina anywhere.

Stephen was sacked from the bank after a while and the Marks moved away to a city where nobody knew who they were.

Chapter Six

2003

I HAVE A CRIMINAL mind. I've committed many crimes.

Starting a talk with that remark is meant to startle the audience and usually does. It may be cheating, but it gets a laugh.

In real life and absolute fact I'd plead guilty to the following petty charge sheet: speeding, parking and other traffic offences. Dropping litter. Forgery – I have written a false name purporting to witness my signature on unimportant documents. Theft: as a kid I occasionally got off the old Routemaster buses without paying the fare; and a few years ago I stole a packet of bacon from Tesco to see what it felt like. (In case you're interested, the answer is, it felt easy but I felt guilty. I put the equivalent money in their charity collection box the next day.)

It's murder, blackmail, extortion, treason which are my bread and butter. You imagine what you don't know. Up until the year 2003 I'd only seen one dead body and even that was in the distance – which didn't stop me coming over all sick and silly when I did, though I must have buried the episode deep down somewhere because it wasn't at all clear in my mind. However on looking back through my archives I found that I'd 'written it out.' It's what most novelists do to dispose of unwelcome obsessions. At the back of a high shelf I keep a box file labelled 'Burn without opening.' It contains various pieces of more or less awful schoolgirl outpourings and private records of events in my adult life that I'd hate anyone else to see. Under the lid is a warning to my heirs: 'If you read this, I'll come back and HAUNT you.' And a copy of the instruction to my executors: 'destroy my private papers'. But you can't rely on them: after Dorothy L. Sayers dropped dead relatively young and quite unexpectedly, her son said she did not really mean it or she would have burnt the diaries and letters herself, and he gave them to a biographer; much the same thing happened to the journals of the secretive Patrick O'Brian.

Unlike those two, I have neither disreputable secrets nor a good memory – in fact a blank one till the age of five. After that it is vague, patchy and entirely dependant on a small stack of old Letts diaries full of adolescent idiocies, Cambridge notepads scribbled with shameful solipsism and the thin 'exercise book' in which I recorded the frustrations of a young mother in the 1960s, housebound, bored and envious. I ought to burn everything I'm unwilling to send to the American library which is housing my other manuscripts and archives and often take the documents out of the box file, dither and then put them all back again pretending they will come in handy if I write a book set in the past. Perhaps an analyst would say that I am afraid of destroying the records of my life for fear of ending that life itself.

They are not a good read. Like many other keepers of occasional journals I only feel any impulse to record my life when there's very little of interest going on it, which means in effect that it reads like a chronicle of wasting time by a discontented person who spent the 1960s – the first decade of my married life – weeping into a nappy bucket like an archetypal *Guardian* woman's page reader, full of an anger which the women's liberation movement had not yet taught me the words to express. But by 1976 discrimination against women had become illegal and I had moved on from pencils and exercise books, past the old-fashioned manual typewriter, to an electric typewriter on which a nightmarish day was recorded – or exorcised.

It was horrible weather that spring, with no indication that the long hot summer of 'the drought year' was going to follow. At the time it seemed changelessly unpleasant with everything flattened and battered by perpetual wind, rain-sodden, the daffodils tattered, the blossom stripped. The weather never deterred my husband, hereafter referred to as 'H' for Husband, Historian or person in Hot pursuit of the county's history from the twentieth-century Duke of Cornwall's Light Infantry right back to prehistoric times. The object of his quest on that particular Sunday was the Early Mesolithic.

H insists that we have an outing. We will go in two cars and meet on a cliff top at the far end of the county, near a village called Trevena. There is a rich mesolithic site, where, at the age of eight, while staying with a great-aunt, he found worked flints and understood they were traces of the distant past. It was the first step on the road towards becoming an archaeologist. One of his fellow enthusiasts rings to say the field has been ploughed for the first time in years. The children grumble fluently, but eventually consent to join in so long as we go to the beach first. H sets off blithe and early. All very well for him. When I go out there are, including my own, ten boots to pull on, five coats to find and a bootful of just-in-case gear to be loaded. And one of the girls gets car-sick. However, by mid-morning we are on the unfamiliar beach. It is deserted. Freezing cold, no wonder nobody else is there. But beautiful. The tide is far out, the sand smooth and brilliantly yellow, the sea a clear and icy blue. The children are soon damp and chilled through. They whine in chorus, until I shut them up with glove-box toffees.

(At this point my ancient journal has an NB in the margin, handwritten, undated: 'Uncharacteristic waffle. Qu why? Prob. to put off moment of writing about what happened. My fingers would hardly hit the keys. Still in shock.')

So we drive off to the place marked with a cross on my map, and I pull in between H's car and one other in a cliff-top layby. It's freezing cold with an icy wind directly off the sea. The last thing I want is to trudge across those muddy furrows but I set a good example. We move forward obediently, with eyes firmly on the ground. We are carrying brown paper bags to drop the booty in. There will be a prize for whoever finds the most, which certainly won't be me, since I seem to be flint-blind. I hate this claggy earth. The effort of getting across it! I think about pavements, and how cold it is and what a bore it will be to clean the kids' clothes and boots.

The field is huge. We start at the road end and move towards the cliff. There's gorse, heather and more mud, though at least there's also a lovely scenic view. I am still stumbling crossly along, bogged down, when the children reach the edge, fling themselves on to their stomachs on the wet ground and peer over the 200-foot drop.

'Look, there's a seal,' one calls, and then another shouts in great excitement, 'No it's not, stupid, it's hundreds of seals.' When I reach them I see it's like one of those optical illusion puzzles, you look down at a distant shingly beach with a scattering of wet grey rocks, and then your vision shifts slightly and you realise that the rocks are actually seals lying on the ground. And there really are nearly a hundred of them; we lose count at seventy-seven. This inaccessible cove below us is where a freighter broke up two years ago. Scavengers swooped down on its cargo of timber planks even before Customs and Excise could say it was theft (the warning a necessary ritual but pointless, given the Cornish tradition of 'wrecking'). Inherited skills or not, they didn't get all the timber. From our precarious vantage point we can see not only the rocklike seals but also a few stray, sodden boards.

Somewhere nearby a man is shouting. Then H says something sharp, I can't hear what, and suddenly one of the boys is yelling. 'Look, look, down there, look at that!' Then I'm yelling too, 'Get back, get back from the edge this minute,' and I'm pulling at them and screaming because I suddenly see that the hump they're pointing at, lying right by the cliffs at the top of the beach, isn't made of wood, it's something grey-brown and wet like the seals and stones, but it's much bigger.

And then the next thing I know is that I'm lying on my back on the prickly, cushiony undergrowth looking at the sky, and all the children are standing around me staring down at my face, and two of them are crying and one is embarrassed and the other is trying to fan my face by flapping his anorak above me. 'You fainted, Mum,' he says in a tone of considerable indignation. Which seems to be true, and it's the first time in my life, and I really feel quite peculiar. I try to speak, clear my throat, swallow and then croak, 'We've got to get help.'

'Dad's already gone with that man, they said there's a phone box in the village over there, to ring – Mum, down there, with the seals, that was —'

Shut up, I tell him, don't say it, not in front of the little ones, and for once miraculously he does what I tell him. One of the girls begins to cry. She is cold, she wants to go home, she's hungry, when will Daddy be back?

But then he reappears and so does the other man, who is wearing green wellies and an oiled jacket and carrying a heavy-looking ex-army rucksack, and he says he was walking round the coast path and was up by the trig point when he saw the person – he thinks it's a woman – fall. Jump? So he ran as fast as he could and he didn't know if he should go back to get his car, but it was right over the other side of the headland – and he was standing there not knowing what to do when he saw us all in the field —

Then we hear an engine above us, coming rapidly closer, piercingly noisy. I have a splitting headache which the roar of the rescue helicopter doesn't help. The boys go back to the cliff edge, lying flat on the wet ground to get a proper view, but I stay back with the girls because I'm still feeling wobbly and peculiar.

By this time there are other people, rubberneckers who've

turned up like magic, from nowhere. I recognise the reporter from BBC Plymouth with his UHER tape recorder, already holding the mike out to the man who saw what happened.

The helicopter can't get close enough to the cliff. Someone's dangling below it but he can't reach the body. The seals' beach is perfectly inaccessible. This is a fearsome stretch of coast. H whispers that it's a traditional suicide spot. No wonder the response seems well rehearsed. But as soon as they are certain that the person really is dead, the urgency to recover the body is lessened. It's obviously going to be a very long job. H is standing with the other man, both with their backs to us, H still holding his bag of flints, the other man swinging his shepherd's crook walking stick

So I say I'll take the children home. And when we get back to the car I realise the one beside ours must be the dead woman's. I feel wobbly again, but look in without saying anything to the children. It's locked, and there's nothing personal visible except for a flight bag on the back seat, unzipped and empty, and then I see a label saying Hertz dangling from the mirror. So we get into our car. The kids quarrel and whine all the way home and it takes us nearly two hours because there's a traction engine rally, but when we get there we make cocoa and find chocolate biscuits and shut ourselves up with the comfort food, the heater turned high, and Watch With Mother, all five of us together.

~

There's nothing else in the folder except for two small newspaper cuttings. One of them was the report of the inquest. The deceased was called Jennifer Galloway. She was an unmarried mother as it was called in those days, when people still talked about illegitimacy, bastards, fallen women and girls who were no better than they should be. She'd lived alone in a bedsit in south London. Her landlady testified that 'She took the room in the summer, I'd not have let her if I'd known she was expecting, no children or animals, that's my rule, but she was quiet enough so I let her stay – on sufferance, mind.'

Her downstairs neighbour told the reporter, 'She kept everything ever so nice, all her books tidy up on the shelf, lots of very modern pictures on the wall, scrawls really, I think she painted them herself, but she took them down before the baby was born, quite right too, they were not suitable for wee ones. She was a great reader. She was always at the public library but she didn't take out stories, she liked heavy books about psychology and such. There was one she said I had to read by an old German called *The Interpretation of Dreams* but I couldn't get on with it at all. She did copy typing I think, tap tap tapping at the typewriter all those months before the baby came and she wouldn't give it up, I'd look in sometimes and there she was working away with one hand and trying to hold the baby with the other. If you want to know what I think, she'd tired herself out, bone weary. No wonder she wasn't thinking straight.'

Another neighbour had refused to speak to the press. You could see that she felt badly treated, having done a favour to her neighbour by looking after her baby only to find herself vilified for having abandoned it. One of her friends had defended her. 'It was very kind of Morag to take two days out of her holiday to look after that baby, considering she hardly knew the mother. There was no way she could wait, she'd been booked on that aeroplane for weeks. It's not like she just washed her hands of it, she knew the mother was on the overnight train and was due back any minute.'

When the baby was eventually found, screaming, starving, stinking, Morag's note was on the table: 'He's been as good as gold, hope your trip went well.'

At the other end of the country, the Cornish coroner had heard Morag explain that her neighbour had begged her to babysit. 'Only two days, it's really important. I'll pay you!' Morag was a trained nursery nurse. Doing this favour to Jennifer Galloway had got her the sack.

An expert witness gave evidence about post-natal depression; he also gave statistics about the number of unmarried mothers driven to suicide by shame.

The inquest was adjourned at that point and by the time it reconvened the mystery had deepened. The newspaper report had winkled out a young woman going by the name Dawn. She had met the dead woman in a commune in Wales which sounded like one of the well-meaning, faintly mystical experiments in group living that sprang up wherever property was cheap. This one was so free and easy (for which read that everyone was always stoned) that a girl could drop in to be part of the shifting population, be known only by the name of her choice – in this case, 'Moondust' – and drop out again a few weeks later with nobody noticing that she'd gone or wondering where or realising that she'd taken with her Dawn's driving licence and purse. Dawn's real name was Jennifer Galloway. She remembered the other young woman though knew nothing about her and was surprised to learn that she had a baby.

Moondust's real name was unknown. The police could find no trace of her before she pitched up at the commune. Nor could they find out where she went after leaving it and before turning up in her bedsit. She must have gone off with a man, or met one soon afterwards, but nobody could find out who, or where, or exactly when. Afterwards a leader writer drew a moral from the story. 'In this country we value our freedom of movement and cherish the right to drop out; our readers will know that notwithstanding the crisis in Northern Ireland this newspaper has opposed the introduction of identity cards. Tragic cases of this kind are the price we pay for our freedom.'

The case remained a mystery. Nobody could explain why the anonymous woman had travelled to the far end of the country, hired a car, driven to a cliff and jumped to her death. The coroner thanked the witness, Mr Jonathan Hicks Polhearne, of Polhearne House, St Budy, and expressed sympathy to him for undergoing the shocking experience. Verdict: suicide while the balance of the deceased's mind was disturbed.

The name was familiar because Polhearne was one of the West Country's oldest houses still occupied by the original eponymous family. The idea has flitted across my mind once or twice that I could make use of it in a history, mystery, twistery novel. But it never struck mental sparks. If you live in Cornwall and spend your time prosaically wife-ing and mothering, the local setting soon feels like a more suitable setting for murder than romance.

The owner became more famous than his house after the secret got out that a bestselling book published under the curious pseudonym, The Artologist, was in fact by Jon Polhearne. It came out in the late 1970s, a time when millions of shelves groaned under their load of teach yourself to change your life books. One more tract about self-improvement and fringe beliefs would have been doomed to obscurity if a talk-show host had not got stuck in a train on the West Coast line and borrowed something – anything – to read from a stranger. He read the book and raved about it on air. This was long before the days of televised Booker Prize dinners and books being seen as glamorous commodities, in fact *Paint, Prophesy, Predict* may have been one of the earliest examples of 'the Oprah effect'. It seemed to hit the twin bull's-eyes of self-help and mysticism. The second edition was produced by a big firm of publishers, whose publicist admitted, years later, that she was the one who, 'by accident on purpose', let out who the author really was. The jacket was covered with passionate praise from influential celebrities (most of whom later admitted they had not read a word either of the book or of what they were supposed to have thought of it): genius, life-changing, influential, mould-breaking, a discovery to equal Einstein and Newton. A review not used in the publicity material said that Eastern philosophy, Jungian archetypes, Freudian analysis, Arthurian legends and the prophecies of Nostradamus had been poured into a bubble bath in which half-educated non-sceptics could soak their souls.

The book is still going strong. Only last week it was included in a Radio 4 list (admittedly rather a long list) of the most life-changing publications ever, right up there with the Bible, the Koran, Shakespeare and the inevitable Tolkien.

I can't pretend to have read it, though I did flick through once and noticed the odd mish-mash of linguistic styles (school essay, academic-turgid, American colloquial, sermonising, and more) that became the basis for a long-running gag about writing by committee in a comedy series of the 1990s called *Homer and Edward at Eight*. (Another reference: Homer to Simpson to Mrs Simpson and the King.) Nor have I met the Polhearnes. Most journalists, refused interviews and reduced to speculating and inventing colourful details, make the present generation of the family sound very peculiar and not romantic at all. The local gossip about our very own celebrity does not sound any better informed. Depending on who's talking, Jon Polhearne is variously a hero, enigma, bounder or con artist. I saw him on TV once, just after his connection with the book got out but well before it 'took off', after which he went into Greta Garbo mode and turned into a famous recluse. But before anyone knew how famous he would become the Devon and Cornwall independent channel got him on to a live show, a one-off, which for some reason hasn't survived on tape.

It featured a palmist, a graphologist and Jon Polhearne as the local guru. At least, the presenter called him a guru, though the word – associated at the time with shaggy-bearded mystics in sandals – did not seem to fit the conventional figure on the screen. The palm-reader was a brightly coloured woman (orange hair, scarlet dress, ultramarine tank top, at least a dozen strings of rainbow beads), and the handwriting expert had a bushy beard and caftan. Polhearne, in a suit and tie, was the one who should have looked out of place. But he exuded a kind of calm, self-contained authority. I couldn't work out how, since he said very little, left 'silence on the air' (which, unusually, the presenter did not leap in to fill) and made a few graceful hand movements, once to block the camera, so momentarily the viewer saw the silhouette of his palm and long fingers, one of them mutilated with two joints missing.

We had only turned on because we had met the celeb whose secrets were supposed to be exposed by the three seers. The first two said nothing that a researcher could not have discovered. Then a girl tied on a blindfold and, under Polhearne's unemphatic gaze, the celebrity actually did begin to daub paint on the waiting canvas. It was amusing to watch the involuntary actions but the alien control was also obscurely disgusting.

Then I realised that I had seen Jon Polhearne before, and after that suddenly remembered when it was. Or rather, my body remembered. First I felt sick; and after that recognised the cliff walker, made up, sleeked down, his hair grey at the temples and receding to leave a peak pointing down the high forehead, and his even, white teeth.

Live shows were in real time in those days so the chorus of oohs, aahs and gasps couldn't be edited. The others had produced snap character analysis, but Polhearne merely uttered a brief, ambiguous warning in a very plummy accent. The scrawl of paint suggested some fatal peril. Easy enough to say, since the celebrity-subject was a well-known mountaineer whose perseverance, courage and interest in heights the others had punctually recognised, and danger was part of his life. Actually, contrary to the painting's message he never did fall – or hasn't yet – and at the age of nearly eighty is still in good shape. All the same, Jon Polhearne seemed indefinably impressive. A friend who perceived coloured auras around people rang up the next

LIMERICK
COUNTY LIBRARY

morning to tell me his had been two colours, something she had never seen before: gold, flecked with black, like a piece of Murano glass. (In spite of my insensitive lack of faith in gurus or auras, I was pleased to hear that mine is hyacinth blue.) We live in an area bulging with nutters mouthing pseudo-unscience and some of them do create some sorts of jobs for some kinds of people, the ancient Polhearne House being kept up and running by the 3P Fellowship and its residential courses. A quick check on their antique website, not updated since 1999, shows their stock-in-trade was changing people's lives through something known as artology, which means art plus astrology. They tack various so-called earth mysteries on too, and a notion they call death divining, which is apparently a kind of fortune-telling. There's no space in my head for understanding any of it.

I am not quite as rational as the above remark implies. That episode at Trevena, for example, was censored in my memory though I must have brooded on it, for one of my books, written some years afterwards, featured a similar death at the bottom of a Swiss mountain precipice.[1] Yet while I am working on my novels and for some time after their publication, I often say, and truly believe while I'm saying it, that every word is pure fiction, based entirely on imagination with no basis whatsoever in life or truth.

So writing this is a new experience and I have to grapple with a technical problem: how to tell a true story at book length, and what should the narrator's point of view be – a question which novelists often dither about. One can sometimes write several chapters before realising it was wasted work because it needed to be in a different voice. This time, for once, I naively thought telling the tale would be perfectly simple, having seen some of these events myself, met most participants and done lots of research. I planned to drive the narrative along with my own process of discovery.

Fifty-seven pages in, I wiped it. Rereading the dry, detailed

[1] Jessica Mann, *Funeral Sites* (Macmillan, 1981)

report made my eyes glaze over. If it did that to me, what would it do for anyone else? The fact is that the notes, or transcripts of some conversations – for instance, with Elliot Rosenwald – make an effective tranquilliser substitute. In the next draft I moved the characters around as in fiction, but facts proved an impossible constraint.

Third time lucky. The narrative will consist of what I saw and what I was told, set out in chronological order.

My personal involvement in this story began with an article I wrote for the *Sunday Express* about the sinking of a ship taking evacuee children to Canada during World War II. Collecting material, I'd conducted phone interviews with survivors, failed to get hold of a study of the subject written by a P. Dilwyn twenty-five years ago, and learnt a lot from a book by Ralph Barker. The story appeared under a reproduction of a September 1940 headline, huge capital letters screaming 'NAZIS TORPEDO MERCY SHIP, KILL CHILDREN.' It began, 'Today is Remembrance Day for the surviving "Children of the *Benares*". Some do not want reminders of the traumatic event in which they lost family and friends. Others have died, emigrated or dropped out. About a dozen will meet today perhaps for the last time, at the Church of the Annunciation in Wembley, where there is a memorial engraved by their fathers and grandfathers, in honour of those who died.' And so on.

That article provoked lots of reaction and a contract to write a non-fiction book about the overseas evacuation of children.[2] Thousands of British children, among them myself aged two, were sent overseas, to live with foster families for several years. I began research by posting an on-line appeal for former evacuees or their families to get in touch. On 13th September 2002 (my birthday, and also the anniversary of the day the *City of Benares* sailed) an email came from a Mrs Constance Thorne who said that her brother was one of the children who died.

We arranged to meet in London. She invited me to tea in

---

[2] Jessica Mann, *Out of Harm's Way* (Headline Publishing, 2005)

Brown's Hotel, telling me it was the only place in town she could possibly stay. I was confronted by a pink damask table covered with an amazing array of carbohydrates, a three-tiered stand carrying scones with cream and jam, cucumber sandwiches, slices of fruit cake and chocolate cake and a plateful of what used to be called fancies. No wonder Connie Thorne was overweight. But she was good-looking with it, clear, very blue eyes, good teeth and enviable hair, silver, thick and wavy. She made no secret of her age or, apparently, of anything else: a woman with a clear conscience, I thought. If she received the traditional warning, 'Fly at once, all is discovered,' she'd probably stay put.

Connie's voice sounded pure Australian but she told me she was born in Cornwall.

'No, were you? That's where I live,' I exclaimed, and we had a 'what a coincidence' conversation as well as the familiar 'are you Cornish yourself' interrogation before I steered her back to 1940.

There were two of them, Connie and her kid brother. He had been selected for the government's overseas evacuation scheme. 'Of course it's very old history, probably before you were born.'

'I was two,' I said.

'Well, I was nearly seventeen. I joined up on my birthday.' Connie chatted and chewed, lifted the teapot lid, summoned more hot water and told me about herself. Her husband – the fourth, it seemed – had died, and she'd decided to move back to Cornwall where she was born.

'D'you know, when I saw the ad for my house it felt like a sign, put out specially for me to see, someone up there was taking good care of me.' She glanced upwards. I didn't ask if she meant one of her dead husbands or God. 'This was just after my Sid passed away, God rest him. You can imagine I was feeling low but that didn't stop his kids coming down like vultures and his people going on at me. I'd got to make up my mind, was I staying on in LA, what about the Cayman Islands property, where were the details of the Long Island mansion, on and on. I needed to find somewhere quick. First I thought maybe I'd better go back to Oz but somehow I couldn't see it. And then one day I said to myself, "Well, Connie old girl, here you are a widow with no kids, not short of a bob or two, it's time to please yourself."

'Always a good idea,' I agreed.

'So I was looking at details of condos in Florida and an island in the Virgins, even thought about a castle in Spain, just doodling on line. I don't know what made me type in the place I was born. But I did, and blow me, up came the realtor's ad for Goonzoyle. Houses ripe for restoration in south-west England, it said, five or six of them. With pictures. "Former nursing home in Cornwall" – there it was, waiting for me. I never actually planned go back but it was the obvious answer, full circle and all that. So here I am, back where I was born, a householder. It won't take me long to get in the swing, I'm a great joiner-in.'

'Where in Cornwall is it?'

'Trevena, near St Budy – d'you know it?'

'I've been there, but it's a long way from where we live.'

'You must come over,' she said.

'That would be lovely,' I replied.

'Though to be perfectly honest I'm a kind of stranger there by this time. Never went back since the war, not till now.'

'You've always been overseas?'

'No. I married an Aussie and went back home with him in '45. Then my second husband, Billy Bob, he took me to the United States, and Sid was Canadian, Sid and Bruce both had Cornish ancestors, metal miners. You ever hear what they used to say? If there's a hole in the ground anywhere in the world there's a Cousin Jack at the bottom of it.'

I said something about records showing that the worldwide diaspora of the Cornish was on almost as large a scale as that of the Irish or perhaps even of the Jews.

'That's right. My husbands were wanderers, lovely men, all

lovely, but none of them ever understood what roots really meant.' Suddenly she burst into song, belting out, 'And shall Trelawny die, there's twenty thousand Cornishmen will know the reason why.'

A bad moment; excruciating in fact. I carefully avoided the stares of other guests and ignored the advancing waiter, but made a show of picking up the notebook and turning the tape on, at which Connie stopped singing and said, 'Now, dear, I've been rambling on, and none of that's any good to you. What d'you want to know?'

'You were telling me about the summer of 1940. What did it feel like, can you remember?'

'Exciting. Well, I was young and people said I was pretty, there was lots going on. Even square-bashing was better than being bossed around in civvy street by an old dragon of a nanny. Of course it would have been different if I'd had family to worry about, but my mother had passed on and poor Dad was a prisoner of war by then. He never came back, died in '43, not that I heard till a year later, but there...'

'The atmosphere must have been pretty scary though.'

'I thought it was exciting, but at that age, what did I know? Some people were terrified, when France fell, and the Low Countries, everyone thought the Germans were going to arrive any minute and we weren't ready, we didn't have weapons, nothing had been organised – it was a shambles really.'

'So the authorities decided to save the children.'

'In the end they did, but only on account of people complaining that the toffs were all sending their precious children off to be safe and leaving the rest to face the music. So the government was pushed into saying they'd pay to send kids to the Dominions. But the whole thing was wrong, in fact it was a silly scheme. They shouldn't ever have gone. Those kids would have been better off staying at home. If only...'

'It must have seemed like a good idea at the time.'

'That's what our Ted thought, he was that excited when I went to the station to say goodbye. He'd got on the list because of Dad being out of the way, and he couldn't stand our stepmother, not once she was expecting, with poor Dad over there – I was that relieved when they said she'd gone off with her fancy man. But Ted was gone by then, went off by train, eighth September 1940. It was the last I ever saw of him. Sailed on the *City of Benares*, poor kid.'

'Such a tragedy,' I murmured.

'Did you know there was a whole family lost that night, five Grimond kids? Augusta, Violet, Constance, Edward, Leonard. I've always remembered their poor little names, alongside poor Teddy.'

'I'm so sorry,' I murmured as she applied the napkin to her eyes.

'Thank you, dear, but there it is, old history now.' Connie Thorne pulled herself together, poured another cup of tea and said, 'It's awful really, I've forgotten so much. If only I could think of more to tell you.' She went through a little list of remembered titbits. Her brother was a cheeky little bugger, a bit of a loner, could be a real lazybones, he should have been born a gentleman of leisure. He was always bunking off school and got into trouble with the attendance officer but you know how some people get away with everything. A bit sly maybe. He was quite a little actor, took off voices like a parrot, and he was that sharp, bright as a button, he could twist you round his little finger if he wanted to, even Dad. Connie's father had been a man of few words, not one to talk about feelings or emotions, but he thought the sun shone out of Ted's eyes.

As she spoke of the long-gone child, Connie's voice took on a tinge of the accent she must have had as a child. I made notes and looked sympathetic, but when Connie said, 'I don't suppose all this will be much use for your book,' she was right; it wasn't. At least, not for that book.

At home I looked up the tragic list of children lost in the *City of Benares*. Ted's name was there, between Joan and Florence Irving and Peter Langton-Lloyd. I photocopied the page and put it in an envelope with a thank-you note which included our numbers and address. Then I transcribed the few useful lines of the interview and added Connie's name and address to the list of people to thank in print and invite to the launch party.

A few weeks after that I got another response to the Internet posting, an email from a Professor Rosenwald which I nearly deleted unopened along with the usual daily avalanche of offers to enlarge my boobs or show me Asian babes. He said he had information for me and would I send my snail mail address. When his letter arrived it was on heavy grey paper with 'Professor Elliot C. Rosenwald' engraved in red cursive across the top, its return address a post office box in Denver, Colorado.

'Thank you for your message. It so happens that I have had sight of your earlier article, and it is for that reason that I have responded to the general inquiry you posted on line since I am already in possession of some, and am seeking more, information, for the purposes of a biography in progress, about one of the children of the *Benares* – one, as it happens, whose name you omitted to mention in your earlier essay. I shall be doing research in the UK next month, hope to be in Cornwall around Easter and should welcome the opportunity to discuss this matter in person.'

Presumably this cryptic hint was meant to be tantalising, but actually it was just irritating. I checked his credentials on line and found one of those boastful descriptions that appear on American university websites, the list of publications padded out with every short book review he'd ever published. He seemed to be an art historian and had written articles about later twentieth-century artists: Barbara Hepworth, Jackson Pollock, Etienne Hadju, Naum Gabo. His titles didn't entice me: '*Getting Inside the Canvas*', '*The Uses of Inspiration*', '*Overt Art, Covert Meanings*'.

I emailed to say we'd be away, which was true because we'd

taken an apartment in Venice for Easter, and that I was sorry, which wasn't. By then I'd already written the draft of my few pages about the *City of Benares*. There might be some details to correct or add in when I eventually got hold of the Dilwyn dissertation. But the tragedy would only form a section of a single chapter describing the evacuated children's journeys all over the world, and the whole book could be only one hundred thousand words long, so there wouldn't be room for much more information about that tragic, abortive voyage.

Chapter Seven

I HADN'T GOT to know Grace Theobald yet when – as she was to tell me later – her 'quote stepfather unquote', Brian Monson, walked out on nine-twelve; the previous day, nine-eleven, his office had closed early and Brian spent his first weekday afternoon at home for twenty years. He and Delia stood glued to the television for the rest of the day as he babbled about his new determination to change his life, now, at once, no waiting till next year when he was due to retire, become a consultant and take on a handful of jobs as a non-exec. What was it all for? Did riches bring happiness? Think of the people dying there, now, before their eyes. Think of old Jim, Brian's best friend from university, who had supported his wife and brought up three kids on a salary less than a tenth of Brian's and was due to retire next year on an academic's pension which was less than the Monsons' annual spend on hospitality and holidays. Or what about Brian's brother Derek, holding down a senior post in an NGO and paid a pittance to sweat it out in some Third World hell-hole. The money Brian had been handed in last year's bonus was more than either of those two would see in a lifetime.

That night Brian had clutched at Delia in a kind of frenzy. 'Death makes me randy,' he said, before falling into a heavy sleep and waking with his mind made up. He was leaving. You have to take your happiness where you can, life is short, he announced. Numb, shell-shocked, Delia didn't protest. Later on she discovered there'd have been no point in arguing. Catch 22: when things are going well you don't worry about your legal rights. When they've gone badly it's too late to acquire any.

When she'd first known Brian, not long out of two years'

worth of hostile divorce proceedings, the idea of remarrying seemed ludicrous. The only one of her six relationships to end in acrimony had been the legal one. One of the very few of her poems to be published was called 'A New Start'. No marriage lines or law/no contract or rules/except of the heart/Together from choice/We shall not part.

At pensionable age and with little pension, the notion of dividing the spoils seemed rather more attractive but this time she had no rights at all, either to Brian's money or to the home they'd shared, which had been rented from the company as a tax-dodge. She didn't suspect him of planning a Delia-dodge. None the less, she was shafted. She'd have to make her own way. It was do-able. Just. She found an ex-council flat near Westbourne Grove and Grace came to help her move in. They scrubbed and sponged, sprayed and wiped. When Delia finished the last can of insect repellent she joined her daughter on the tiny balcony.

'A plague of flies combined with exhaust fumes – will this place be all right for you?' Grace said anxiously.

'It'll clean up lovely, wait and see.'

'I didn't realise there'd be so much traffic. Noisy, isn't it?'

'Yes, but remember those hoots from the river traffic?' Delia said brightly, though the penthouse had been silent and still compared with an ex-council flat on the Hallfield estate overlooking a main road.

'I do hope you're going to be OK.'

Delia had firmly decided to be perfectly fine. 'It's kind of you to worry but please don't. Desist. Refrain.'

Grace, at thirty-five, was a sensible, sometimes formidable woman. A curator at the William and Mary Museum, she also had a business sideline in buying and selling vintage clothes. As a teenager she had the hobby of hunting for treasures in charity shops, which led her on to a career and an authoritative academic reputation.

Grace sometimes shared her house with a man, sometimes

apparently lived alone. Delia never inquired. On moving day, Grace had turned up unannounced with kir and champagne, said, 'Let's celebrate, this place feels good,' and was upbeat about the accommodation, tactfully pretending not to notice her mother's private belongings: the vibrator which rolled out of an unzipped washbag, a tortoiseshell cigarette box containing condoms, the filing basket of envelopes addressed to herself in Delia's own handwriting – rejected poems, returned by editors to sender. Instead Grace was complimentary about Delia's wardrobe. She selected garment bags stamped with upmarket logos, poked edges of material out to finger and uncovered some of the dresses to examine full length. She was too tall for them herself except for one Shirin Guild coat which Brian called Delia's tent, and hated. Grace held a blaze of primary colours against herself and said:

'I love this Lacroix.'

'Is that what it is? Brian chose it.'

'He's got a good eye.'

'D'you want to take them off my hands?'

'Oh not yet, Mum, hang on to them, the fabrics are gorgeous. And this one – look at the piping. I'll have them for the costume galleries one day, I'm thinking of putting on a fin de siècle show at the Will and Moll.'

Delia had never been very interested in clothes and rather thought that from now on comfort would be the criterion. But she liked to see Grace's enthusiasm even if their thought processes and tastes didn't intersect. Delia was in grey sweats, while Grace had explained that her dress was a Westwood, unsaleable because a previous owner's cigarette had left holes in the dangling sleeves.

'This is quite boring, I'll deal with the rest another time,' Delia said.

Grace was never one to leave a book half read or a job half done. 'No, look, those are the last boxes, let's just finish it off.'

'That lot's your grandfather's, from his place when it was cleared out,' Delia said. 'God knows why I hung on to them. He won't be wanting them, that's for sure.'

Grace opened lids on to musty tweed, stained flannel, creased ties. Both women, embarrassed by the squalor of Stephen Mark's leavings, without comment and in tacit agreement sealed the boxes up again and put them beside the front door to go out with the trash.

'This one says "Keep This", in Grandad's writing, better just check,' Grace said, as she opened the cardboard flaps of the last carton. 'Oh look, there's a case. DM – it must be yours.'

'That's my old school case, I haven't seen it for...not since I went to college. Fancy Dad keeping that.'

Grace pulled the case out of the cardboard crate and opened it to see damp-stained Puffin books, faded green hardback Arthur Ransomes, a carriage clock, some inaccurate watercolours of garden flowers, a mini menagerie of chipped china animals. 'All for Oxfam?' She threw accurately into the charity-shop box.

'Let's dump the lot, this is all just junk.'

'You never know, there might be something worth keeping. Look, you can't possibly chuck the family photos – oh my God, look at this, you dressed like a dowager.' Grace turned the pages, giggling over 1950s teenage fashions. 'We're quite alike, really, me and you as a teenager, the same square chins and bony cheeks.'

'My hair wasn't as thick as yours, and mousy, not dark.'

'I only remember you blonde. And our eyes are different, mine are the same as Dad's. Oh, this is sweet – is that baby you?'

'Must be, who else?'

'I wonder if there's one of your mother too.'

'Oh, I'm sure there must be, I'll look later. Here, hand it over.' Delia closed the album and put it in the bookcase. 'Is that it?'

'Nearly through, there's one more thing at the bottom here, this envelope. Delia Mark, Lower Fifth. Maybe it's your school reports.' Grace shook the envelope and some picture postcards fell out. They were black and white or sepia pictures already stamped with a one penny ultramarine showing George VI in profile. 'St Ives, a lighthouse, St Michael's Mount. Look, you wrote this one to someone called Miss Alison Jones. "I've made a new friend called Rosina. She is very posh and her house is 500 years old. I stopped a night there in a four-poster bed." Four exclamation marks. But you never posted it.'

'You know how that holiday ended.'

'Of course. Sorry.'

'Come on, we'll find an eatery in Westbourne Grove.'

'Wait a sec, there's something...' Grace slid out of the envelope a sheet of heavy off-white paper with a serrated edge showing it had been torn from a sketchbook. Unrepresentational shapes in thick watercolour were splashed across the page. 'This isn't bad at all. It looks sort of familiar, but I can't think what it reminds me of. Who's it by?'

'Don't ask me.'

'But you must know where it came from?'

'I forget.'

Grace was afraid of her mother's ageing. Suppose she went Stephen's way; or rather, don't ever suppose. She said irrelevantly, 'Vitamin C and E supplements, that's what you're supposed to take to ward off —' She stopped before saying Alzheimer's. Then, looking at her mother's face, she recognised that Delia had been lying. She did remember but didn't want to say. This was the forbidden territory, not to be discussed, policed by the spectre of Grace's long-lost, unknown step-grandmother, lurking in the unknown background of family history.

'I'm bored of this, let's go,' Delia said.

'Let's try that Chinese on Queensway.'

'Good idea.'

'What about this picture?'

'Do you think it's worth anything?'

'Could well be.'

'Let's sell it then. Can you…?'

'OK, I'll try.' Grace slid the picture into a gaudy spotted canvas bag, designed, she had told Delia, by Orla Kiely, and added, 'Dinner's on me.'

Chapter Eight

IN 1999 ROSINA and Matthew Reid retired to Cornwall despite their intention, while house-hunting, to stay safely east of the Tamar. Then they saw their dream house. It was, admittedly, in Cornwall but on the south-east coast, at the other end of the county from Polhearne, an art deco cube perched on a cliff top. The architecture was not back in fashion quite yet, but the garden had been famous once, though long neglected. Together the Reids set to work restoring and extending the flat landscaped area within its windbreak of trees and a 'hanging garden' of narrow terraces with steps down the steeply sloping cliff. Though they knew nobody in the district when they moved in, Rosina did not expect to keep her maiden name secret. Still, she was amused to answer the bell and find a Cornwall Nationalist Party canvasser on the step who announced that Rosina was a 'Rich White Settler' in a colonised country and the natives wanted her out. 'Racism's a criminal offence,' Rosina replied, slamming the door on him.

Before long the Reids were part of local life. Even I, living a long way off, was often told, 'You simply must meet Rosina, you'd have so much in common.' That seemed unlikely to me. I only have to touch a plant for it to shrivel up and die, while she was a committed gardener who won prizes at horticultural shows. But we were both computer bores, nerds according to our children, or – in advertiser-speak – silver surfers, though neither of us has grey hair – or we don't show it if we do. Rosina and I both have websites. Hers includes a comprehensive on-line camellia archive.

Elliot Rosenwald evidently assumed a woman in her sixties

would be set in old-fashioned ways. He wrote her a formal letter on heavy engraved paper.

She brought up the template she had created some time before and tapped in 'Dear Professor Rosenwald.'

'Thank you for your letter requesting information about my sister Mrs Lucia Hicks Polhearne —'

She inserted the word 'late' before 'sister'.

'— and her husband. I am afraid I am unable to help you. However your access to material that is already in the public domain will enable you to...' and so on.

It was the standard brush-off, composed a few years back when the 1950s came into fashion and students, desperate for an original subject, began to hunt out obscure artists from a period which was still in living memory. Rosina thought they would have trouble finding anything worth saying about paintings which she considered derivative and artificial; she found the shapes puerile and the colours unpleasant, his greens too khaki, his reds too mauve, like someone with a filter over his vision. But she owned one.

Lucia had sent it as a wedding present with a note. It was the first communication exchanged with the family in years. 'This is to acknowledge the announcement of your marriage. I am sending a painting Jon did the year he came back from America, even though you have turned against us, but Father and Mother still feel unable to forgive you...' Forgive! Father! Rosina had repeated, weeping in Matthew's arms. How could she!

They never hung the picture because they hated it. Her parents had refused to have any of Jon's work in the house because Father believed that artists were 'not our class' and a relation who painted was one to be ashamed of. Jon gave up painting when he married Lucia and became a gentleman of leisure at Polhearne, living with (and on) Father and Mother until Father died and Mother started living with them. Rosina was not invited, nor asked herself, back.

She had a pang of sadness when the children were born, but Matthew had enough relations for the two of them so it didn't really matter. At least so she told herself on the increasingly rare occasions that Polhearne came into her head, though unanswerable questions sometimes crossed her mind. Was it peculiar of Matthew to be so uninterested, not persuading her to bury the hatchet, in fact never even pinning down exactly what the hatchet was? And had Father remained an autocrat once there was another man in the house? Did Mother, as a widow, defer to her son-in-law? Did Lucia ever try to assert herself against her husband?

Rosina and Matthew went to Polhearne together only once, for her mother's funeral. They went up and down in one day, which meant twelve hours in trains. They sat at the back of the hideously familiar church where Sunday after Sunday Rosina had whiled away the time imagining a different life. As a child she'd believed that getting married was her only escape route and planned the ceremony without visualising the man: slipper satin and lilies. She had not been at Lucia's wedding. On the day she was ill, prostrated by aches and pains which were diagnosed as flu, sweating out anger, disgust and shame.

Mother's coffin was covered with white camellias. The new vicar was young, his voice reedy. Then Jon popped up in the pulpit as though by magic. He looked every inch the squire. His reading was in an appropriately grave tone. Rosina grabbed Matthew's hand. The accent and intonation made her shudder.

'He reads well,' Matthew whispered.

'It's a take-off, he's learnt to speak exactly like my father.'

Afterwards Lucia was as chilly as Rosina, Matthew monosyllabic and Jon kept his distance. Rosina exchanged a few nods and handshakes but she had become a stranger. Only the aged Mr Tremellen gossiped about Lucia's semi-detached marriage and Jon going off without her for weeks at a time.

'Who with, that's what I'd like to know, he won't be on his

lonesome, not him. Just like his old grandad, like I always said. Here.' He beckoned Matthew who bent to put his ear within whisper range. 'Old Mr Hicks, he was an old ram, right enough. Round Trevena way they called him the Town Bull.'

Reaching the front of the queue, Rosina said a formal goodbye. Matthew asked Lucia if she was going to keep the house.

'Of course, Jon would never move.'

'It must cost a fortune to run.'

'But there's an umbilical cord. We feel rooted. Unlike my sister.'

It wasn't worth discussion, or correcting mixed metaphors either. Rosina said, 'I wouldn't care if I never see it again so long as I live.'

'Don't worry, you aren't invited.'

The Reids left on that sour note, and did not meet Lucia again till 1980. By that time Jon was famous, and probably rich enough to keep the house going easily. The Reids were based in New York. Rosina was pregnant for the third time, not on purpose though that did not seem to be any consolation at all a month later when she miscarried. But just then she felt on top of the world. 'You always make me nicer than I really am,' she told Matthew, and he said, 'No, other people used to make you nastier than you really are. You can't be unhappy and nice.'

'Unhappy? Moi? Jamais. Never.'

'In Paris, you were. I saw it in your eyes.'

'Listen, mister, I was having a wonderful time! I modelled for Jacques Blanc, my picture's in the Galerie Nationale! People will mention me in their memoirs. I was a poet's muse, I was free! Think of the evening we met. Wasn't I having fun?' A party in Jean Ballamie's house in the Marais, Rosina in a tiny, tight black dress, with long loose black hair, her face all black-rimmed eyes, her figure mostly long black-tight legs, dancing, laughing. A man whose name she didn't know took her by the hand, whispered in her ear, gestured to the stairs. She was following him, neither willing nor unwilling, when the strange Englishman insisted he'd been promised the lady's company now. Neither the other man nor Rosina cared enough to argue. What difference did it make? But the Englishman didn't want sex. He wanted to talk, and then to talk some more, and then to woo her gradually, a slow process that no other man had ever thought necessary, and when at last they were in bed together it was unimaginably different. The experienced, unshockable Rosina believed she'd tried everything. Nothing left to learn, no male instinct or attribute she didn't know.

Except for love. She hadn't believed in it. Never expected it. Which, as Matthew said, just showed how wrong she could be.

'Happier now, anyway,' he said, and Rosina agreed. She loved New York.

At a gallery opening they overheard an English art dealer mention the Polhearnes. They were coming over. He was going to sell the Romneys. The dealer talked about death duties, critical that no attempt to avoid them had been made by the late Mr Polhearne, but gleeful because it meant sales and big commissions coming his way. Then he talked about fine old families dying out and the handicapped grandchild.

That weekend the *New York Times* ran a profile of Jon. The sale of the pictures was not mentioned; the journalist's interest had been provoked by a forthcoming TV programme about 'Chuck', whose life had been changed by Jon's book. He was a plumber by trade. His mother had died leaving him, among other things, a case of books from the 'Mind, body spirit' section of the local shop – their titles ranging from *Discerning the Mist*, *The Witches' Yearbook* to a teach-yourself book about *Guided Imagery to Connect with Angels*. He eventually read *Paint, Prophesy, Predict*, and was inspired to buy himself a box of paints. What happened to him then, the journalist wrote, 'is cloaked in mystery'.

Chuck set up his painting gear, and then 'basically I slipped into a trance, an altered state. I was no longer conscious of myself from within, I saw myself from the eye of a stranger. I was out of it, completely out of it, I don't know how long for. But when I woke up I saw that my hand had painted the face of a man, a strange man, and I knew – not his name – but what he was and what was going to happen to him. I'd never gone in for thinking about spiritualism or the supernatural or religion or anything like that. But this was prophetic, because the very next week that man's photograph was in the news. He had gone into an Australian school with a machine gun and massacred fifteen children.'

After that, the article said, the former plumber began to paint and predict full-time. When he first started he saw only a fleeting flicker, but with training and practice he learned to understand the images that he could summon up in waking dreams, recognising their energies and aura and significance. In this way, driven by forces 'of which we know little', he created spiritual images that brought people comfort, hope or even foreknowledge.

The first showing of the television programme – its subject, according to the pre-publicity, a seer, and according to reviewers, a charlatan – coincided with Jon's visit to New York. He put up his hands against camera lenses and wouldn't speak to any reporters, not a word about himself, his book or his Romneys. A *New York Times* profile writer struggled to reconcile the contradictory ideas of an influential and bestselling author who remained obsessively discreet.

'In a world where money is made through self-advertisement by people who hire personal public relations experts, Mr Polhearne of Polhearne has a unique selling point: modesty. This English aristocrat with his stately home in romantic south-west England, his London-tailored tweeds and his ancient name, might seem like the last person on earth to be a guru, guide or spiritual leader and as a matter of fact he never claims to be any of those things. His Oxford accent is never heard in public and he has never published another word. The more he is silent, reticent, unresponsive, the more people believe that he has the answers, proof if ever there was proof that less is more.'

Rosina said, 'Not a single mention of Lucia, you notice, or that he's taken over her name as well as everything else.'

'I think we should ask her round,' Matthew said. 'I'll leave a message at the Plaza Hotel.'

'Have her here? No! I couldn't. She wouldn't.'

But in the end, under pressure, Rosina could, Matthew would and Lucia did. She had changed; the 'jolly hockey sticks' girl was a brittle, anxious and obsessed woman who talked about nothing but her child. Polhearne was hardly mentioned, their parents not at all. Jon's name was uttered in a respectful tone. Rosina did not talk about him, but Matthew showed polite interest. 'What's he up to apart from writing the book? Did he take on all the jobs your father did? Chairman, trustee, magistrate, patron, all those local duties?'

'He never wanted to be involved with that kind of thing, he likes a quiet life,' Lucia said.

An easy one, she should say, Rosina thought and later listened to Matthew pondering about the effect of childhood trauma. 'That time after the shipwreck, in the water, alone with a dead body, expecting to die any minute, it could knock the stuffing out of a chap for ever. It's surprising he managed to finish writing a book. I wonder if there'll ever be another one. More likely he'll give it up, just like painting.'

'Do we have to talk about him?' Rosina asked.

'No. But people will, now he's famous. He's interesting.'

'Maybe. But not to me.'

When Lucia left for the clinic in Arizona where she was certain that this time Kit would be cured, Rosina said, 'I didn't feel I knew her at all, she could be a complete stranger. We never got on all that well as children but at least she was always a good sport, a jolly, bouncy girl, not at all the way she seems now.'

'She told me she was dreadfully hurt when you went off.'

'She knew why.'

'People said you were jealous.'

'I wasn't, I never wanted to inherit —'

'Jealous of him. Jon.'

'No!'

'They thought you had a crush on him, she says.'

'I hated him, I hated the lot of them, I still do.'

'Oh Rosina, you can't when she's so sad.'

'What about me? I was sad! I don't want to talk about it. But if I had ever envied Lucia, which I didn't, nobody could now. She seems defeated, beaten.'

'Also eminently kickable and evidently kicked,' Matthew said.

'Oh Matthew, no, surely not – she would never let – not nowadays!'

'She implied that she deserves it.'

Rosina surprised herself by throwing her glass (a good one, Steuben crystal) at the wall. It smashed and she burst into tears. Gasping, she wailed out, 'How could she? After Father?'

'I think she blames herself for Kit.'

'She couldn't. All those miscarriages, and then this – punishing herself. It's as if she's in some ghastly treadmill, round and round without escape.'

'Battered wives often blame themselves.'

That morning, Rosina had said a cool goodbye and Matthew went down to put Lucia in her cab. He remarked on a bruise, and Lucia said, 'It's just that I'm so unsatisfactory, it's my fault.'

Matthew quoted the words. Rosina interpreted them. 'She thinks she's no good in bed. Too inhibited. His fault but she blames herself.'

After Arizona Lucia took Kit to Toulouse, had no luck there and the following year spent some months in Budapest. They exchanged postcards and Christmas cards. The idea of reconciliation would surface only to be pushed under automatically and remain unexpressed. The two women met occasionally over the years, almost as strangers, in public places, their conversation polite, their voices cool.

Then suddenly, it was too late. Rosina did not even know Lucia was ill until a death notice appeared. A private cremation had already taken place.

Rosina wondered guiltily, Why didn't I try harder? Why didn't Matthew make me? Poor Lucia. And poor Kit. Never expected to survive even till his teens, he was a middle-aged baby, still in residential care and unaware that his mother was dead, or that he'd had a mother at all. As for Jon: an enigma. A cipher, wrapped in a riddle. A recluse holed up in a wing of the house, having let the bulk of it to his nutty acolytes for some sort of centre. He received rent from and was looked after by his followers, but never got involved in the courses they ran, never even met the students, much to the disappointment of paying guests. Some wrote newspaper articles complaining about it. If Kit's care home also complained of neglect, nobody published that.

Rosina shook herself away from that line of thought. 'Get on with it, girl,' she muttered, turning back to the Rosenwald letter. Then Nat padded silently in. He was an archaeologist who earned an irregular and puny income from intermittent short-term contracts because every university job he applied for had too many over-qualified applicants. He had come to Cornwall, was taking yet another higher degree, and said he was doing Rosina a favour by keeping her company. Morwenna, a high-earning banker, came down specially one weekend to accuse him of copping out. 'He's just scuttled back to Mum and home comforts, Mother, you shouldn't let him get away with it.' Rosina thought the price worth paying. 'I'm glad to have him back. I'd be even gladder if you came too.' Morwenna giggled, and said, 'In your dreams,' and left early in the afternoon with the excuse of beating the traffic.

Nat was doing forensic archaeology in Plymouth, acquiring a

qualification that could be applied to earning a living. 'How was your day?' Rosina asked.

'Good. One of the classes was about how forensic archaeology got going. Did you know it dates from when archaeologists saw the police searching the Yorkshire moors for Brady and Hindley's victims?'

'That was before you were born.'

'I've seen the shots. The windswept Saddleworth moor and a line of heavy boots trampling over the evidence, remember?'

'Vividly,' Rosina said.

'But you probably didn't notice how they destroyed the clues in the very process of searching for them.' Nat began to speak in a lecturing tone. Resigning herself, Rosina thought as she often had before that her son was one of nature's schoolmasters and if only she hadn't made the mistake of advising him to go to a teacher training college he might even have been one. 'You see, Mum, they should be reading the landscape without corrupting the traces interred in it, maybe looking from the air or using dog searches, but if not you've got to walk lightly – lightly's really important – to try and tell if there's been a clandestine burial, and if so exactly where it is. If there's a body buried the ground collapses eventually and you see a depression. Or there might be some artefacts on the surface, or abnormal vegetation.'

Rosina wasn't going to be taught about plants by Nat. 'The soil's enriched by aeration,' she said briskly.

'Or cadaveric putrefaction.'

'Ugh.'

'Actually most of it's ordinary field work, nothing disgusting,' he assured her. 'Someone's put the turf back without matching it up, that's a giveaway. And you get an ordinary planimetric map drawn, and once you can see the topography in broad outline you can work out where burial sites might be, which is what the cops hunting for Brady and Hindley's victims should have done.'

'I just hope you won't get much hands-on experience,' Rosina said.

'Oh Mum – I can't live on you for ever.'

'You'll be living off other people dying instead.'

'Yeah, well, no worries so far, today's dig was just a mock-up, the trainers buried animals for us to find.'

'Yuk.'

'No, it was really interesting, specially with so many of the sciences involved, not just the DNA, there's pathology, entomology, odontology too, you've no idea how many details can be significant. So we found it and excavated and measured and took photos and records for going to court. And then we had to collect the remains and put them in labelled bags, because in a real case I'd have to make sure they get to the morgue.'

'After which someone else takes over, I hope.'

'No, I'd clean them up, and lay them out in anatomical position, and then check that the pathologist keeps samples. Apparently the best are a molar tooth and a mid-shaft section of femur but they aren't always available.'

'Well, I'm glad you're so cheerful but it doesn't sound like archaeology to me at all,' Rosina said rather sourly.

'It's just an extra qualification, Mum. I don't suppose there'll be much call for my forensic skills down here but if there is, someone's got to do it.'

Rosina hadn't noticed the time. 'Nat, I must get on.'

'What are you up to?'

'I was putting off an American about JH and started wondering why I still do.'

'I've been waiting for you to notice.'

'What d'you mean?'

'I can see why you were discreet while Lucia was around, though I'd have thought she'd be pleased to dish the dirt considering what a shit he is, but you don't have to keep quiet about him now.'

'It's become an automatic reaction.'

'What's this one asking for?'

'It isn't clear from his letter. He's an academic, just says he wants to come and talk.'

'Say yes, it's cool.'

'D'you think?'

'If a poor starving scholar can waste his time on that lot we might as well waste ours on letting him in.'

Chapter Nine

'HI, IT'S CONNIE THORNE?' The tone rising like a question, one that I could answer. I often get muddled with the names of the many interviewees for my book but I didn't need reminding who Connie was.

She said, 'I've got lots to show you, come soon, come tomorrow.'

Prompted by her call I spent the rest of the day tidying up the section on the wreck of the *City of Benares*. Next morning I set off early, took far longer getting down to St Budy than expected – local traffic must have doubled in five years, Cornish roads aren't up to it – found my way to Trevena but then drove down and up and down the hill from the village, passing an obscure gateway three times, before realising it had to be the lane leading to Goonzoyle. It was flanked by Cornish hedges, which means dry stone walls overgrown with grass and, in this case, a swathe of primroses smelling swooning-sweet, but the surface was appalling, pitted with water-filled holes and with scant remnants of ancient tarmac protruding above a stony base. I drove cautiously along to an overgrown gravel sweep. The house was built in a dip, presumably to give it some protection from the wind, so the sea was out of sight. That had probably knocked six figures off the price.

The house was even more peculiar than the gazetteer made it sound.

'*Goonzoyle Manor. Rebuilt for Isaiah Hicks Esq.*'

I'd looked Isaiah Hicks up. He was one of those men, born in poverty in the eighteenth century, who managed to make themselves. At the time Cornwall was still a place apart,

separated by distance from modernising progress. Metaphorically, it had been stuck in the Middle Ages right up till the
Civil War. Its inhabitants (male), apart from a few hereditary
landowners, were small farmers or labourers, plus the odd
tradesman in the few tiny towns. Then quite suddenly up popped
a new native middle class, getting rich on the lucky local
combination of underground minerals, cheap human labour,
water power and deep water harbours to take the stuff away.
Boys who went down the mines as labourers ended up as mine
captains, sent their sons to public schools and acquired
substantial houses such as Goonzoyle and proceeded to
embellish or ruin them, depending on your point of view.

*'Late C19 incorporating earlier features, with C20 extensions.
Shale rubble with rag slate, granite, brick and tile features and
Delabole slate roof. Rectangular with short north-east wing
which includes earlier walling. 3 storeys. South-west front has 6
windows above 4 windows, bay to west, central doorway, porch.
Smaller attic windows to gables. Turret (formerly tower) to north
corner. Internal hall, 6 pillars, Italianate plaster mouldings, tiled
floor, probably C19.'*

Before the energetic Isaiah got his mitts on it this house might
have been gracious or at least comfortable-looking. But the
'earlier features' had been swallowed up behind an unhappy
combination of great oblong granite blocks with decorative lines
of red brick inserted above each row of windows. The windows
themselves were of varying shapes, some tall sashes, others with
rounded or arched tops, some narrow, like arrow slits. The
bricks in the chimneys were set at decorative angles. A Cornish
shield of fifteen besants – circles set in rows of five, four, three,
two and one – had been carved above the date 1871.

During the long years that had passed since the architect and
client had indulged their flights of fantasy, the gaudy frontage
would have been regarded as marvellous, then hideous and soon
unforgivable, in quick succession. But popular taste goes round

in circles and a new generation admires the high Victorian style, so now Goonzoyle had been designated a listed building protected from demolition or change. I thought it was perfectly hideous.

There was a small portico with a triangular roof which was not much protection from horizontal rain and flurries of stinging sleet, and a front door newly painted in glossy black, though the brass lion's head knocker was tarnished. The bell was a kind of antique pulley, but nobody responded when I rang and knocked. I was just wondering whether to go round the back when an enormous four-wheel drive pulled up behind the VW and Connie Thorne jumped out, followed by a small black and white dog, soaking wet, prancing and yapping.

'Hello, welcome, nice to see you, hope you've not been waiting long, I've been up to Bodmin for a sale. Digger! Digger, here, boy. This is Digger, I hope you don't mind dogs, stop it, Digs, get off her coat, he's a Jack Russell – down, Digger! – he was at the animal shelter, I've rehomed him. Come in, come in, what are we doing standing here in the rain? I'll just get this out of the – such luck that I caught sight of it, they'd got it under a rolled carpet, I had to buy a couple of deck chairs in the same lot, but it's exactly like the ones that used to belong in here, isn't it wonderful? Oh, thanks, if you don't mind, that's really kind.'

I helped to lug Connie Thorne's find out of the car. It was an indisputably ugly domestic object, two sets of stags' antlers mounted on an oak board to make a gruesome kind of coat rack. 'We'll put it down on this rug, that's right, I'll get Spike to help nail it up.'

The entrance hall was elaborately tiled. As the terrier dashed wetly around, its paws skidded on the smooth surface. A dim light came through a high stained glass window with medieval-style lettering, flowers and faces signifying something though it would take a while to work out what. Connie's appalling new acquisition would fit in here perfectly. She said:

'I'm so thrilled by all this, it'll be lovely to show you everything. Did I tell you about my plan to track down the family portraits and heirlooms? I'm going to find out all the details about them, in fact that's what Spike's doing as we speak, he's been at the County Record Office but he'll be back soon, I'd like for you to meet him.' The dog was dashing round sniffing for intruders. 'Here, Digger, heel. God, it's like a monsoon out there.' Connie flung off her coat with a shower of water on to the brown and yellow floor. 'Put yours here too, and we'll go and warm up.'

Connie followed the dog and I followed behind Connie's ample jeans and paint-stained sweatshirt into the unimproved squalor of the rear part of the building, along a passage with cracked lino on the floor and walls painted in hospital green, through swinging fire doors, on through an industrial sized, disused kitchen with grease marks on the walls and a sinister smell and into what must once have been a pantry or scullery which was now set up as a temporary den, with a two-ring cooker, three plastic chairs at a picnic table and a trolley standing in for a store cupboard.

'I'm getting my new kitchen installed next month, till then it's camping out back here. Smoke?'

'I don't, thanks.'

'Sure? You needn't take any notice of the No Smoking signs.'

'What kind of institution was it?'

'When they requisitioned it in the war there was a hospital for wounded officers. Then the National Health took it over for geriatrics, then after that it was leased to a women's refuge but not for long, too expensive for a charity to keep up. I can have every night in a different ward or a bay or an expensive private room. The outside's protected but you wouldn't believe what they've done inside over the years, the poor old place has been properly mucked about with.'

The smell of bottled gas reminded me of excavation camps but the coffee beans which Connie ground in a handmill came from a bag labelled Fortnum and Mason, and the biscuits she offered were best Belgian chocolate.

'The house must have been very grand,' I said.

'It was smaller in my time, just what you might call a "gentleman's residence". All the extensions went up after the war and I'm going to get rid of them. It'll be a great improvement.'

'It's still a big place even without the extras.'

'Yes, big, but welcoming, that's what I remember, I used to think the house was saying, come in, be comfortable, it's warm and cosy here. D'you know, all these years on, I can still see the dining room shining, the polished table, and the silver, and the rows of glasses. They lived above their means, though I didn't know it at the time. Sid left me nicely, thank you, so I'll be able to restore everything, you'll see, I've already found some of the original furniture, I guess someone saw me coming! You'd never credit it, but the actual Goonzoyle dining table came up in at a sale in Par this summer, it had been over Bodmin way, and I got dead ringers for the chairs in an antique shop in Truro, they're being recovered with burgundy velvet now. And I found a couple of photos of the other rooms, the library and the drawing room in about 1900, some with the family in, they were in the Cornish Studies Library in Redruth, so I'll be able to make everything fit.'

'Don't you have your own family photos?'

'Oh no, dear, my family didn't have – oh, I see what you mean, you didn't think I was the daughter of the house, did you?'

'I thought that's why you wanted to research your ancestors, isn't that what you told me when we spoke?' I'd imagined her consulting family research centres, parish registers, baptismal records and archives of The Latter Day Saints. Or she'd join the queues in the Record Office, where people searched eagerly for evidence to show they were descended from someone interesting, a highwayman or pirate or criminal hanged at a crossroads.

Connie said, 'I should have explained. This was the big house, my dad was the outdoor man, gardening, handyman, jack of all trades. The Hicks family lived here then, I don't know if there's any of them still around. Me and my brother, we were just the kids with their noses pressed to the window wishing they could live like the posh people.'

A gaffe; I was embarrassed. 'I'd understood you said it was your childhood home.'

'I wish. But no way. I was the kitchenmaid at fourteen, promoted to housemaid, no less, when I was just fifteen, before I got a job up in Devon, under-nursery maid, just a slavey really, nobody'd do it nowadays. We lived in a tied cottage, one up one down and an earth closet. It's difficult to imagine now, how we all squeezed in, me and Ted, our dad and Nancy. Only then the war came and Dad went and so did I, and Nancy took off with her fancy man.' She paused and added, 'Old history.'

I said, 'Who lives in the cottage now?'

'It's long gone but it was over there, look where I'm pointing, behind those trees.'

I put the steaming mug down to look through the small rear window into a muddy yard. 'I'll find the plan for the courtyard,' Connie said and left the room. She'd left a pile of paper topped with a typed list on the table and being magnetised by the written word – even if it's only the cartoon on a cereal packet or ingredients on a ketchup bottle – I unintentionally and automatically scan-read at a glance a list of names beginning Philip Hicks, Edward Hicks. These must all be previous residents. Isaiah Hicks, Jabez Gilbert, Thomasina Gilbert, Philomena Mary Gilbert. Coincidentally, I knew about her, having reviewed a biography by a specialist in women's studies from the Midwest. Philomena Mary was an 'English Miss', travelled to Russia in the 1860s to work as a governess and in the process turned a Grand Ducal family into lifelong Anglophiles.

When Connie came back holding a roll of paper I said, 'I do

apologise, I shouldn't pry.'

'It isn't private, in fact I've been saving a copy for you to look at when you've got time.' She scrabbled a heap of paper into a folder. 'Here, put that in your bag, will it fit? Good. Take a look when you've got time. I thought your husband might be interested too, this is the first step in a history of Goonzoyle, who lived here and so on, Spike's been busy on it.'

'Very useful for you to have a researcher, I must say.'

'Researcher, au pair, lodger.'

'Did you advertise?'

'No, we met when he was going round the coastal footpath. He came down here to join the 3Ps at St Budy, but he said it was on its last legs, only a couple of people there.'

'What's it like? I've never known what goes on there.'

'He's not said much, except that it was full of dead animals.'

'Dead...?'

'Hunting trophies. My second husband had them, but not as many. Spike made a list.' What looked like a shopping list, held on the fridge by a strawberry-shaped magnet, was headed Trophy Heads. An even, backward-sloping handwriting listed skull mounts, cape mounts, skins and sets, of deer (red, roe, fallow and muntjak), springbok, impala, nyala, otters, stoats, possums, foxes and various birds. 'They're all over the place, up on the walls.'

'It sounds nightmarish.'

'Spike said it was really creepy.'

'You wouldn't expect them to go in for shooting at a place like that.'

'They told him most of the trophies were shot years ago, before the war and some before the first war, but the trouble is being a veggie, it upset him. It's supposed to be all to do with death being part of life, and something about embracing destiny, I didn't get all of it. But I don't think Spike did either. Anyway, I'd told him to look in if he was nearby again, so when he pitched up with his backpack I asked him to stay on, and am I glad!'

'You didn't let a perfectly strange man move into the house?' My voice must have expressed horror, because Connie patted me soothingly on the arm and said:

'No worries, we're not so uptight in Oz, I know you don't even pick up hitch-hikers any more here. But Spike's been staying a couple of weeks now and I've not been found murdered in my bed yet.'

'But Connie, d'you know anything about him?'

'I know he's from Scotland, that's obvious the minute he opens his mouth, and I know he's sweet and kind and good fun. Is that enough?'

'Hardly – he could be...'

'An axe murderer? Actually, he's got a history degree from Glasgow and he's a carpenter handyman, and he came on here from Polhearne. OK?'

I quelled the impulse to interfere, telling myself she knew what she was doing and in any case it wasn't my business. Instead, I remarked, 'There was an article about what they do there in Tuesday's paper. Was he what they call a postulant? It seems to be another word for apprentice.'

'I suppose he must have been, he'll be back soon, he can tell you about it.'

'Connie, you did get some sort of reference, didn't you?'

'You ought to trust people more. I go on instinct. Actually, isn't that him now? Spike! Come and meet him.' The heavy stereo beat filled the air as a Peugeot soft top in canary yellow pulled up with a spraying of gravel beside Connie's battered four-wheel drive. Spike: mid-twenties, tall, jelled spikes of gravity-defying blond hair, fray-edged denim shorts, a skimpy vest and bare feet. Rings and studs like polka dots scattered on all visible skin, which is to say, the skin I saw at first glance before averting my eyes. It's not that I disapprove of body piercing, just that it makes me feel sick. Which may well be what it's meant for.

It had a quite different effect on Connie. She looked soft and pink and sparky. They kissed cheek to cheek. He handed her a couple of supermarket bags, and then started opening the roof, apparently to take the surfboard. 'See you later,' Connie said to him, and to me, 'Look, he's done the shopping.' I followed her back along the passage, and realised she smelt of Patou's Joy, but also there was an unmistakable whiff of sex and sweaty young man on her. First I wondered what it felt like rubbing up against skin combined with all those little lumps of metal; then phrases such as 'toy boy' and 'fortune hunter' flashed through my mind. But when Connie faced me again in the kitchen, she looked so bright and lithe, so rejuvenated, that I thought, Better than a face lift any day. Why shouldn't she?

But what an idiot I'd been. I wasn't shocked to think of Connie, at her age, having sex with a boy in his twenties, in fact it seemed much less exploitative than the socially acceptable opposite, and nobody turns a hair when old men have young women as their arm candy. What did shock me was my own surprise.

'Did you see the new motor?' Connie asked. 'We got it yesterday.'

'Lovely – but will it have room for your saleroom finds?'

'I'm keeping the other as well. Spike's very practical, he's had to be.'

'Has he?'

'The poor boy's on his own since his mother died. Adoptive mother. Actually, you can tell him – in fact that's why I asked you over – or partly, of course, I wanted you to come over anyway.'

'What's he —'

'He's on the track of his birth parents. Apparently his real mother died when he was tiny and he was put out for adoption.'

'He's got the names, has he?'

'I don't ask, he'll tell me when he's good and ready. Look what he's found about the people who lived here, this is all in chronological order. He's got back to Goonzoyle in medieval tithe maps, that's the first mention so far, there was a family called Pentreath, right back in the early 1600s. Then Gilberts, up to Jabez who only had daughters. The older one was the heiress, Thomasina. She married Isaiah Hicks and scooped the lot.'

I told Connie what I recalled about Philomena Mary's adventures and promised to pass on my review copy of the book.

'Great! She must have taken after her grandpa, Isaiah Hicks was nothing unusual, educated at a posh school up country and well off, but Thomasina and Philomena, they came from enterprising stock. Jabez was a self-made man, he was down the mine at the age of ten like his father and grandfather and great-grandfather before him and worked his way from having nothing to being a mine captain. And his great-grandson was a colonel of a regiment and he married the Honourable Blanche, a lord's daughter.'

'Social mobility in action.'

'So now I've got Spike finding out about mining and miners, and Methodism. And while he's on to that I'm getting on with my rebuilding.'

She unrolled her architect's drawing. The plan showed the back yard bounded by its old stone walls, but with the cobblestones lifted and paving stones laid. The garden designer had visualised tubs of orange trees and terracotta pots of lavender and rosemary with espaliered fruit trees against the walls.

Connie said, 'You can imagine the change from the old days. That's where the rain-water tank was, I can still remember pumping the water up into a bucket, you had to heave on an iron bar, up and down, for ages.' The dog was whining. 'Digger needs to go out. Want to come and have a look now the rain's slackened off a bit?'

We both fetched our coats and went out into what had become a general moistness. There was standing water on the ground. I could almost feel the movement of my hair as it was frizzed into corkscrews by the damp air. The dog barked sharply, turned round in a rapid pursuit of its own tail and then dashed off like a rocket.

'He won't go far.' Connie said.

This rear courtyard of the house had been a cobbled quadrangle, bounded by the back wall of the house and on two sides by long single-storey sheds with paint-peeled doors hanging off their hinges. The far side had been protected from the weather by a high stone wall, now mostly tumbled into a weed-grown heap. Beyond it was a muddle of unmanaged trees and scrub.

'Jeepers but it's cold out here. Digger! Here, Dig-dig-digger! Where's he gone? Digger!'

Connie's shouts were blown away on the raw south-east wind. Being at the back of the house one couldn't see the sea, but it was only half a mile away down the hill and I tasted salt on my lips.

'Digger, come on.'

'Should we go and see if he's got stuck?'

'We'd hear if – but yes, we'd better.' I felt I had to follow her out of the courtyard and along a narrow, muddy path fringed by dripping, prickly bushes. Through them I just caught glimpses of the sea, the sand dunes, the square tower of Trevena Church, a mine chimney, its dark finger pointing upward like an awful warning.

'Have you got a lot of land?' I asked.

'Just the garden and a half-acre field, more than enough for me. Digger! Wait – ssh.' She held up her finger while we listened out. 'There, can you hear?'

She began to push her way through pathless undergrowth, so I plunged in her wake into the prickles of gorse, brambles, blackberries, stinging nettles and a good deal of random plastic litter. We could hear yapping now, oddly muffled, and it was difficult to tell what direction it came from.

'Digger, it's OK, sweetie, I'm coming!'

I was so close on Connie's heels that I came right up against her broad wet back when she suddenly stopped. There was some kind of hole in the ground ahead, virtually invisible in the undergrowth. 'He's here, but I can't see —'

I suddenly grabbed Connie's arm tightly. 'Hey, come back, that could be a mineshaft.'

'There's none of those round here.'

'They aren't always known about. Haven't you read news stories about cottages collapsing into forgotten shafts?'

'Yes, in the States, but surely not here. Digger!'

'The trouble is that he's small enough to squirm into tiny spaces.'

'Oh, God, what shall I do? He sounds – he's in trouble. I've got to – I can't leave him. Digger, I'm here!' Her voice had lost its vigour and certainty, so I said:

'I'll call the rescue services, shall I?' I had to walk up to a ridge to make the call. The view was spectacular from there, with the cluster of houses in the village below a grassy slope, and beyond it sand dunes, sea and the white beacon of a rock lighthouse. Something in the dripping greenery smelt sweetly fresh.

The story needed repeating several times: the dog chased a rabbit, I explained patiently, it squirmed under bushes and fell down a mineshaft. I wondered what image the girl in the call centre was visualising from her desk somewhere in far-off India. But she passed on enough urgent information for rescuers to come rushing. They looked like people who loved their work and there were a lot of them, more, surely, than would turn out for an animal in any other country.

By mid-afternoon we were still there, standing in a renewed downpour. I'd been back to the house to collect a couple of umbrellas, used the bathroom and hovered guiltily in the warm kitchen. Then Spike came in.

'Hi, what's going on?' A Scottish accent with Estuary extras. He took a water filter out of the fridge and drank from the jug.

I explained awkwardly, my tone not quite right since I don't know the language of the generation after my children and before my grandchildren and am not as unselfconscious as the outgoing and spontaneous Connie, who took in hitch-hikers without qualms and, trusting people, found them trustworthy. I'd never have given a lift to this rather dangerous-looking young person in the first place.

Spike bounded athletically out of the door and ran up the path. I followed more slowly, cautious on the slippery mud, to find a growing cluster of people, some in uniform, some wearing plastic badges. They'd come from the Fire Service and the Cornwall Mineshaft Rescue Unit. As I stood there a rescue helicopter from the Royal Naval Station at Culdrose descended in its whirlwind on to the hillside, the owner of the neighbouring farm arrived on his tractor and a tourist told everyone in turn that he was a keen caver and would go straight to the rescue now as ever was if only the fusspots and busybodies would give over with their health and safety regulations. But officialdom had decided that specialist equipment had to be brought over, and a safety crew must be standing by in case anyone got into difficulty. 'The safety of our personnel is paramount at all times,' one of them recited.

I suspected they were really waiting for the news media to turn up.

People stood round chatting in low voices like mourners at a funeral. Some prowled impatiently. A man who had been examining a pile of stones walked towards a clump of his friends with something in his hand. 'Look.'

'What's that? Let's see, give it here.'

'Terribly rusty – careful.'

'I think it's a First World War bayonet, my old dad had one.'

Connie slumped to sit on a crate labelled 'Breathing Apparatus' under a large yellow and black umbrella printed with the words 'Duchy of Cornwall'. A man with a yellow jacket and hard hat worn over a dark suit started telling her about the variety of what he called 'present physical safety hazards'. The possibilities included other openings into the shaft, unstable high walls or mine buildings that could easily collapse at a touch. You could get lost in the tunnels, fall down other internal shafts or meet disease-carrying, predatory animals that lived in the old mine. You could find, touch and be made sick by old explosives, drums of chemicals or being exposed to toxic mine tailings. There might be poisonous gases or low oxygen levels.

'Nobody ever said there was a shaft here, I'd have remembered.' Connie was by now pale and tearful.

'That's all right, my lovely, you weren't to know,' a man in uniform said. Spike tried to drape a blanket round her shoulders, but she pushed it aside. I noticed that in public they were being very discreet. She took a deep breath and said crossly:

'It should have shown up when my lawyer did the searches.'

'They aren't all recorded, these old shafts.'

'Don't they have names? Wheal Rose, White Alice, South Crofty, Wheal Prosper – so what's this one?'

'It might never have been a proper mine, see, could be a trial shaft, they dug them out, those old tinners, but most of them came to nothing.'

'So they left booby traps behind,' I muttered.

After a while some sausages were chucked into the black hole. Later they reached the stage of shining a light beam on to the dejected little animal. It was quite dark by the time a man kitted out in full climbing gear began to lower himself down under carefully rigged searchlights. Connie was allowed to go close enough to see for herself that the jagged rocky shaft was wet and filthy. Digger barked furiously as the strange man came closer. Suddenly a cloud of creatures swirled out of the shaft like a brief tropical storm: bats.

The climber had attached a throat mike and was giving a running commentary as he descended. 'Doesn't sound very glad to see me, does he? It's all right now, good boy.' A jury-rigged speaker broadcast his words to the crowd, now getting on for forty people. 'He's seen me. OK, doggie, here's the cavalry to the rescue.'

'Is he all right?' someone shouted.

'Yeah yeah, he's fine, bit dazzled by the light. He's – uh oh. He's vomiting up, must have been something he ate, were those the same sausages we all had? Another metre to go, and – we've landed! One small step for me, one giant step for... Oh.' His voice stopped.

'Dan. Dan, are you OK?'

'What's going on? Dan!'

Dan answered in a different tone, not jolly and pleased with himself, as he had been before. 'Can you hear me up there?'

'Loud and clear.'

'OK, well, I've picked up the dog now but looks like he's done a bit of digging. It's soft, you know, down here, dusty, muddy, like it's a kind of overlay above shingle.'

'OK, mate, sounds as per usual.'

'Only the dog's found something. He's dug up bones.'

'Cattle. No worries. They fall in all the time.'

'I think these are human bones.'

One of the officials had taken his mobile off its belt clip. He pressed one key three times and spoke.

'Hey, can you hear me up there? They're definitely human.'

'We'll need an archaeologist.'

'No, this is something else – it's a police job. There's bits of clothing too.'

Somebody was saying, 'Are you all right?'

Embarrassed, I gabbled, 'Sorry, so sorry, I'm fine.'

I didn't know what could have come over me. I'm a crime novelist, and those were only old bones.

I wiped the cold sweat off my face. 'Just a dizzy moment, please forget it.'

'OK, cool,' Spike said.

Someone was shouting, barking an order. 'Don't touch, don't

disturb the remains. Pull him up, get him out of there.'

'Who can it be?' Connie whispered.

We stood and waited. I felt shaky, and couldn't think why until it came to me that this was a reminder of that other occasion, back in 1976. I'd encountered death at the bottom of a long drop before, and not far away from where we were standing. My subconscious had made the connection more quickly than my brain.

Connie was shaking; suddenly she looked a hundred years old. The farmer called across with a kind of dour satisfaction, 'So now you'll likely be selling up again.'

Connie looked at him blankly.

Spike said, 'Cheer up, Connie, it's not like they're anyone you know.'

Connie stared at him with an expression he might not have seen before, disapproving, on her dignity, no longer a lover but a dowager quelling a cheeky child.

'There she blows,' the farmer called, and pointed his stubby, grimy finger. Someone in a yellow hard hat emerged from below, holding the dog. As soon as Digger touched the ground he made a dash for his mistress. She picked him up and hugged the whimpering, wagging bundle. Then, ignoring Spike's outstretched hand, she walked slowly down the path towards Goonzoyle.

Chapter Ten

WHEN ELLIOTT ROSENWALD returned to Oxford he found the letter from Rosina Reid in his pigeonhole at the college where he'd been given a 'visiting fellowship' for the period of his sabbatical. On further consideration she might be willing to cooperate, but perhaps he could first explain why he was interested in Jon Hicks and what line his book would take.

Could, he thought, but won't. His exposition was going to burst on the world like an unexpected thunderclap, which was what it had felt like the day Simon Kelly first came to see him.

In the spring of 2002 Elliot had published two short articles about the St Ives artists of the early post-war period. He was reluctantly coming to the conclusion that he'd squeezed the subject dry, said all there was to say. It was time to move on. He settled on the East Anglian painters of the later twentieth century as his next subject, and arranged to spend a month of the summer vacation in London, where he would collect material for a grant application and research proposal.

He found a summer rental in north London's Dartmouth Park through an advertisement in the London Review of Books. Late one afternoon, returning from Tate Britain, he was annoyed to find someone waiting for him. Propped against the door of his third-floor walk-up was an almost insultingly grungy young man. The weather was hot, the man was sweaty and smelly. What's wrong with washing? Elliot wondered, taking in the studs and chains, Doc Martens, four-letter slogan on the shirt and dirty backpack.

'Professor Rosenwald? Hi. I've brought something for you to look at.'

This wouldn't be the first time a would-be artist had doorstepped Elliot Rosenwald. He said, 'What makes you suppose that I would do so? It is my settled policy never to give advice on work.'

'You'll be interested in this.'

'Anyway, how the hell did you find me? You can't just turn up here and —'

'There was this article I saw, in the *Standard*, it was about how you're the authority —'

'Is that what this is about? You have something for authentication?'

'It's in here.'

Elliot wasn't going to let a stranger into his apartment. That bag could have anything in it. 'No. You have to leave now.'

The young man swung the backpack down on the lino floor, knelt to unpeel the velcro fastener and revealed that inside the modern waterproof fabric was another bag made of faded green canvas fastened by leather straps. After a short struggle with the rusty buckles he opened the flap, revealing a stack of papers and what looked like a sketchbook.

'What is this?' Elliot barked.

'Take a look, you'll be interested, honest.' The documents were on pale blue, tissue-paper thin paper of the obsolete foolscap size, carbon copies of something typed on a manual machine, with pencilled corrections. The words were so faded as to be very difficult to read.

'You don't expect me to decipher this, do you?'

'No way, just see if anything looks familiar. It's worth your while.'

The pages felt at once fragile and dirty. Elliot bent down to touch, fastidiously, with the tips of his finger and thumb. 'And this? What is it?'

The younger man opened the sketchbook and held up a page to show him before quickly snapping it closed. 'Looks familiar?'

'You're asking me to identify a picture at a glance?'

'No, I just want to catch your attention, Professor Rosenwald.'

He'd done that all right. 'Now this.' He held the typescript up to display it.

Elliot kept a poker face as he put on his reading glasses and squatted – taking time to be gratified by his own suppleness – to examine the typescript's first page. 'This looks like —' he began, and stopped himself making the suggestion. 'What is this?'

'Thought you'd be interested,' the man said triumphantly, and swooped to snatch the book away.

'I haven't seen enough.'

'A taster.'

This typescript might, just might be gold dust. Elliot said, 'Will you entrust me with it?'

'It'll cost you.'

'Why don't we go in and sit down.' His mind flitted over the bed he'd left unmade that morning. Would he think —? No. He wouldn't. Elliot had learnt from experience. He was proved right, as the visitor passed the tumbled bedclothes without a glance, cleared the breakfast crumbs away with a sweep of his arm and put everything down on the table.

He opened pages marked with yellow stickies and held them for Elliot to see. 'The ability is not capable of acquisition, it is inborn.' The word was crossed out, and 'innate' written above it in pencil. 'It will not be found in persons who are in thrall to the usual mental methods of Clairaudience, Clairvoyance and Clairsentience, nor by self-named mediums. It manifests through art itself. And who can say what dreams may come when the artist is in his altered state, what dreams and nightmares, what visions he may paint, of moments still to come, poised, inevitable.' The last typed word had a line through it, with 'unavoidable' written above in cursive letters.

Elliot felt – what did he feel? Shaken? Thrilled? No, he felt like a man who needed a drink.

'Recognise anything?'

Elliot peeled his tongue off his soft palate. 'That's from *Paint, Prophesy, Predict*. Is this provenanced?'

'First off, what about the pics? Are they any good?'

'Good – no; but interesting, yes, quite, to social history more than art history.'

'Not signed though.'

'The sketchbook appears to be the work of a minor artist known as Jix – very minor, interesting only because of his association with the artists' colony of St Ives for a short period in the 1950s.'

'Gotcha! I knew it! I knew they were Jix, aka Polhearne. That's got to authenticate the typescript, wouldn't you say?'

'If they were found to be connected throughout, perhaps. But you're going too fast. You came by them – found them, that is – in what way?'

'Right, it's deal-time. This lot is full of corrections. The para you saw, those words were innate and unavoidable in the published version, I've checked, and there's other examples too, longer ones, some whole paragraphs changed. This has got to be a carbon of the original version and the sketchbook's something else. I did think of offering the collection back to him, but he didn't answer my message. Anyway, there's more money in it from someone else.' He didn't add, 'like you'. Instead after a pause he said, 'Don't you agree?'

'Were they in a sale? A shop?'

'The deal is, you authenticate and then I say where they came from. You write your book, go on telly, get your tenure or whatever the hell else you fancy. I get the money.'

Elliot felt literally nauseous with tension. The word 'deal' was hovering on his lips and, rather too quickly, he said it aloud.

The other man was unexpectedly canny. He produced three copies of a contract: dates, deadlines, the details of the deal, agreements about copyright and confidentiality, and the number of security photocopies to be made and how they would be kept secret, and a very substantial advance payment. Elliot had to raise the money by selling one of his clever finds, a little painting by Lee Krasner, wife of Jackson Pollock.

It was going to be worth it. There would be fame, fortune and a tenured professorship in it. Meanwhile, hard work: Elliot, so prolix in conversation, was terse in the notes he dictated into his recorder or put in his memo. As he scanned a copy of Rosina's letter, he spoke aloud to himself.

'Family piety, query. Mem: tread softly. Important appear to show reverence J's art/respect his writing. Promise serious analysis, using requisite comparanda. Mention analagous work.'

And that was where he'd stop.

Aloud, though alone, Elliot said, 'The rest will be silence. So far.'

Chapter Eleven

THE PAPER CROWNS were, one might say, the crowning horror, and that was exactly what Delia would say one of these days, to me among others. Even at the time she could see herself, hear her own voice, turning the incongruous image into a titbit in the tale, repeated because bad moments turn into good stories. She could imagine it already, crisp, neat phrases designed to entertain, without waffle, all inessentials omitted, including the shock, the pain. She'd be glossing over the sheer, nasty, shaming squalor of the moment when she saw her father shrinking back, cowering in uncomprehending terror from the uniformed police.

They arrived in full view from the lounge. Grace, who'd been restlessly prowling, was the first to notice their light flashing and siren at full blast. The car sped in with a scattering of gravel and an emergency stop beside the undertaker's limo which, with tactless practicality, seemed to be parked permanently at the ready outside the 'retirement home'. The residents were probably past noticing. Nor had most of them reacted to the birthday cake with its nine candles, one per decade, or to the mini explosions as the care assistants pulled the crackers. Few of the inmates were strong enough to pull them apart.

'I'll be your strong right arm, shall I?' one of the helpers offered. Stephen had forgotten how to speak English before he forgot how to speak at all and even the language of his youth left him. His head nodded up and down, repeatedly, as it always did. The volunteer was a well-meaning girl, kind and gentle. She'd have to be, spending her weekend in the nursing home. When Delia murmured that her father wasn't keen on loud noises, she nodded understandingly and dissected the scarlet crepe paper carefully, discarding the phosphorus strip. She pulled out a plastic racing car, unfolded a flimsy pink zigzag of tissue paper and perched it on the scaly, brown-spotted dome of Stephen's skull. The gaudy bits of paper perched on grey hair or bald pates seemed incongruous and insulting, a reminder that these inmates were in their second childhood.

Mrs Collingwood, who owned this 'home' as well as half a dozen similar establishments in other parts of the Home Counties, had led off with 'Happy Birthday'. She was a well-maintained woman in her forties, with unlined skin, blonde curls, manicured nails and impregnable make-up. Grace clocked her suit, last year's Escada, worn with a Marks and Spencer shirt and a knock-off Prada bag.

'Happy birthday to you...' The staff joined in. Grace said loudly, 'Happy birthday, Grandad,' and then zipped her lips but Delia and two younger women who were visiting relations that day exchanged embarrassed glances and muttered a few words. 'Happy birthday, dear Stephen...' Most of the inmates remained uninvolved, though a couple automatically raised cracked voices, and one tiny, hunched woman suddenly emitted a clear, resonant tenor.

'Our Norah was in the Bach Choir,' Nurse Mavis told Delia, and doubled the volume to add, 'Weren't you, Norah?'

The voices trailed off. Only Norah's rich notes, which seemed to have no apparent connection with the singer's wizened face, soared joyously above the interruptions as doors slammed and feet tramped and messages on the officers' personal radios broadcast their non-stop mutter. Two tall, young, strong men in uniform came in, exotic intruders from a world long lost to most of the people in this room.

Mrs Collingwood's eyes had darted round her employees, assessing which was likely to be the quarry. She knew herself to be guiltless, and almost by definition, so were the inmates. Cool and commanding, she said, 'Good evening, officers.'

'Detective Sergeant Lynch, ma'am, Thames Valley CID.' He held up a card and was already pocketing it when Mrs Collingwood held out her hand.

'May I?' She read it carefully, glanced from photo to face a couple of times and handed it back. 'You understand I have to be careful.'

'Quite right, madam.'

'Now, how can I help you?'

The policemen's hard stare moved round the ancient residents, sitting where they had been put on wipeable leatherette chairs except for those whose days were spent in wheelchairs. 'I'm never going in a wheelchair, I won't be a burden,' Delia's father used to say. But here he was. And the police had come for him.

'Which of these gentlemen is Mr Stephen Mark?' the sergeant asked. The eyes of all who were conscious and could hear swivelled towards the old man's blank, affectless face. The policemen moved to stand over him, not listening to Delia's protests: her father couldn't walk or talk, he didn't understand a word the policemen said. Grace left the room to call her lawyer. She could be heard pitching her voice clearly to some recalcitrant secretary. The officers eventually realised that there was no point in asking Stephen questions, whereupon they insisted on reading out the formal words.

'Arresting you on suspicion...'

'This is ridiculous. Can't you see my father's —'

'...of the murder of Sheila Mark...'

'Here, Mrs Theobald, here's a chair.'

'You have the right to remain silent...'

'Like the old man could talk or something.' A woman's derisive mutter.

'Are you all right, Mother?'

'...may harm your defence in court.' The end of the recitation.

'Someone get my mother a cup of tea,' Grace commanded. 'And you, open that window.'

'Dad.' Delia's voice came out as a whisper. Her father hadn't moved. He was still sitting with the daft hat on his head, but his eyes were staring, watery, pleading. He knew something awful had happened.

'Dad. They've found...'

The care assistants' whispers hissed round the room.

'Did you hear what he told Mrs Collingwood?'

'They found a body.'

'Do they think he did it?'

'Mrs Theobald. Are you all right, Mrs Theobald?'

Grace said, 'Mum, it's OK, the lawyer's on the way. Though God knows what this is all about.'

'I...yes, sergeant, I'm all right. Considering. But you can't – he can't – you can see for yourself that he's...'

'No point in moving the old man, that's for sure. Not today, that is.'

'Of course it's all a mistake.' As Delia spoke she realised that nobody believed her. She wasn't sure she believed herself.

'Nobody's moving anywhere,' Grace said clearly, looking at Mrs Collingwood. You could almost see the proprietor bite back her impulse to get the suspect off her premises. But higher authority had told the arresting officers not to take the old man into custody – yet.

The policemen had finished. Leaving, they looked abashed and ashamed, as visitors to this hopeless place always did. Once in the hall their footsteps speeded up and then they could be seen outside, taking deep breaths of free air, stretching their arms, reminding themselves they were young and strong and wouldn't ever be shut up in hot rooms in cold-hearted institutions, this wasn't how they were going to end up. No way. Never.

Chapter Twelve

ROSINA WISHED SHE had never answered Elliot Rosenwald's letter. His subject was one she would still rather not discuss. He left several messages before Nat picked up the phone, said, 'Yes of course, she's just here,' and firmly handed it to his mother. She listened to a lengthy speech. Then she said:

'I really can't help, I've been out of touch with Jon Polhearne for far too long.' It was decades since they had last spoken, at the end of a holiday which terminated in acrimony and officialdom. However wild Rosina recognised that had been, she never could think later what mad impulse had made her agree to join a shooting house party – of all things – at the invitation of a virtual stranger. He owned a Victorian mock-up of a medieval castle in the style known as Scottish baronial, in the Borders, near Innerleithen. The idea was alien to the world she lived in at the time. But she was invited along with her friends, nearly all French or Italian, drop-outs or hippies, veterans of the sit-in, protest march, water cannon and prison cell. Thirty years on two of them had been the subject of biographies and one was having a retrospective exhibition at the Design Museum. There was a dress designer, and a violinist, a lawyer and an accountant – they were a couple – a Moroccan boy who was officially the violinist's servant and a model travelling with the dress designer who was unofficially the Moroccan's girlfriend. They'd been found in bed on day three by the violinist who indulged in a hissy fit sufficiently epic to turn into one of those 'Do you remember the time when?' episodes. The deafening histrionics went on all day.

Looking back, Rosina thought how virtuous her children's lives were compared with her own at their age. How innocent they still were in believing her to be innocently unworldly. How incredulous they would be to learn of that very far from innocent Scottish episode…

The visitors found their function was to liven up their host's weekend. Seeing himself as a twentieth-century cross between the Marquis de Sade and Dashwood of the eighteenth-century Hellfire Club, he had made plans which might lead on to some other fantasy but began with orgies.

That was cool, or would have been if he'd just meant the usual group sex with the usual drink and drugs. But he turned out to have a vicious streak. Early on he'd shown them round 'the policies' where his initials were carved into trees, some done in childhood and distorted as they had grown, others freshly gouged out of the living trunk. His guests didn't guess that the rough wood was a surrogate for smooth skin. He gave them a lecture about pruning and tying back as he walked them round the famous fruit garden with peaches and apricots trained against its ancient pink brick walls. You couldn't tell that he was dreaming of tying back and cutting a girl's peachy limbs.

The trip came to its inevitably unhappy end which involved hospitals, the police and a barrage of offensive, vituperative publicity along the lines of running the participants out of Scotland, a conclusion which they avoided by leaving town. The others flew back to Paris directly from Edinburgh, relieved to get away.

For some forgotten reason – probably that she'd quite simply had enough of the lot of them – Rosina went on her own by train. Walking towards the Flying Scotsman through Waverley Station, crowded and jostling, she attracted attention, as usual. She had long since abandoned the self-protective mannerisms of most British females of the time. In France women didn't behave as though every male was a dangerous predator; here they observed the implicit rules that Rosina had grown up with, taking care not to be provocative. Girls knew automatically that they shouldn't even meet the eyes of a strange man. Rosina stalked, head high, toes pointed and bottom in, *The Times* and two glossy magazines under her arm, towards the train and met the eyes of people old and young, the ugly and the smart, the admiring and the disapproving – and the men who took her gaze to be an invitation.

The train pulled out the minute after she boarded so she walked through its crowded coaches looking for a vacant seat. She was a few yards behind a couple on their way to the first class, a tall man in a 'British warm' coat that reminded her unpleasantly of Father, with a short blonde girl who tittuped along behind him, moving her hand to stroke his head or pick a hair from his collar and then hanging on to his arm again.

Rosina found a single vacant seat but it was beside a child who soon drove her to escape. She moved along to the smoking carriage which was full, so she decided to perch in the first class and see if a smile and a fluttering eyelash would do the trick. She read a headline about a murderer's conviction and put the paper aside thinking, That's enough blood for this week. Then she leafed through the *Tatler* and in an article about country pursuits illustrated with images of Castle Howard, Chatsworth and Charlecote she turned the page on to a picture and paragraph about Polhearne, shot by an expert architectural photographer who made the house look dreamily romantic, with the owners arm-in-arm and smiling at the front door. It was still a private house at the time, long before the 3P community moved in.

Rosina closed the magazine as though it burnt, pushed it under her seat and picked up an abandoned copy of *The Scotsman*. Her own photo was in a group mug-shot on a middle page. She heard the ticket collector enter the carriage and waited as he progressed towards her, clipping, telling or selling. Leeds? Change at York. Plane to catch? Don't worry, madam, we should make up the time. Blocked toilet? I'll report it. Upgrade a ticket? The man in the British warm had to buy a ticket, and the guard filled in a form, spelling out the words. Edinburgh Waverley, London King's Cross, thank you, sir. The hand held out for credit card and ticket had an amputated stump for little finger.

Rosina was shaken by an instantaneous ripple of lust and, with it, a surge of unspecific shame. It was an automatic reaction, it didn't mean anything. Stop it, Rosina, she thought, forget it.

His back was to her, she hadn't seen his face, nor he hers. Would he recognise her? The guard was at her table. Rosina handed him her ticket, summoned up her flirtatious, fluttering wiles, but her heart wasn't in it.

Someone was saying, 'My dear Johns, how are you?' Jon didn't correct the slip of the tongue as he half-stood for the older man. 'Good news about the place in Regent's Park. Well done. Been up shooting?' Jon murmured something, but Rosina, by then, was being firmly escorted out of the coach to rejoin the lower classes.

She didn't worry about the child and his gummy fingers during the rest of the journey. She was too shaken, and disgusted by herself for being so. Why had she reacted physically to a man she hated, when others left her cold? It was disgusting, obscene, taboo. Scrubbing at her exposed skin in the lavatory cubicle, she tried to calm herself down. Drawn almost involuntarily by curiosity, or by something else, Rosina moved up the train again as it drew into the terminus, but couldn't see him, or the girl, in the crowds on the platform. They must have got off at Watford. She thought, Thank God for that, and joined the queue making for the tube. At the bottom of the escalator he materialised beside her. Like a camouflaged soldier, he was in a kind of protective colour, so much part of the rush-hour crowd as to have been invisible.

'Got rid of your floozy then?' she said nastily. He shepherded her out of the human flow to a corner where a violinist was busking Vivaldi.

'Is that the word you'd use?' Even his voice sounded like Father's now. He moved and she stepped backwards sharply before realising he was just touching the folded package of newsprint protruding from his pocket. On top was *The Scotsman*. Floozy. Tart. Whore. He wasn't saying the words, they were in her head and the image that went with them was her own. He said, 'You've got chewing gum on your coat, here,' and put his finger on the material covering her breast. She felt her nipples spring erect and jerked herself away.

'Don't touch me.'

'OK, OK.' He held his hands up, palm forward.

'I'm leaving.'

'Maybe you'd better take this.' He handed her the package, the newspaper and folded inside it a magazine. She looked down and up – and he had already gone, melted into the crowd. The busker started playing Mozart and Rosina jumped as though she had touched a live wire. Which way had he gone?

The violinist said, 'Your bloke took the up escalator.' Rosina ran in the opposite direction, down to the deeper underground. On the platform she shoved the newspaper into a bin. The magazine with it had the delivery address pencilled at the top. '107 Chester.'

Years afterwards, when Rosina had turned into a different person, someone who could hardly believe in the existence, long ago, of the wild, alien child she had once been, she found herself walking along Chester Terrace, Regent's Park and the buried, ignored episode surfaced in her memory. Mrs Matthew Reid, wife, mother of two, prosperous, conventionally dressed, self-confident and sunk in the contentment of monogamy, saw a row of brass name plates were screwed to the side of Number 107's black front door. McKinnon, Druce, Schwartz. She had tugged out the old-fashioned bellpull and heard a distant tinkling, the click of the pulley that unlatched the street door and let her into a stone hallway and towards the steep scrubbed staircase. A man with a grey handlebar moustache was leaning over the first-floor banister.

'Oh! I was expecting my meal on wheels.'

'Sorry, I was looking for Mr Polhearne.'

'Never heard of him.'

'Oh, I thought this might be Jon's place.'

'Oh, that bloke. Jon's not been here since the squatters.'

'The...?'

'That place was left empty for months at a time, which is a wicked waste, I admit that, but it doesn't mean I welcome layabouts as neighbours. I had to call the council, and police – the trouble it caused you wouldn't believe. And once they were gone he sold it without putting in an appearance. I heard he'd upped sticks and gone to Ireland —'

'Mum? Mother?'

'Nat. I'm sorry, I was miles away.'

'You brushed the American professor off again – I thought you were going to talk to him.'

'There's nothing I can say, I can't help with that research.'

'What's wrong?'

'Nothing.'

'I know you don't like talking about Polhearne.'

'I don't have anything to say.'

'Now I've said the forbidden name I meant to tell you. I got a letter.'

'Who from? What about?'

'Don't worry, nothing personal. It was an enforcement notice. Something to do with tree preservation at Polhearne.'

'Why did they send it to you?'

'Last resort, it looks like. They can't get any joy out of the people who are there.'

'He's got about forty years left of the lease.'

'He's only a kind of lodger, the tenant's the charitable trust.'

'Oh, them.'

'Yes, but their lease falls in, if they renege, or don't maintain it properly, didn't you know?'

Chapter Thirteen

I HAVE BOUGHT pictures at the Camelot Gallery in St Ives, though not very often since the place became so fashionable, the art so expensive and our walls so crowded. In fact we ought to be selling, not buying more, but then we see something irresistible, as I had in the Camelot that Christmas, when I guiltily splashed out on a little Joan Eardley, dated 1960, which had strayed a long way from its Scottish home. The gallery is run by a woman I can't ever introduce, having known her too long to admit I've forgotten her name, a clever fine art graduate with a fisherman boyfriend and a good instinct for serious buyers.

As she wrapped the picture up she told me about the provenance. It had belonged to the widow of a Scottish doctor who moved down to live near her children in Penzance. 'There's quite a lot of work from that period surfacing and coming on to the market now, pictures that people bought quite cheaply when they were young. Then the next generation has different tastes and turns the art into money.'

'This gallery's probably full of stuff that's got a similar history. Perhaps it should be called a virtuous circle,' I said. 'What about that John Wells over there, for example?'

'Yup, and look over there, only just in this week, the woman who brought it was quite young, she said it had been in her family since the 1950s. I've got someone quite keen on it, I think.'

She told me about the man who had come in the day before. It had been a busy day, but early afternoon was a quiet patch and she stood in the doorway for a breath of fresh air, keeping an eye on a man's progress along Fore Street. He'd looked like he'd be a big spender when she first spotted him, wearing a suit – a pin-striped suit! In St Ives! And he had shining shoes too, as well as a neat buttoned-up polo shirt. But he'd gone into all the other shops and galleries along the road and never came out carrying any parcels. Maybe Hepworth would be his bag. She placed the limestone egg with the oval cavity temptingly in the window before retreating to her desk because punters were sometimes put off by an over-eager welcome. So when the door buzzer sounded she just said, 'Good afternoon,' and went on pretending to work, observing with sidelong glances as he moved round the exhibits.

Not sculpture then, and not contemporary painters either – he walked straight past the Jackson and the Howard and even the precious new acquisition, a little, late Barns – Graham. Then she thought, Bingo – he's an abstracts man, as he took a moment to examine a geometrical Heron and a Riley lithograph. When he paused in the back corner of the room she murmured, 'Anything I can help with?'

'Thank you, I was contemplating this work. Guess it's a Jix, right?'

'We're pretty sure it is.'

A flat oblong of canvas, dull green with scarlet slashes and stripes, with words written in tiny pencilled capitals on the back: 'The Whipping Post.'

'A curious title.'

'I wondered if that line's a whip. It could be blood, those splashes of red...or...'

With a glance asking permission, the man unhooked the wooden frame and looked at the back. 1954.

'It's a late one,' she remarked. 'I've always wondered why he stopped painting, some sort of block, do you think?'

'I believe it is in doubt whether he ceased to make art or merely ceased to exhibit it. There were some highly disobliging reactions to his work. Many a man has gone into hiding on failing to achieve the success he hoped for.'

'It certainly must have hurt to be called "a man whose ambition is not to make good art but to be a famous artist",' she said, putting on a posh accent. 'You'd be shy of showing your stuff. Maybe there's years' worth of unexhibited work put away somewhere.'

'If so it would not be to your advantage. Scarcity keeps the value high.'

She said, 'We could come to an arrangement as to price.'

The visitor produced a tiny camera from his top pocket. 'May I...?'

'Go ahead,' she agreed, disappointed.

He put the camera back in his pocket and took out a notebook in which he wrote rapidly. 'I should be interested to see any other work by this artist.'

'Well, in that case it just so happens that...' She stepped across the room and gestured. 'There's another one come in the other day.'

'Unsigned. Do you know its provenance?'

'No, the owner didn't say, just that she'd brought it down to Cornwall because she thought there'd be more market for it here. Have a look in better light, I'll put it here.' She stood in front of the easel beside him to look at the painting. It was on paper torn from a sketch pad with the indents of the metal rings along one side, foxed at the edges, and not quite flat, thickly covered with irregularly shapes of bright colour. 'It doesn't look like it was framed, or even kept quite flat.'

He recorded the details and said, 'I am grateful and shall consider the possibilities.'

She thought, He's got a client, he's going to call and check. Aloud she said, 'I don't know if you're interested in art and astrology too?'

'Psychic art. What have you got?'

'The original Artology,' she said triumphantly, opening the desk drawer to take out a package wrapped in protective film. A rare copy of Polhearne's *Paint, Prophesy, Predict* in the small first edition by an obscure regional publisher, it had been waiting for Mr Right to pay the earth for it. 'We had a painting that was inspired by the 3Ps, there's quite an unusual history attached, though I probably shouldn't say anything.'

'I understand your caution, given that we are talking about an art or technique which purports to foretell future events, and indeed has been claimed to influence them. Please believe my full recognition of the fact that this touches on the subject of a dangerous notion whose consequences can be, shall I say, unpredictable.'

She said, 'This canvas I'm talking about was called The Tarot. The story goes that this bloke read the 3Ps and then went to learn more about it, he'd never painted before, but he stood in front of the canvas for the first time in his life and went into a trance. Later on he described it as an altered state, or a change of consciousness, like he'd fallen asleep and in his sleep he was watching himself from a stranger's point of view. And when he woke there was this picture on the canvas.'

'I was not familiar with that particular episode, but it sounds very like those described in the book.'

'Except that this time the picture analysis showed that its components were all from a Tarot card – the Hanged Man.'

'And did the painter die?' He was a portentous, slow-spoken man, so it didn't immediately register that he'd made a joke. The girl said solemnly:

'No, but the person who bought the picture did. That's why it came on the market.' She didn't add, and perhaps didn't even know, that the owner had died at the age of ninety-one, but she'd got the American interested anyway, which was good because a nice little commission on the sale price was just what she could do with right now. 'I'll bring it in from our associate dealer if you're interested.'

Disappointingly the American didn't take the bait. Carefully stowing his camera in its carry-bag he said, 'I believe that one of the tenets of artology is that taking a picture's photo makes it lose its power. But that depends, I think you'll agree, on there being any power in the picture in the first place.'

I heard about the American professor's gnomic utterances because I was in St Ives the next day looking for a work of art to give a couple who had everything. Their post-wedding party was later that week. Rosina Reid was there. I recognized her though we had never been introduced. From behind she looked lithe and young and like a trendsetter of the Quant generation in a shift dress, with black, glossy hair cut in the kind of geometric bob that had freed women from the permanent wave. The front view showed a woman who was old and had developed the face she deserved, the clear skin creased from smiling but no frown lines between her semicircular cobalt blue eyes.

We were in a circle of women, all talking about the mass movement homewards of families at Bank Holiday weekends and food: buying and heaving it home, cooking, having a cook in, getting ready-made from a supermarket.

'I might as well be running a boarding house except it's me that writes the cheques,' said a woman in spectacular diamonds who smelt of dogs.

Someone else asked, 'What about you, Rosina?'

Her voice was clear but deep. 'It's kitchen duty for me too.'

A weatherbeaten artist from Bude said, 'I say, Rosina, that's a bit of a come-down after Polhearne, I bet you grew up with regiments of cooks and bottle washers.' It was the first I knew of her connection to the famous name.

A fluffy woman in time-expired hippy clothes said, 'Tell you what, Rosina, there's a real favour you could do me. I'd give anything to meet your wonderful brother-in-law.' I noticed that the others in earshot shifted their stance a little, like people dissociating themselves; none of them spoke, and the brash woman went on loudly, 'You're so lucky to be related to him, I think he's simply marvellous, my absolute hero. If you could just introduce me?'

Rosina said quietly, 'We don't see very much of each other, I'm afraid,' and then, elegantly making the next phrase sound unconnected, 'I really have to get back.' She moved towards the door. I lingered, listening to the post mortem.

'Bad luck, Peggy, foot in mouth time or what! Didn't you know the Polhearnes had a falling out?'

'How was I supposed to guess that?'

'They don't speak. Haven't for years.'

'Well, it's not like it's a secret who she is.'

'Most people have probably forgotten. It's not mentioned.'

'Rosina told someone I know that she's divorced from the Polhearnes.'

'How can you divorce your relations?'

'Metaphorically, Peggy, not really.'

'I still don't see how I could have known. All these family feuds and things you aren't allowed to mention – I do think the Cornish are quite hard to get on with sometimes. I thought it was a compliment, all I meant was that he's a prophet, a real star, and that house must be so beautiful, you'd have thought she'd be pleased.'

'A prophet! Honestly, Peggy —'

'Well, you've got to admit he's in touch with parts of the consciousness most people don't know they've got. I told you about the course I went on —'

'Which of the many?'

'About enlightenment transmission, the causeless —'

'Oh God, don't let her get started,' a guest muttered. The other woman interrupted before Peggy could recite her piece.

'Yes, dear, you've told us all about it. That was the one with causeless love and limitless joy, right?'

'Anyway, my old father says the man's a bounder.'

'Difficult for them though, with Lucia so preoccupied by that poor child.'

'Never could stand the feller.'

'Course he did grow up in the USA.'

'My brother says the Polhearnes chucked Rosina out when she was only about fifteen, he knows that for a fact because his father-in-law knew the aunt who took her in, otherwise she'd have been on the streets.'

'I heard she ran away from home.'

'I wouldn't be surprised, the old man was notorious in the neighbourhood.'

'Really? Her father? Poor little girl!'

'Actually she was quite a goer, according to this chap I know.'

'I've heard she was cut off without a penny.'

'No wonder she has to do her own cooking then.'

Chapter Fourteen

REMEMBERING HER SHARE in the conversation the next morning Rosina thought of Mr and Mrs Tremellen who 'lived in' when she was growing up, as did old Nanny who never left her room from the time Rosina was five until she was taken away six years later to end her days in the old people's home at Goonzoyle. Cleaning women came in relays and Mother used to bemoan the fact that it was a sad come-down since she arrived as a bride and met twelve indoor staff. But whether it was wartime or post-war, the Polhearne ladies didn't cook or clean. That was one of the differences between them and the disinherited daughter.

Rosina thought of herself as 'the one who got away'. She was a wife, a mother, a friend, a gardener, but in her own mind still a refugee like the mother and daughter Aunt Muriel had taken in when they escaped from Germany before the war, who had stayed on ever since as cook and cleaner. Frau Weiss was always afraid she would be turned out in the cold again, and worked like a slave, silent and inconspicuous. Tiptoeing as usual, she had come into the room without knocking when Rosina was getting dressed, gasped and gone for Aunt Muriel but Rosina had locked the door. Even so, Aunt Muriel was the one who fetched her from school at the end of term. She announced that she was taking Rosina to Zermatt for the holidays and would deliver her to the finishing school in Paris on the way home. 'You can come to Edwardes Square whenever you like, darling, that bedroom's all yours.' Muriel died eighteen months later, and Rosina never went to Polhearne again. She still did not know what Muriel had said to her parents.

It had been a pity not to see Mrs Tremellen again. Rosina sent her Christmas cards, with the address typed. If father had seen her handwriting on the envelope he actually might have turned the Tremellens out. And what would Mother do then, poor thing, Mother who had never cooked a meal in her life? And what would Father say now, if he knew a daughter of his managed without resident help? Something shocked and shocking.

Rosina corrected her wandering thoughts. Father would think it served her right. 'That girl will end up in the gutter,' he'd told Mother. 'I forbid you to speak to her.' As though I wanted to! she thought.

Stop. Stop it, Rosina. Take your mind off it. But with a force 6 wind off the sea and pouring rain she couldn't turn to her usual remedy of hard labouring. There was no point in doing housework either to spite her dead father or for its own sake. Rosina employed a team of contract cleaners who turned up once a fortnight and left everything gleaming. The downside was their virtuosity in tidying up. She spent hours of her life trying to second guess them, and occasionally suspected they were hiding things on purpose. One could hardly complain that they were using their initiative, but oh lord, wherever would they suppose that scissors or magnifying glasses or a fountain pen should be put away? As soon as they left Rosina always moved the cushions off the diagonal, rearranged the mantelpiece ornaments and made a messy stack of the magazines and papers which had been placed in overlapping piles, hotel-style. Today the *Western Morning News* was at the top, its front-page lead the news story about the arrest of a suspect in the case concerning the skeletons at Goonzoyle.

Rosina had heard far more than she wanted to know about them already. It wasn't the yuk-factor that was the problem. Rosina was always perfectly cool about the nasties that other people cringed from, blood, spiders, rodents, snakes, hauntings, dead animals. In all their years of living overseas and travelling abroad, the Reids were determinedly unsqueamish, proudly remaining unsentimental about cats, dogs, donkeys or any of the sad creatures which other Brits rushed to rescue. Rosina had seen human remains in very nasty stages of decomposition without a qualm. But this was a different matter.

It must have been about ten days ago that Nat had received a call inviting him go to the police station in Buriton. It was his first professional assignment. That evening he came home all excited and insisted on giving her a blow-by-blow account of using his new forensic skills.

'Actually, Mum, you'll never guess where it was.'

'It'll say on the news, won't it?'

'I didn't tell them there was a family connection, though it seemed funny seeing it like that for the first time – it turned out to be Goonzoyle, wasn't that where Grandmother's family came from? You probably went there when you were a kid.'

'It was already an old people's home,' Rosina said. She wasn't feeling a hundred per cent well. 'Is it terribly hot in here or am I imagining it?'

'Are you OK, Mum?'

'Fine.' Not for the first time in her life she felt glad that whisky looked like ginger ale.

'The house is full of institutional stuff lying round still. I can't say I'd want to take it on, but the woman who's bought it seemed keen. She took me through the house, but my actual site's up a lane. It's pretty exciting for me, this job.'

Nat wanted to tell Rosina what they had found. He made her promise not to pass anything on and laid out hundreds of photos, the record of his work. 'It's really great experience, Mum, they might easily have got the prof down from Plymouth instead. I think they're using me instead because I'm cheaper. But I'm doing a proper job.' She had closed her ears to most of his speech but to that last remark replied that she was proud of him.

Under his direction the trench was geometrically squared off, textbook tidy. He kept a sharp eye on the team of inexperienced workers as they scraped away at the soil with flat little masonry trowels, soft small brushes and all the other gear conventional archaeologists used on real excavations. On the third day Nat worked alone, because it was the final phase and that was the expert's responsibility. His only company had been a uniformed constable, a young woman who stood silent for hours, hands behind her back and a vacant, absent expression on her face.

When Nat got back he shovelled in the shepherd's pie Rosina had left in the warming oven and then set up his computer and a white screen in the drawing room and began to show off every enlarged detail.

'Look, Mum, this shows it really clearly, d'you see there's fragments of material still, a summer dress. She had stuff in her pockets, looks like they'll be able to identify her.'

'How...' Rosina cleared her throat. 'How long ago did she fall – in fact, did she fall? Nat, it wasn't murder?'

'The pathologist's the one to say about that, someone could have pushed her, but my guess is she just fell. Easy to slip down, and it'd be quite hard to hear her shouting from —'

'Oh Nat. It doesn't bear thinking about.'

'Anyway, we can tell it happened after the war. I wondered if it was actually a Hicks relation – a distant one, not close enough for me to declare an interest.'

'There weren't any Hickses there by that time.'

'Sure? It was late Forties, maybe 1950, her clothes had utility marks – what's wrong, Mum? You feeling OK?'

'Nothing. I'm tired, that's all.'

'Oh good. Look, those belong to the other one.'

'You don't mean – there can't have been another? Not two...' Rosina said faintly.

'I wish you'd concentrate, Ma, I told you all about it. The

police thought it was a suicide pact to start with, but it turns out the second one – look, here on the picture, you can see the skeleton's cleaner – it's been there quite a bit longer, a good ten years.'

'Before the war?'

'Yes, very likely, there was a coin underneath, an Edward VIII threepenny bit, so it couldn't have been before 1936. An expert's going to check some metal traces, might be part of a corset. Actually the coin's quite worn, so I think it's early Forties, and it's fascinating because – look, Mum, see those little white dots and dashes, all inside the pelvic girdle? She was pregnant, I think that may be an almost full-term infant.'

'Actually, Nat, stop. Too much information,' she'd said.

Nat looked wounded. Even at thirty-two he felt it should be Rosina's pleasure as well as duty to take a meticulous interest in everything that concerned him. But he said kindly, 'OK, it's cool. You should have seen the woman who's bought Goonzoyle, we got talking when I went down for some water and she really flipped.'

'I wonder why she wanted that big house.'

'Her problem. Anyway, she asked what was going on so I explained about the time frame, and told her about the Edward VIII coin. She started singing "Hark the herald angels sing" only it went on, "Mrs Simpson stole our king" and then she said she remembered his abdication and all the fuss. Why did people care? Then I said about the foetal skeleton and she suddenly started panting, like she was suffocating, actually it was quite frightening.'

'What did you do?'

'Luckily I didn't need to, that bloke was there, you know, the Scottish punk I told you about. He was cool, said she was hyperventilating, emptied some saffron buns out of a paper bag and made her breathe into it. Have a bun, they came from a bakery in Buriton.'

'I don't blame the poor woman, I'm feeling pretty uncomfortable already and that's without any gory details.'

'Lucky you aren't the hyperventilating type, then.'

Chapter Fifteen

ON SATURDAY MORNING a friend rang and told me to turn on Radio 4. A folksy presenter was talking to a very aged man. I deduced that we were back to 1940, because he was just explaining about his desperate need to get to New York to see his fiancée because she was an American citizen and as such wasn't allowed to travel to Britain.

'And you've been reminded of all this, you told me, by seeing pictures of children in Baghdad.'

'Children should be spared from war, and naturally one can't help thinking of that just now, with what's going on in Iraq. Saving the children, is what we should do. It's what we were trying to do, when we loaded them on to that ship.'

'The *City of Benares*. How did you come to be there?'

'I'd just qualified as a doctor so I was waiting to be called up. But what really mattered to me then was getting married. The problem was that I was in Northumberland and she was in New York. Then one day I had a brainwave. If only I could get across the Atlantic and we could get married then she'd automatically become a British subject and I could put her on my passport and we could come home together. So I applied to be an escort for the kids who were being sent overseas to escape the war.'

'They must have been really grateful for your offer,' the presenter prompted.

'Oh no, there were thousands of people applying. They had a very thorough vetting procedure, though quite a primitive one, it included asking one's relations – that was my stepmother in my case – if I'd be likely to save myself or the kids first if the ship was torpedoed. All they asked me was whether I'd be able to cope with seasick kids and was I prone to seasickness myself.'

'And did you get any training?'

'There wasn't really time for that, the whole evacuation programme was being set up in a terrific hurry.'

'There must have been a lot of panic around.'

'I wouldn't say panic, too much stiff-upper-lip, but people certainly thought invasion was imminent. You see, that summer, with the enemy poised on the other side of the English Channel, with the Low Countries and France under occupation, we were just waiting – and trying to save the next generation. People were pretty frightened for their families.'

'So you were going to rescue them. How did it begin?'

'I reported to the mustering centre in Liverpool, and fifteen little ruffians were handed into my charge by a teacher who had brought them up by train, so I was plunged straight into it.'

'"It" being...?'

'Well, there were heavy air raids in Liverpool at the time, which was bad enough, and these were children who hadn't been away from home before, so there were tears and quarrels and fights and nightmares and some were sick and some wouldn't eat, and there were some kids who didn't have the clothes on the lists they'd been given – that turned out all right because Marks and Spencers provided a whole lot – and then we discovered that half the kids had left their gas masks behind and their boxes were full of sweets and food instead. We had a lot of community singing, *Roll Out The Barrel* and *Run Rabbit Run* mostly, neither of them very suitable if you come to think of it.'

'And did that go on for long time?'

'We were there for five days before we got loaded on to the ship. SS *City of Benares*. But then we thought things were looking up. She was one of the Ellermann line, quite a new ship, only commissioned three years, designed for the India run, so although the officers were British the crew were Lascars – Indians. Most of these children had never seen anyone with brown skin before, any more than they'd seen such luxury, gold taps – of course some of the kids had never seen any colour taps in their lives before, nor starched napkins, three course meals, stewards in white uniform waiting at table, there was even a film producer on board, a woman – what was she called? Sorry, it's gone. But I do remember she was making an official documentary of the voyage and all the kids wanted to get into the pictures.'

'So at first the work wasn't too hard for you.'

'No, and I'm lucky because I don't get seasick and I wasn't hard at work, the kids didn't need me every moment of the day. They were nice lot...'

If this was on television the camera would have focused on a wrinkled, sorrowful face, but as people always say, on radio the pictures are better. The warm, Liverpool voice said gently, 'you were fond of them.'

'I was, yes, you couldn't help it.'

'And you had a soft spot for one in particular.'

'I did, yes, a little chap from Cornwall. I can't help thinking now, it's what I've often thought, if he'd stayed at home he'd probably still be living to this day.'

This presenter wasn't frightened of silence on the air and allowed the old man to collect himself before prompting, 'You got to know him well during those days, did you?'

'He was such a bright little chap, brave too, took it like a trooper when he got hurt. He never said much but there wasn't a lot went on he didn't notice, he was curious about everything, learning all the time. He'd come from a very poor home, a working-class lad, but you could see him watching how people behaved, little things like what you should do with a table napkin, or how you manage a table full of cutlery. He didn't make the same mistake twice, the first time we sat down at a laid table he used his fingers and gobbled but at the next meal he could have been sitting next to the King. I had fifteen boys in my party, and he was the only one who wanted to use the ship's library, or took an interest in the pictures on the walls – Indian scenery mostly so I didn't know much about them myself. By day three he was instructing me, he'd been told by the crew what the pictures showed.'

'And he was on his way to Canada.'

'He was supposed to be going to work as a labourer on his uncle's farm. He wasn't looking forward to that, but I didn't think he'd be there long – if ever there was somebody who'd make his way in the New World, he was the one. It was the night before it happened. I was wandering around, went up to one of the other decks, and there was Ted with his nose pressed against the window of the first-class lounge, watching and taking it all in. I'd seen him the day before in the sickbay, so I knew he was not supposed to be there, but we chatted a bit, the way you do when it's late and you know it's time for bed, and that's when the confidences slip out. I told him about my fiancée in New York and he told me that he was going to be a gentleman too one day – I'm afraid that's the kind of language we all used in those days. He'd have managed it, you know. I wrote to the Children's Overseas Reception Board afterwards, to tell them about him. Some years later an American student came to talk to me, must have been late Seventies, nice enough chap with a Welsh name, what was it, Selwyn, Elwyn...'

'Don't worry about the name. He was doing research, was he?'

'That's right, so I told him all I could remember about the ship, its facilities. He was a good listener, showed a real interest, wanted to know everything I could remember. He said he'd mention the boy Ted because his thesis was about evacuees and the class system but I don't know if he ever did.'

Just as he was beginning to describe the moment when the torpedo struck, my phone rang. I had to pick it up because I'd promised to meet someone at the train station when they called, and by the time I was in the car the programme had moved on to a woman from Norfolk who rubbed on radishes as a cure for boils and spots. All the same I called Goonzoyle on the mobile.

'Connie, have you been listening to Radio 4 this morning?'

'No.'

'Well, I happened to hear this programme. Connie, you'd have been interested. I don't know quite how to say this...'

'I don't understand.' Her voice sounded a bit quavery, but I went on, and explained about this final sighting of her lost brother. 'I suppose you might have heard from this old man before, he probably got in touch with your family in 1940. Shall I let you have his name and the programme details? I mean, he obviously was talking about your Ted.'

Click. I stared stupidly at the silent telephone. Connie Thorne had hung up on me!

Had I offended her by mentioning her little brother? No, that couldn't be right. But then why had she given me the clearest, most unmistakable of brush-offs? What on earth was all that about?

I really didn't have the faintest idea.

Chapter Sixteen

MINE BONES FIFTIES MISSING WOMAN.

Rosina had taken in the screamer headline with a glance as she bent to the doormat, but without putting her glasses on couldn't read any more. Holding the paper in front of her, flat like a tray, averting her eyes from the bold typeface, she'd walked through the hall and into the room she still called Matthew's library. Lying on the desk was another document she didn't want to read, a circular sent from the Department for the Environment, Fisheries and Rural Affairs, entitled 'Phytophthora Ramorum'.

It was more than half a century since Rosina had done any Latin or Greek but she could still translate the word phytophthora: it meant plant destroyer. She had heeded but not needed the warning. Like every other gardener she had spent many months on tenterhooks of terror lest her rhododendrons should start showing signs of SOD or Sudden Oak Death. The newly rampant, devastating fungus had been recognised first in San Francisco Bay and had reached Cornwall last year, and raised the spectre of the last time millions of trees died when the English countryside was laid waste by Dutch elm disease.

It didn't bear thinking of. Nor did the news item about the identification of Nat's skeletons. One was that of a woman who had been missing for decades; her husband had always been suspected and now, though very old, was under arrest. The piece was illustrated with a shot of the suspect's daughter, Mrs Cordelia Theobald, socialising with her partner, Mr Brian Monson, described as 'a prominent financier', and her daughter Grace Theobald. Rosina felt quite sorry for the girl; the last thing one wants is a misspent youth revived in embarrassing pictures, like this one of a leering man and a wild-eyed girl holding a glass and a joint, tongue to stuck-out tongue. Rosina, whose own behaviour when young would have made an embarrassing paragraph, looked briefly, sympathised and pushed the other details literally and emotionally out of sight. It was absolutely nothing, nothing whatsoever, to do with her. And she'd been too busy, with the garden open on two occasions, once during an afternoon in aid of the Red Cross, the next day a private early evening show-round for a group of American camellia enthusiasts. Things had to be made presentable but doing or directing the work had seemed equally arduous, perhaps because it was in the same week as a bridge-and-supper fundraiser for Macmillan nurses.

No wonder I'm whacked, Rosina thought. But in fact she wasn't physically tired, she just didn't feel herself. I'm a bit off colour, she thought, an old-fashioned expression her mother used. Or she'd say, 'You're under the weather.' Euphemisms. Facts were in disguise if they were referred to, or simply unmentionable. But Mother knew what was really wrong. She must have known. Mustn't she?

Rosina, stop, just don't go there!

What's come over me?

Working too hard, that's all. There was no choice, without Matthew. The work needed doing and spring was always the busiest season especially this year because there had been more visitors than usual. People were scared to fly so they had holidays in Cornwall instead. Cowards, Rosina muttered, might as well be frightened of using the motorway. I'll go away after the last open day. Turkey. I'd like to see Ephesus again.

'Mrs Reid!'

Rosina turned the newspaper over to stop being reminded of its headline, went into the hall and saw a woman, silhouetted against the light in the porch, its inner glass door a little open.

'Mrs Reid? So sorry, I did ring but —'

'The bell doesn't work, you have to knock.'

'I thought you must be in, the door's open.'

It always was, though Rosina didn't say so. She went closer, her own feet silent on the faded carpet runner she'd bought in Morocco the year Morwenna was born. The dogs nosed along at her heels. Useless as watchdogs, old, wheezing and smelly, they had been Matthew's pets, spoilt by him but perversely much fonder of Rosina who didn't really like them. A preference for working dogs was probably the only point of agreement with her father that she had ever found.

In the shaded hall Rosina didn't recognise the caller but presumed she was a friend of Nat's who might have come here before and would be offended if his mother had forgotten. Rosina said warmly, 'Come in, nice to see you, but I'm afraid Nat's not here, he's working in —'

'Mrs Reid, I'm not here to see your son, I don't know him.'

'Ah. In that case...'

'You won't know my name, it's Grace Theobald.'

In the sitting room's brilliant marine light Rosina could see she wasn't after all a Nat-girlfriend type, which was nearly always fluffy, juvenile and blonde. Grace Theobald looked high-powered, in severe sludge-coloured tailoring worn with a frivolously patterned and girlish bodice and an art nouveau necklace.

'But —' Rosina stopped herself finishing the sentence with 'I was just reading about you'. 'Haven't we met before somewhere?'

'Let me give you my card.'

Rosina took it and read, 'Grace Theobald, MA, DipMus, PhD, Department of Costume and Fabric, The William and Mary Museum.'

'Costume – are you a dress designer, Dr Theobald?'

'I don't do it, I just know about it – vintage clothes, the underpinnings, old fabrics.'

'For exhibitions?'

'Yes, at the museum, but I've got a business buying and selling them too. I've found some good things in this district before now. But that's not why I —'

'Maybe that's where I've seen you.'

'I think you're seeing my mother in me.'

'Your —?'

'I know it's a terribly long time ago, you were only teenagers, but she thinks you might remember —'

Rosina interrupted, almost involuntarily, as though compelled to put off a dreaded moment. Something within her didn't want to hear what it was she might remember. She said:

'I never offered you something to drink. What would you like?'

'Anything soft, please – I'm driving.'

'Come and see what we've got.'

Grace followed, as always automatically noticing clothes and fabrics. Rosina's house was furnished conventionally, moderately good antiques combined with Habitat and Ikea, but there were plenty of things Grace would willingly take away. The Festival of Britain fabric, yellow and green skewed pots on scarlet linen, on a cushion in the kitchen, a Clarice Cliff jug used to hold pens and pencils on the desk. Knotted at Rosina Reid's neck was a devoré scarf by Workers For Freedom and she was wearing a Jil Sander silk-tweed jacket, admittedly with the wrong shoulder line for this year but still unexpected in this context. But then, as Grace had found in five minutes on Google, Rosina hadn't always been a country lady. The obituaries of her husband described an international money-man's career. Matthew Reid had spent his whole working life in capital cities, Paris, Sao Paolo, Montreal, Washington at the World Bank, and his final entry in *Who's Who* for 1996 gave an address in South Kensington.

His wife's details were only included as far as they were relevant. Matthew Reid had m Rosina Valentine Polhearne, dau of Gerald Polhearne Esq of Polhearne, St Budy, Cornwall, 1d

Morwenna Mary, 1s Nathan George.

Rosina led Grace to the kitchen. 'Sorry about the mess.' She gestured at last night's empty silver-foil trays of supermarket fish pie and, at the other end of the long rectangle, the intractable piles of papers, photos, torn-out recipes, bills, instruction manuals and heaven knew what else that had been piled on the table for so long. 'My son says we should tell people it's installation art.'

'What a wonderful room,' Grace said. 'I'd love to have a big Aga.'

'The house I grew up in had an eight-oven one, so this actually seems quite small to me.'

Rosina opened the fridge and recited the soft drink contents. 'Apple juice, fizzy or flat, cranberry, mineral water...' She was putting off explanations, almost automatically, without intention. She set out glasses, poured sparkling water, took a sizeable gin and tonic for herself, carried the tray back to the drawing room, all the while doing what Nat called 'burbling'. The weather, the previous month's destructive wind, the fact that the camellias were long past their best and these were the last till next year: she named them one by one, lovingly.

'Lady Vansittart, white with pink stripes, then this pure white one's Pope John XXIII, and here's Camellia sasanqua, slightly scented, rather like nicotiana, and this one is Quintessence.'

'I like the very pale pink one. And this bright pink's lovely too.'

'That's Leonard Messel. And this one's called Sweet Jane...' Rosina's voice died away. She thought, What's wrong with me? and then, Stop it. She drew in breath and said, 'Now tell me what I can do for you.'

Her visitor felt as awkward as Rosina herself. With a visible effort of will Grace Theobald put her glass down to speak, and even then she came out with a series of false starts.

'The reason I've come – it's complicated – I'm not sure how to put – what I'm wondering is...'

'Spit it out.'

She took a deep breath, unconsciously stroking a rather enviable velvet scarf. 'Your name used to be Polhearne, right? Rosina Polhearne?'

'Yes.'

'OK, here's the thing. Do you remember someone called Delia? Delia Mark?'

'Delia...'

'When she was thirteen. She was in Cornwall for the holidays. Easter 1951.'

Rosina let a silence fall. She didn't nod or shake her head. But she noticed her hands were trembling, so clasped them tightly on her lap.

'I'm her daughter. And I need your help, or rather, we do. Delia and Stephen. Her father. You know the bodies they found in the mineshaft down near St Budy? One's been identified, it's the remains of my grandfather's wife who went missing that holidays, missing without trace. Stephen's spent all these years being under suspicion, and now – but Delia's certain he's innocent. I am too, he simply couldn't have done it. Not him. So if you could only think back, anything you remember, any detail at all...'

Under the authoritative tone there was a desperate plea. Rival responses flitted on to Rosina's tongue and evaporated unuttered.

I don't want to be involved.

I should help.

Don't go there!

Stalling again, Rosina turned back to the panacea: food and socialising. 'You'll stay and have some lunch? Why don't you walk round the garden while I get something together.'

Grace looked like someone who was trying to analyse the subtext. But she set off obediently until she was out of sight of the house, on a grass terrace about six feet wide, below the top of the cliff. She sat on a step, in the sun and out of the wind, dictated some notes into her voice-activated recorder and then simply took in the view. What a place to live! It was like a lighthouse. Or perhaps, with this lush growth going down the side of the high cliff, more like hanging gardens. Where were they – was it Babylon? No, Nineveh. Where quinqueremes came from... She closed her eyes.

Rosina had set out lunch in a small paved area outside the kitchen, explaining it was the one part of the garden which didn't make her feel she ought to be working. Serious gardeners' gardens are short of outdoor chairs and had no such luxuries as sun umbrellas or barbecues, she explained, gesturing Grace towards an old wooden table placed in a sunny corner with no view of the sea but pleasantly out of the wind. There was scented jasmine climbing the slate-hung wall, and a border of herbs in terracotta pots. Rosina briefly admired her own artistry, thought how disgusted her parents would have been at the idea of lunch al fresco and switched off the intrusive image.

'Help yourself, Grace. It's an Italian salad, oranges, olives, fennel.'

'It all looks wonderful, fancy getting all this together without notice.'

'D'you like prosciutto – or are you a vegetarian? And help yourself to bread.'

'Delicious. And focaccia. What a yummy combo. I'll have learnt as much through meeting you as my mother did all those years ago.'

And there they were, the subject broached. Rosina shivered, and thought, A ghost on my grave. Aloud she said, 'Learnt? Delia?'

Grace put her knife and fork down and pushed the plate aside so that she could rest her chin on her folded hands. She looked intelligent and determined, Rosina thought, but beautiful too, the new breed of woman. I wish I was in my thirties again and that sort of person. The sudden pang of envy, unexpected and sharp, shook Rosina, who liked to think she'd had her share of fun and now was contented with her lot.

'You had a huge influence on her, from the moment you first met at Trevena.'

'That much I do remember. I used to bike over to the beach.'

'All alone?'

'Children wouldn't be allowed to now, but there wasn't much traffic around and nobody ever admitted the existence of paedophiles, in those days things were left unsaid. Swept under the carpet, that was the expression.'

'Do you think that was better?'

'Better? Certainly not! The harm done by ignorance, the suffering – things should be out in the open.' Rosina's voice carried an undertone of – Grace couldn't tell what it was, but could see that some emotion had interrupted a calmer train of thought. Rosina went into the kitchen, and came back with a bottle of cold wine. Her expression was controlled again: the public face resumed.

Grace said, 'You were telling me you went over to Trevena. I've been to see it, the beach is really idyllic. Sand and little pools and cliffs, and that view…'

'I don't know what it's like now but it was a perfect beach in those days, before the Torrey Canyon went down. I heard that the detergent they used to clean the oil spill did permanent damage to the beach flora and fauna.'

'Delia was sitting on a rock making a list for a nature-study holiday task when you came up and started talking.'

'Did I?'

'She said you just clicked right away.'

'I was probably glad to find a pal. I went to a boarding school so I didn't know many girls my age, unlike my sister, she always knew the neighbours because she played tennis and rode. But I think I must have been mooching round on my own. A sulky adolescent.'

'Delia was just keeping out of the way. She was on holiday with her father and stepmother and they only had a small caravan.'

'Her stepmother.'

'Yes. Sheila Mark. The deceased.'

'I'm very sorry,' Rosina said formally.

'Thank you, but of course she died long before I was born. We'll probably have to organise some kind of funeral, which is a pretty ghastly thought.'

'Are you allowed to until —'

'No, not yet. And I suppose it's not much of a problem compared with everything else that's happening.'

'If there's anything I can help with...' Rosina felt the offer impelled out of her mouth against her will, and was greatly relieved when Grace replied briskly:

'Thank you so much, it's great to know you're there, but it won't really be a problem. And it's not as though I knew her. She was my grandfather's second wife, much younger than him but too old to have fun with Delia, no wonder she was thrilled to find a friend. And all the more so when you had her over to your place. I tried to go and see it but nobody seems to be allowed in. I was disappointed because Delia's told me such a lot about it, says she spent a lot of that holiday there.'

'I have such a bad memory.'

'Well, it did, it made an enormous impression on her. The little I could see certainly looked wonderful so I can understand why she's never forgotten it, especially with her own parents being foreigners.'

'From...?'

'Czechs, both of them, though not Grandfather's second wife. But he had an accent, which always meant they were outsiders. Brits seem to have been pretty insular in those days. So Delia never wanted to be like them, she was always looking to see how other people did things. Your family for example, though it was pretty scary, she'd never met the landed gentry before, or come across servants, her family didn't even have a cleaner.'

'They weren't really servants, just some old people who'd been there for years. Family pensioners.'

'Delia didn't know the difference so she was terribly shy of them, afraid they were thinking she should be on the other side of the green baize door with them. She said she slept over once and she was put in a room with a four-poster bed and a wash basin in the room too, with running hot water – that was something new in her life. And the next morning, the housemaid came in to light the fire and draw the curtains. And then there was – a butler perhaps, or handyman – somebody who stood by a hot plate on the sideboard at breakfast and scared her rigid.'

'Poor useless old Tremellen? My parents kept him on as a kind of pensioner, and I suppose he did look a bit peculiar because he'd been wounded in the North Africa campaign. Was she really frightened?'

'Yes, but she simply loved it too, I didn't know about it till the other day but after all this time she can still remember the tiniest details, even the stuffed animal heads on the walls and a tiger skin rug.'

'Big game hunters brought them all back.'

'And she can recite every single detail of the food.'

'Which year did you say this was?'

'1951.'

'But food was still rationed.'

'That's just it, she was used to marge and one egg a week but you had cream and butter, a whole silver dish full of curls of the stuff, and lots of different home-made cakes, and eggs for breakfast.'

Rosina said defensively, 'It certainly wasn't black market stuff, Polhearne had a home farm in those days.'

'Oh – please, that never crossed my mind, it's just something

Delia told me, that she'd never seen so much food before.'

'And she's remembered all this ever since?'

'Everything about Polhearne's engraved on her heart. It wasn't just the rooted Englishness she yearned for, it was the whole set-up – the class thing, you know? D'you remember that hymn, about the rich man in his castle, the poor man at the gate, and God ordering the estate?'

'Of course. All things bright and beautiful.'

'It must have been hard for poor men who wanted a castle too. I think just then, the post-war period, must have been on the cusp, not egalitarian yet but lots of aspiration going on. So Delia noted everything, she wanted to pass for posh. Your mother told you off for saying sorry when you'd sneezed, because it was common, and you were scolded for cutting the bread on your side plate with a knife and believe me, Delia's never done either since. Bread's broken, sneezes go unexcused. She sticks to your mother's vocabulary too, looking glass, writing paper, chimneypiece, she's given up on luncheon and bust bodice —'

'Was that one of my mother's words? I don't even know what it means.'

'A bra, but you weren't allowed one, your mother thought nice girls didn't, so Delia left hers off too.'

'I suppose I should apologise.'

'Apologise? Delia absolutely loved it all, she took it all in, when she told me about it she even reeled off a list of the family portraits.'

'Which is more than I can.'

'A melancholy cavalier with dark eyes, a lady with a white wig in blue satin, some pink girls in mauve party frocks, with a spaniel. Yes, she remembers it all, and never said a single word to me about it until now. It's why I'm here. She can't get away so I promised to ask you. The question is, what are your memories of the day, the last day of the holidays, the last time you met

Delia? I don't want to sound dramatic, but for Stephen it's vitally important. Life or death.'

'That sounds serious.' A giant stood in the doorway, six three if he's an inch and broad with it, Grace thought. This must be the '1s Nathan George b 1970.' As he moved closer she realised that some of the height was accounted for by a thicket of brown curls. Ruddy face, grey-blue eyes, unshaved and wearing ancient clothes. He probably hasn't looked in a mirror for a week, she thought. But he had an observant gaze, now rapidly changed from polite query to suspicion.

'You look like you're completely wiped out, Mum. Is there a problem?'

'No, everything's fine. This is my son Nat. Dr Grace Theobald, Nat, she's here because of your skeletons.'

Nat Reid batted the dust off the seat of his jeans before flopping on to a cushion covered, as Grace had automatically noticed, with a chinoiserie design fabric: Baker, mid-seventies.

'I didn't have a chance to tell you, Dr Theobald —'

'Grace.'

'And I'm Rosina. I should have explained that Nat's been professionally involved with the case.'

'Oh. Are you a policeman?'

'Actually I was called in as a civilian adviser.'

'Does that mean there's a conflict of interest here?'

'I think my job's done. I'm a forensic archaeologist.'

'Well, I hope that doesn't mean your mother can't talk about it.' Grace's tone sounded more aggressive than she'd intended. 'I'm sorry, I didn't mean to – it's just that we, my mother, my grandfather, we're in real trouble here.'

Rosina said, 'They've charged Grace's grandfather, Nat.'

'With murder,' Grace said.

'They say he killed his wife,' Rosina said.

'Only one set of remains has been identified, someone called Sheila Mark,' Nat said.

'My grandfather's Stephen Mark.'

'Oh, right. I heard about him actually, but they said he was completely out of it. Unfit to plead.'

'That's not the point.' Grace was horrified to find her voice thickening. She blinked rapidly, several times. I can't cry! she thought, took a deep breath and went on, 'My mother's sure he's innocent.'

'You must be pretty sure too, if you've come all the way from – where?'

'East Anglia,' Rosina said, in a tone intended to warn her son to cool it.

Grace said, 'He was chucked out of the home, and Delia couldn't get him in anywhere else, none of these places let trouble in if they can help it, so now he's in her flat and can't be left alone. Which is why I'm here.'

'Crap.'

'Nat, don't,' Rosina said.

'Sorry, Mum, but it doesn't explain anything. I mean, so you've got a problem, but it's nothing to do with us, is it? So what's my mother supposed to do about it exactly?'

Grace's voice was its authoritative self again as she said, 'I can certainly tell you what I'm hoping for.'

'Yeah, what?'

'I'd like your mother to tell me what happened the day Sheila died.'

'Hey, get real, we're talking about 1950 here —'

'1951,' his mother said.

'Whatever. You were just a kid.'

Grace said, 'So was Delia. My mother. She'd made friends with your mother on the beach at Trevena. You were there the day Sheila went missing, Rosina, you saw Delia there.'

'If she was there herself why doesn't she remember what happened?' Nat demanded.

'She thinks you saw something on the way to meet her. You

never had a chance to talk about it, and of course you couldn't actually do what you'd both solemnly sworn, to stay friends and write to each other and visit each other, none of that was possible after what happened. Delia and my grandfather moved around a lot and you lost touch. But Delia never forgot you. I was telling your mother what an impression she and her family made, and that wonderful old house.'

Nat never told anyone that Polhearne belonged to him because the fact that he was technically the landlord seemed irrelevant and unreal. He would be old before the lease fell in and when it did he wouldn't have enough money either to keep the place or to endow it as a gift to the National Trust.

Grace went on, 'I'm so hoping your mother might remember that day at Trevena. Delia remembers you saw something, or recognised someone.'

Rosina felt her knees brace as they had all her life when she was going to disobey an order or refuse a request, like, as Mother once said, a stubborn pony.

'Why's this the first time of asking then?' Nat said aggressively. 'Isn't it a bit late?'

'There was no need, not until now. Sheila still might have been alive.'

'I don't remember anything about her, I'm afraid.' Rosina's eyes were still very clear and blue. Meeting them, Grace wondered if the flushed cheeks were caused by broken veins, exertion or embarrassment. Rosina felt her face heating up. She knew it was from shame, an old and obsolete emotion.

She'd buried it for a long time, putting the past behind her, first as a druggy drunk wild child, then, going to the other extreme, transformed into a monogamous matron. But there had been a bad patch after Morwenna and Nat left home. Matthew was abroad or out all the time. Rosina's periods stopped, just like that, suddenly and symptomless. She felt increasingly 'surplus to requirements'. Since in fact nobody did need her just then, the feeling was not entirely irrational, though never admitted.

Rosina began to do something unusual. She found herself thinking about her own life; and became aware of a fact which, not being naturally introspective, she'd never quite registered: there were blanks in her memory. She could summon up the young child she had been and return in memory to the day nursery, with the fire and the tall brass bars of the fireguard, and the rocking-horse she'd fallen off, and the den she made under the table behind the dangling red cloth with bobbles round the edge. She could still feel the sand in her toes, thorns in her hands, smell the gorse or daffodils, visualise the beach and the sea; she remembered blackberrying, riding her fat Shetland pony, playing 'Für Elise' in the drawing room, wearing a starched white party frock and her lovely patent leather shoes, when ladies came to tea. She could recall herself in Aunt Muriel's tall house in Kensington. But her real life began when she went to be 'finished' in Paris, aged fifteen going on thirty-five.

She had actually made an effort to fill in the gap. Years later she was still ashamed to admit that she'd even tried hypnotism.

The clinic was shabby and casual, with steep stairs leading up past notices about several varieties of massage. The hypnotist was at the ready in a small room at the top of the house. Rosina sat in a low-backed wicker 'conservatory' chair which got her in the small of the back. The hypnotist, a fatherly middle-aged man from Delhi, said he had been doing this for thirty years: he was also clairvoyant, an NHS provider and BUPA recognised. Operations could be carried out without anaesthetics, with him in attendance. He could recover memories, winding the tape of memory back, or forward for precognition. Hypnosis worked with everybody if they let it.

'I enable you to relax, Mrs Reid, but you will remain conscious throughout. If anything brings on trauma, I'm trained to put you back into the normal state. So now close your eyes and sit comfortably.'

Rosina had been taught in antenatal classes the 'visualise muscles and relax them' routine: forehead, neck, shoulders and so on down. She'd always failed.

'Imagine yourself in a train, sitting all comfortably in a seat by the window, you're looking out at the stations, each has a sign showing your age. You're going backwards through the years. You have a long way to go, you're really in charge of that train, the moment you press that button, you can stop if you want to, talk if you want to – go back to forty, remember what it was like, thirty-five, thirty, twenty-one...'

Rosina was stonily awake, and still not so much as a twinge of memory revived. It was embarrassing to be silent when he was trying so hard. Politely, she spoke of her first child's birth, marriage, meeting Matthew. What preceded that was not to be spoken of to this person or anyone else; and before that, adolescence was a blank. Opening her eyes she said, 'Nothing, I'm afraid.'

'Maybe there are certain things that prevent you seeing. If something very eventful happened to you, no way can you forget it, there's highly charged emotion and the moment you enter into that zone, you get a sudden shock, your mind is suddenly alerted. No, it's like an electrical charge – the memory is still there somewhere but it could be like a battery, with voltage too low to feel, rather than high voltage. You may have discharged the pain.'

If only. Feeling less like herself than ever, Rosina did something else she could never admit, even to Matthew, and started seeing a therapist. That talking cure or time passing or hormonal changes – something, never mind what, did the trick of making Rosina herself again. But her memory remained vague, a distanced, watcher's view of a few odd moments. A girl with pigtails. In church. On a bike. At a little writing desk in the room at the end of the north passage – and her mind swerved away. A door slammed shut. Was that a literal memory, or a metaphor?

The smell of meat, a sudden wave of nausea. As always Rosina pushed the thought away again, smoothed the covering over, patted it down to the bottom of her memory store. A reinterment. No archaeologist of the mind was going to get anywhere near that buried layer.

'Mum?'

Nat. And Dr Theobald, with her bothersome questions and reminders. The less Nat thought about Polhearne the better. The days of an eponymous mini monarch inheriting ostentatious, unearned status were gone.

'Nat, didn't you say you had to be in Truro?'

'You needn't drop hints, Mother. You want me to bugger off, say so.'

He left in a cloud of self-righteousness and gravel. Rosina said, 'I'm afraid I have a very bad memory, it always amazed me that my husband could produce an autobiography full of details from his childhood —'

'Was it published? I'd like to —'

'It was only privately printed, just for his family, I really doubt if it would interest you – but the astonishing thing to me was that he had this almost total recall, everything that ever happened or anyone said... My memory's like a sponged blackboard.'

'That's awful! I mean, for you. But it's a pity for me too. You don't think you might find some diaries or photos to jog your memory?'

'I think anything I'd left behind was put on a bonfire when I left home.'

Grace was shocked. 'Surely your parents would never have done that without asking you.'

'I left on bad terms, it was a "never darken my doors again" situation.'

'Oh.' Grace longed to know why. But all Rosina said was:

'It was worse for my sister Lucia. Poor girl, if ever anyone needed moral support – first she had a series of horrid miscarriages and stillbirths and then when she did have a son at last he turned out to be mentally deficient – nowadays they call it learning difficulties but it wasn't just difficulties for poor little Kit, he wasn't ever going to learn anything.'

'Is he still…?'

'Yes, I'm afraid so, in a home in Somerset. I know it's awful to put it like that but they said he'd only live till his teens and he's survived his mother. But that's a digression. Now Grace, give me your number, I'll have a think and be in touch.'

Rosina walked out to the car with Grace and saw it was completely full of clothes in clear plastic bags. 'Goodness!'

'It's treasure trove, designer clothes of four decades, I found them all in the Cancer Relief in Liskeard. Somebody had just brought them in from a house clearance in Polperro. Nobody seemed to have any idea what they're worth so I handed over a donation as conscience money and took the lot before anyone else could snap them up. Look at this slub silk, it's a Jacques Heim, late Fifties. And here's a Sixties Dior – isn't the pink lining wonderful with the black velvet?'

'I love that fluting,' Rosina said jealously. 'I really must start looking in charity shops.'

'Or you could sell your own things on to dress agencies.'

'I don't think anyone would buy my old clothes.'

'Sure they would, if they're like that lovely jacket you've got on.'

'Ancient, though.'

'It would be snapped up, honestly.'

'Grace.'

'Yes?'

'What did your mother look like?'

'I brought this for you. Look.' It was a small, square, black and white photo. Two girls, side by side, face the camera. They are wearing fitted tops that mould round the beginnings of breasts, with wide belts and full, flowered skirts. They squint into the sun, smiling, holding hands thrust high in the air. Behind them is a hedge, with a girl's bike leaning against it.

On the back, in a schoolgirl's cursive, it says, 'Delia and Rosina, April 1951. Trevena.'

Chapter Seventeen

I HAD LEFT home in good time to get to speak at a lunchtime event in Buriton Library so pulled into a lay-by to go over my notes on child evacuees, a subject which (unlike my lifelong specialty of women plus crime fiction) I couldn't yet talk about in my sleep. Engine off, mobile on – and it rang immediately.

'It's Spike.' I hesitated and he said impatiently, 'Simon, yeah, at Goonzoyle?'

'Oh yes, of course.'

'The thing is, yeah, have you got Connie?'

'Got – what d'you mean?'

'See, she's gone missing.'

'Oh my God.' My mind sprang to cliffs and quarries and long falls. 'How long's she —?'

'I dunno, see, I only got back late, and the house was quiet so I just thought she'd gone to bed, but then when I got up —'

'Is her car there?'

'Yeah, but she never slept in her bed or anything, she could have been gone for days.'

'Have you been away?'

'I had to go to London.'

'I suppose you've looked everywhere? I mean —'

'She's not at the bottom of the old mine if that's what you mean.'

'What about the house? Does it look —'

'Like there's been a fight? No. Listen, I looked all over.'

'No phone message?'

'No.'

'Tell you what,' I said, 'I'll come by this afternoon. I'm giving a talk, so I've got to get on but I'll see you later. About four, OK?'

The talk went well, particularly as in the audience were two people who had themselves been overseas evacuees. Driving back towards Trevena I thought about my most recent conversation with Connie, on the same subject, when to my surprise she brushed me off with a response so brusque and unfriendly that I was worried I'd offended her. With any luck she would be back by now, and I could put things right.

It was getting on for four thirty by the time I made it to Goonzoyle. The 4x4 was parked beside the yellow sports car and the front door was open so I went in and found Spike sitting gloomily in the big hall with the dog on his knee. I said:

'Oh good, you've got the dog. Does that mean Connie's back?'

He followed me along the passage into the kitchen, still arranged in the camping-out style I had seen before, but untidier. 'He was at the farm next door. Connie often leaves him there.'

'That's all right then, you might have called and let me know there was nothing to worry about.'

'Nothing to – listen, it was last Monday night. Today's Friday.'

'So she's gone away, what's the problem?'

'She wouldn't, not without telling me.'

'Well, she obviously has. Don't fuss, Spike, you're not Connie's keeper. Or husband or son.'

'It's not like she's a young woman.'

'She's old enough to please herself, anyway,' I told him unsympathetically.

'But she had things on this week, someone from the planning department, that kind of thing.'

'You did search everywhere, Spike, did you?' I asked, imagining an old lady falling at the far end of the big empty house, calling out, trying to crawl, and gradually growing still and silent where she lay.

'Look for yourself.'

When I came before I had not realised the full desolation of an abandoned, neglected institution. Connie had set up camp in one or two corners, her little kitchen which seemed to be the nerve centre of her establishment, a room with a row of brass bells high on the wall, that must have been a servants' hall, with a couple of comfortable chairs, a huge flat screen television and a state-of-the-art computer, and up a narrow back stairs the room she'd taken over as her bedroom. It was not what one would call cosy or even comfortable because little had changed since the room was a hospital ward, except for the fact that it had a very expensive, very large double bed and a set of 1930s bedroom furniture Connie had probably bought at one of her famous sales. The pink patterned duvet and pillows were rumpled. An unbuckled backpack lay beside the bed, its contents, mostly not very clean clothes, spilling out on the floor.

The walls were still painted in the thick shiny dark cream colour so popular with public administrators, but flaking and scratched after years of use. Under a pretty kelim rug the floor was brown lino.

I glanced round, feeling shy, and said, 'Do you know if anything is missing? I mean, would you know if she packed a suitcase?'

'I dunno, d'you want to have a look?'

Inquisitive though I am about other people's lives, I've never gone further than looking at what has been left on view, not being one of those women who ask to use the bathroom in order to snoop in the cupboards. Gingerly I pulled open a drawer and found it contained an impressive array of expensive cosmetics. I automatically picked up a Chanel lipstick and wound up its apparently unused redness. Spike was standing at the opened wardrobe, looking helplessly at the row of hanging clothes, pretty, soft, pink and blue cashmeres and silks, emanating a delectable flowery scent. There was a box of Patou's Joy and a bottle of Chloe's Narcisse on a 1930s walnut dressing table, and two boxes of condoms were on one of the tables.

'Does Connie take any medication, are there usually bottles of pills here?'

'What?'

'People of her age often do.'

'I never noticed that,' Spike muttered. 'I don't think Connie needs to.'

'Oh, well, that's good,' I said. 'What about spectacles – reading glasses?'

'Not that I know of.'

'Well, either she's a phenomenon or she wears contacts. I just wondered if we could tell whether she'd packed anything. Do know where she keeps luggage?'

He seemed to so I followed him along the cheerless corridor, painted in institutional green up to dado height and cream above it. We passed the open doors of other equally inhospitable rooms and I wondered how Connie thought this barracks could ever be made into a cosy home again – if that was what it once had been. It could well have seemed so to a poor and naive girl, but it didn't look likely to me.

Passing the open door of a bathroom I noticed bars for heaving yourself out of the bath or off the lavatory, peeling paint and cracking floor covering, with an incongruous pile of fluffy, colourful towels and a stack of even more expensive-looking soap. It was obvious which was Spike's room since it shared the invariable characteristic of a young person's den, being carpeted in discarded clothes and smelling faintly feral; but I also noticed that the single divan bed was without sheets and blankets and evidently unused. On further, and to a whole room devoted simply to suitcases. 'Can you tell if there's any missing?' I asked, but guessed that I could answer my own question, because there was a tidy oblong gap between a large suitcase and a small overnight bag. 'Look, you see, obviously she's gone away but not for very long or she'd have taken a bigger bag and told you she was going.'

'Actually,' he mumbled, 'we had a bit of a falling out.'

'Did you? What about?' I shouldn't have asked him that, and regretted it the moment I had. I really didn't want to hear about lovers' quarrels. In fact he said:

'It was about hunting out my birth parents.'

'Connie didn't approve of it?'

'She used to be OK with it but I gave her an update and she lost her cool for some reason. I guess she was jealous.'

I found it an unpleasant experience going around this gaunt, uncompromising establishment. Even if it were true that it had been a cosy family home all those years ago, the institutional atmosphere had completely taken it over, and as Spike and I went along endless passages, up and down staircases, pushed open heavy fire doors, shone torches into shuttered rooms, I realised that I simply couldn't imagine these intractable spaces transformed back into a private house. The estate agent who succeeded in offloading it on to Connie must have celebrated the unexpected sale. The single redeeming feature was the view from the rooms which had originally been the main bedrooms. Hidden from the ground floor by hedges and the lie of the land, it spread spectacularly out before our eyes: the green fields sweeping down the slope towards the village of Trevena, a cluster of small houses around the tall grey oblong of the ancient church tower, and beyond it the fields shading into the yellow of sand dunes and then the beach, white surf, blue water and the gleaming beacon of the lighthouse tower. It is a favourite, famous, much reproduced Cornish view from any angle but perhaps best of all from this one, even enough to make this gloomy pile worth buying though it wasn't the reason Connie had done so.

'She really isn't here,' I said.

'Told you.'

'You did.' I followed Spike through the empty house back to the kitchen and said, 'If she'd left you a message where would it be?'

'On the fridge.'

An array of fridge magnets held torn-out recipes and the odd photo on to the enamel surface but there was nothing that looked like a message. 'Did you look and see if anything had fallen off?'

He crouched down and peered underneath. 'Nope.'

I picked up papers and put them down; the design for a kitchen layout, an advertisement for contract gardeners torn out of the local paper. A flyer for the village fete; scribbled on the back was a London phone number followed by three digits. 'Look, Spike.'

Like the fictional detectives I write about, he dialled, and pressed the speaker button.

'Ramada Hotel, Gatwick.'

'Is Mrs Thorne staying there?' Spike asked, and said to me, 'She's at an airport hotel!'

'I thought she said she'd only ever stay at Brown's.'

'It's funny, I was up in London myself.'

The Four Seasons tinkling stopped and the woman's voice said nobody of that name had booked in.

'What about trying room 503,' I said, and the telephonist must have heard, because a moment later someone said, 'Yes?'

'Is Mrs Thorne there?'

'Mrs Thorpe?'

'Thorne. Constance Thorne,' Spike said.

'Just one moment, please.'

I said to Spike, 'They're getting her.' But it wasn't Connie's voice that followed.

'Who is that speaking, please?' It was a man's voice.

'Tell her it's Spike, I'm in Cornwall.'

'Your full name, please?'

'Is she there? Who is that?' Other voices could be heard in the background.

'Detective Sergeant Hanson, Thames Valley police – would you...' but I didn't hear the rest because Spike had dropped the telephone like something that had become red hot.

Chapter Eighteen

THE DAY BEFORE had been still and sunny. 'I can't remember a prettier spring,' Rosina said, charmed by the success of a planting scheme – a vista of camellias arranged so that reds, pinks and whites seemed to shade naturally into each other on the slope. The primulas and the azaleas were just coming out too, surrounded with swathes of primroses and daffodils, white magnolias underplanted with white tulips. 'You and your colour-themed gardens!' Nat said, but kindly. He knew and she denied that she wouldn't be able to keep up all her three acres much longer. How could one give any of it up? In fact Rosina had been toying with the idea of just taking in a little extra part of the rough ground, visualising it with herbaceous plants for the summer, blues and lilacs, grey foliage.

It was easier to be sensible on a rainy day. Nat had gone out early. Rosina was good about not being nosy, which meant that he usually told her what he was doing, but there'd been no explanation for the cleaned car and careful shave, or for the bunch of variegated tulips which he was putting carefully on the back seat when Rosina happened to glance out of the landing window. Wretched boy, he's picked all my double pinks, she noticed, at once vexed and forgiving. When she went down to the kitchen she saw he'd left a post-it on the coffee pot. 'Out all day, back late.' A girl, she thought. Pity about the weather. Instead of yesterday's busy blue sea, today there wasn't a boat in sight on the steely water, and rain was mercilessly battering and stripping the flowers.

Rosina sat at the desk in Matthew's study, Grace's photo propped under the light. Delia and Rosina, April 1951. She looked at herself with a magnifying glass. Bobbysoxers. That was the word. Not like modern teenagers, with their shiny hair and teeth. We were lumpy and plain with greasy hair, always trying to hide our breasts and stubbly legs, afraid we smelled nasty because so many other girls did, secretive about bodily functions as though other people didn't menstruate or crap. We were ashamed.

I wonder whether we'd recognise one another.

Rosina stared at the other girl's picture. Was it a lie, was it self-deception, was it denial? For the black and white image didn't connect with any emotion or reaction archived deep in her conscious mind. Rosina was notoriously truthful, it was a family joke. 'Let me put them off/ say I've got flu coming on/ pretend the train's late. Rosina cannot tell a lie,' Matthew always said.

But now she wondered if she was really being honest with herself, and brought up into consideration an episode that was not forgotten but hidden, its concealment lying by omission, and all the more perverse because she'd maintained her reticence in conversation with the only person in the world from whom it was perverse to hide things. Not Matthew, who only wanted to know as much as Rosina chose to tell him, but Meera, a psychotherapist. Rosina's therapist. What had that been about then? Even at the time Rosina couldn't have answered that.

You choose to go to her, nobody makes you. You overcome your lifelong habit of feeling slightly supercilious about psychotherapy, you realise it isn't pure self-indulgence after all because suddenly it's the only thing between you and going stark staring mad.

Quite voluntarily you turn up at her house once a week and pay a small fortune for your own good. And then you tell untruths. You might just as well set fire to the twenty-pound notes. The payment, for some reason, was never with cheques or plastic, the routine included a stop at a cash machine on the way to Belsize Park.

You're sitting in her anonymous room, and your voice is going on about your childhood. It's difficult to get your head around this one-sided talking, not turning the conversation to her, in fact not knowing anything about her. She's as neutral as her beige carpet and cream chairs and just as unforthcoming. You don't discover anything at all about her, despite a lifetime's experience of being interested in other people, or purporting to be, of automatically getting other people to tell you about themselves. By the time the pudding comes round you could almost write a dinner-neighbour's biography. Just as well that few people return the compliment, given your patchy and edited memories. Meera had talked about selective amnesia and the human ability to forget unwanted thoughts. 'You can block the memory but it has not gone completely away. And its consequences survive.'

All that Rosina could dredge up were the traditional infancy flashes, boring and always regrettable when included in biographies. 'Who was it said they always skipped the first chapter?'

Meera stared unresponsively. She didn't care for literary allusions. So you persevered, dredging away.

'I know they say, give me a child till he's seven. The Jesuits, wasn't it? I can't remember anything much before I was seven except those traditional things like hiding under the nursery table or being made to eat up disgusting dinner or hiding when I heard Father coming...'

'Go on.'

'That's all.'

'Why did you hide when you heard your father coming?'

'Oh, I don't know, no particular reason.'

'Was it a game?'

'A game? No...' Why was that question enough to switch the taps back on? 'Sorry, I'm cleaning you out of Kleenex.'

'That's what it's there for. So not a game?'

'I expect I didn't want to go sailing or something. Have I told you about the dinghy we kept on the river? It was an Arthur Ransome sort of childhood, landing on beaches you couldn't reach on foot and making bonfires out of driftwood and heating baked beans up in the tin. It's funny, we were more free in one way because people weren't afraid of nasty men. Not that there weren't any nasty men, I suppose, just that they were never talked about. Actually I was probably too innocent to realise they were nasty men, the first time somebody flashed at me I had no idea what I was meant to be looking at. So mothers weren't afraid of strangers as they are now, I think they were more frightened of people one knew.'

Without speaking, Meera handed a fresh box of tissues across. 'Thanks. I don't know what's come over me, it's not like me to cry. All this introspection – it's not healthy.'

'You said your mother was frightened of people one knew.'

'No, no, I can't have... Can we stop for a moment?' The water tasted of chlorine. After a while Rosina went on, 'I just meant that in those days we were kept under control more than children are now, we had to do as we were told.'

'By your father?... The father you used to hide from when you heard him coming?'

Did Rosina answer that question? She couldn't remember. Perhaps she had been saved by the bell. Meera was very strict about timekeeping. A session could end in mid-sentence when the hour was up.

She was unrelenting in her questions too, homing in on gaps, pouncing on omissions. Which was quite right. It was a waste of money and time and effort if you didn't tell her the truth about everything. At least everything that was relevant. That you were certain you really remembered.

Whatever it was those sessions of conversation did, however they worked, they'd done the trick. Real life resumed. And you never did tell Meera or Matthew or anyone else about going back to Polhearne.

Years ago; Jon's book, though in print, had long since stopped being news. He of course still kept mum, an adamant invariable refusenik: no PR, no interviews, no comment, which left journalists free to write about him uninhibited by any personal knowledge, but by this time very few bothered. One might notice occasional references and remarks; one woman saying the 3Ps had changed her life; another voicing her suspicion that there was something not quite right about it. An article in a travel section, describing residential retreats (Polhearne not recommended), mentioned rumours. Nothing substantiated, all so delicately expressed that no mud would stick, but repeating local gossip in delicate hints that Jon Polhearne was conning a gullible public. But he'd found a very canny 'unique selling point' as a guru who never gave advice, or made speeches or public appearances; who, having made a fortune with one book, had the restraint not to follow it up with another. Even the residential centre at his home was run by others without Polhearne's involvement. 'I don't think he does anything at all. He doesn't seem to do any work, there's no writing, not even any involvement with the centre except for taking rent from it. They say he goes shooting with his county neighbours instead,' was one unattributed quote. 'This February will be spent far from a crumbling mansion in soggy south-west England visiting the palaces of Rajasthan with an oil billionaire, a former ambassador and a Scottish duke.'

A mystery man, even a hollow man, the writer summed it up; something fishy there; Lucia his stooge, his feed. It was openly suggested that he married her for money, but also that after twenty-five years together she had invested her own life in his fame and success. It remained necessary for his wife to believe, and to believe that others believed, that he was a man without blemish, though hints were dropped of several blemishes in his personal life. 'A man who believes with such overweening, repugnant vanity that he is great, will also believe that he can do pretty much what he likes and all the more so when everyone around him seems to acquiesce and agree.'

Looking back to that secret, unadmitted day, Rosina could see that she was already working up to the nervous breakdown that had sent her to a psychotherapist. She was alone in the holiday cottage they owned at the time, in Dorset. The children had left, Matthew was in Dubai, and it was Rosina's birthday. St Valentine's Day. She had a flash of remembering her birthday party as an infant: a frilly dress, a pink sash, dancing shoes. Then the idea came to her out of the blue: I'll go now, today, on my own. Since their meeting in New York she and Lucia had exchanged the odd postcard, so she knew Lucia had taken Kit to try a new miracle cure, so-called, in Spain. Jon was in India with his grand companions. She decided, Now's the moment to go back to Polhearne.

It was signposted. That was new. She saw one of those brown heritage markers to show tourists where to go. Polhearne Study Centre. Even then she thought it was pointless, and almost generally acknowledged to be. Drop-outs got to live in a stately home and paid to keep its owners living in their inheritance, a bargain presumably of mutual benefit whose actual motive was never acknowledged by either party.

Stone eagles still perched on the old granite gateposts. On one side, a discreet carved slate plaque said 'Polhearne', and on the other was a notice about the 3P Fellowship, opening hours and charges. Rosina had never seen the cast-iron gates which had been taken down in 1939. She remembered a photo of them in some album, elaborate curlicues of metal topped with a gilded Cornish chough. Later she read about the scrap collections of the

Second World War, when Britain's streets and squares had lost their traditional cast-iron railings, uprooted and sent away to be turned into aeroplanes along with aluminium saucepans. In fact it was the wrong kind of metal, unsuitable for the manufacture of anything to do with the war effort. The collection had been undertaken either out of stupidity or for purposes of propaganda. Much of it was dumped at sea, some had been taken to secret quarries and stores all over the country where the historic metalwork was stashed, wasted but waiting to be reunited with its original home.

So these elegant black and gilt wrought-iron gates might possibly be the original ones, or, if a copy, then a very expensive one.

The drive had been resurfaced, though quite some time ago. Still, it was very different from the unmade road that used to be so treacherous on a gearless pushbike. The cattle grid halfway down the drive was gone. There were the huge yew trees, flanking the footpath and facing the formal gateway, always described as among the biggest in Britain and now, surely, even bigger, their wide, high canopies green-black against the wintery sky. Lucia and Rosina: by tradition, Mrs Tremellen said, the twinned trees were called after the daughters of the house.

And then, sweeping round the bend, one came face to face with the house itself. Rosina's foot involuntarily left the accelerator, as she stared at the strange but familiar, loved and hated frontage. Then somebody behind hooted and she drove on, following signs that read 'Visitor's Parking' and took her round, past the old stable yard and on to a tarmac surface marked out with white lines, where the pigsty had been.

Walking back towards the visitors' entrance at the back of the house in what had been the Tremellens' apartment, Rosina read the numerous finger posts directing people to the lecture theatre, the dream workshop, the art studio, the kiln, the visitor centre. She followed the last and found herself in a small museum set up in the disused laundry. The exhibits were about the house and family; a family tree of the Polhearnes going back to before the Norman conquest, and the Hicks family tree too, much less complete and much shorter but showing Mother's background and Jon's too. Rosina's name was on it, with equals Matthew Reid, but Morwenna and Nat weren't there. Seeing that omission was the first moment when Rosina felt any emotion about this return visit. Damn it all, they should jolly well be included. Not even a photo! But then there wasn't one of Rosina either except as a baby in a long frilly christening dress, wearing a white bonnet and held in the arms of the Siamese princess, at that time resident in Cornwall, who was her godmother. Bending over the glass case Rosina identified Lucia and Mother and then moved to the next display showing earlier ancestors. Some curious objects were on view. Father's OBE, Grandfather's VC, an early sepia photo of a shooting party, a row of seated women in huge hats, and behind them men in knickerbockers, with guns. A propeller from a biplane that ditched in the drink in 1918. A silver platter on which the visiting Queen Victoria had been served her Cornish cream tea. A tailor's dummy clothed in a brocade dress with large panniers and a fichu. Some faded scraps of linen labelled 'Flag taken in surrender by Captain Paul Polhearne at Waterloo'. A sword, a riding whip, a mahogany writing box.

They could do with a pro, Rosina was thinking when a soft voice said, 'It's time for our dream voyages, please to join us.' It was a gentle command, but so authoritative that there was no question of not obeying it. Rosina went out into the courtyard following the sage, an elderly man dressed like a monk in a homespun robe. She observed that the windows had been treated with the ugly brown wood stain that so many people had taken to using because it was said to resist the weather better than paint. It didn't suit the grey stones of the long low house. It could all do with a lick of paint; the house was in better nick than it had been during the post-war years of austerity but it looked a bit rundown and uncared for. 'How many people live here?' she asked,

'All the year round, about a dozen.'

'Including the Polhearnes?'

'Ah, no, they are quite separate in the west wing. If it's Jon you've come to see I'm afraid you'll be disappointed. I'm conducting today's session.'

Rosina smiled politely, and was taken aback when the man appeared offended and said huffily, 'I'm extremely well qualified, I am expert in the pre-Christian mythologies —'

'Pre-Christian?' she said faintly.

'Occult, pagan, Egyptian, Amerindian.' They progressed very slowly, the man, rather like the tortoise he resembled, inching along on the cobbled path and not stepping on the turf in the middle, as though it was a sacred lawn in an Oxford college. His panting old voice went on relentlessly: 'And I have studied among other philosophies Vedanta, Zen, the I Ching, the tarot, astrology, shamanism and of course artology. As far as dreaming is concerned, I am naturally a disciple of our proprietor, and through his instruction and inspiration help seekers after truth to discover the necessary technique for lucid dreams. Your hand will be guided to record the truth your gods and guiding spirits reveal.'

Rosina had been looking through ground-floor windows. Bedrooms and a television room and the pillared hall. Not looking where she was going, she barked her knee on a square chunk of granite.

The mounting block. Next thing, she realised that she must have blacked out. Not for long, a couple of seconds perhaps. She was beside the trunk-sized stone, her leg bleeding, feeling rather sick, her skin tingling and smarting, and with the old man standing on the cobbled path and peering at her. Mrs Tremellen would have said she'd 'come over all queer'. And Rosina remembered exactly why, and where the ghostly sensations in her body had sprung from, and what the sound in her ears was, a rough, shouting voice, 'You naughty, wicked girl, you must be punished.' At his mercy, tummy against this rough stone. Waiting, buttocks clenched. Red-faced, drops of moisture on his forehead, in his hand the black riding crop and behind him Mother, turning away.

'I must go.'

'Please stay.'

'I've got to leave, now.' She left the old man standing and ran out through the arched gateway, escaping from Polhearne – again.

The sessions with Meera started quite soon after that and over a period of months the demons were pushed back behind bars; but she'd never told Meera about that return visit.

They had talked about dreaming and prophecy, even a little about Jon. Mentioning his particular brand of soul-doctoring made the trained psychologist's lip discreetly turn down and Matthew's expression, 'rival witch doctors', flitted across Rosina's mind. But Meera was interested in the breach with Jon and Polhearne, probing it, coming back to it repeatedly, obviously supposing it had contributed to Rosina's present state. 'I've no feelings about Jon at all, not personally,' Rosina truthfully insisted. 'I don't think he makes my sister happy, he isn't kind to her, he lives on her money and I think he married her for it, but I don't feel any emotion about him. Really, truly.'

'And the house? Your childhood home? You never went back. That's quite a drastic reaction.'

'Honestly, Meera, it wasn't a little Eden that I was cast out of like Eve. I never got on with my parents so they were glad to see the back of me. And Lucia and Jon had to be on their side, they were living there.'

'And hoped to inherit. Was it in their interest for you to be out of the way?'

'Could be. But I'd not have taken a penny in any case. Not from...' Rosina's voice stopped.

After a silence Meera said, 'There we are again.'

'Look, it's a beautiful place, a historical treasure and I'm very happy that it's being preserved for other people to look at. But it wasn't a happy house. Lucia's welcome to it, or Jon for that matter. I left from choice and if I'd been the heir it would have gone on the market that very day, I'd never have moved back.'

'It wasn't a happy house?' Meera prompted, and Rosina returned to dredging up memories of childhood because that was how people neutralised them. Confront the past, accept it – and then forget it.

So now, in her own home, Rosina stared at the photo of Delia and Rosina, April 1951 and thought, if Sheila Mark's disappearance was all over the papers, even in *The Times*, why didn't I know about it? It must have been on the wireless news too. No TV then, the first time I ever saw it was the coronation – 1953.

I must have been sent straight back to school as soon as Delia's mother disappeared. We didn't look at *The Times* at that age and the house mistress would disapprove of anyone reading a different paper. Current affairs were for older girls. So it's quite possible that I didn't hear the news. But what happened before term started?

Shut your eyes and try free association. What comes into your head?

Father, his face taut, glistening, as it did when he was furious.

A platform. It's dark, I can hear the hiss of gas lamps. The train's coming. The wave of relief surging through my body.

Mother. Crying when she says goodbye. She's putting it on. She doesn't really love me, if she did she'd take better care of me.

Running, I've dropped my things and my hair's untied and the brambles and bracken and gorse are scratching my legs but I'm running as fast as I can, I've got to get away.

Chapter Nineteen

I'D BEEN WAITING for ages. More than an hour. The waiting room at Buriton police station was furnished with uncomfortable benches screwed to the walls. It was stuffy and smelly: disinfectant, principally, with a whiff of vomit. The only distraction provided was a two-day-old copy of the *Western Morning News*. I had read every single word at least twice: the front page headlines (Big Cat Sighted On Moor), sport – quite a lot of which I didn't understand, news in brief (tree felling in village churchyard, unnamed local woman dies in London hotel, junior minister visits Eden Project), the small ads – sales from cars to pets, services from massage to window cleaning. I'd done the nonogram, the crossword, seen what I could have heard if only this room had a radio. I have never been good at waiting.

Could I just leave? Or at least go out and buy a book?

But I was too unsure of myself in this unfamiliar situation, especially with a not quite clear conscience. Could this be about a packet of supermarket bacon? A false name written in faked handwriting purporting to witness my signature? Crime writers often meet police officers. They give us tips, try to curdle our blood, and let us think we have a kind of private line to officialdom. But this was different. Was I in trouble? What did they think I'd done? At least they'd assured me it was nothing to do with the family but I couldn't think what else this could be about. I felt increasingly nervous, which no doubt is the room's desired effect.

Then someone else was shown in, a soft, burly man, with big bifocals, strands of grey hair plastered on to his pink skull and cushiony lips.

'If you wouldn't mind waiting here, sir.'

'I have no objection, this is an interesting experience for me.' His voice was southern American. He looked at me, I gave an unenthusiastic nod and he exclaimed,

'I know you!'

'I'm sorry, I don't quite —'

'From your author photographs! This is a lucky chance in a strange circumstance.' He extracted a visiting card and I saw that he was my correspondent, Professor Elliot Rosenwald. I didn't ask why he was there but he soon told me. He'd had a similar phone call to the one I received the previous evening. Would I come down to the police headquarters in Buriton and give information? Wondering what would happen if I said no, I said yes. Appointments were made, mine for ten, his for eleven – and here we were. I asked if he had been told what for, though I had an uneasy feeling that I already knew. This was something to do with Connie and/or Spike.

'I do not know and am willing to possess my soul in patience. Meanwhile I should wish to improve the shining hour by taking this unexpected opportunity of speaking with you if you permit.'

'Of course. I think you said you're interested in the *City of Benares* episode,' I said, and added that I was sorry to have been away before and this was a lucky encounter.

Elliott Rosenwald brushed the metal seat with his handkerchief before lowering himself on to it, took out a mobile phone and turned it off and straightened his tie. He chose his words leisurely, using twenty when ten would do to tell me that first of all, I needed to understand where he was coming from. He was working on a comprehensive study of the artistic circles of the 1950s, obviously including the artists' colony, so called, in St Ives, despite some frustration of his quest by a certain lack of cooperation from a few surviving artists, one of whom in particular was unwilling to speak to scholars, writers (he begged my pardon for making a distinction between the two, clearly thinking I'd take it personally) or reporters.

'Who is this secretive artist?' I asked, and he said:

'You will have heard of Jix.'

'Rather brutal post-war abstracts?' I said, thinking each to his own and leaving out the adjectives that sprang to mind, ugly, second-rate and second-hand.

'Indeed, though in his case my area of interest is in the environment and the cross-fertilisation between the artists he met and in whose circles he moved.'

He seemed to be avoiding the word 'derivative' so I didn't use it either, instead murmuring, 'Social history rather than art history?'

'In this particular case, perhaps, for – and I apologise if I am offering you well-known information – he exhibited in New York during the early 1950s, at the artists' cooperative gallery, and the show was praised by the critic Harold Rosenberg. And of course he was able to encounter other artists at the club on 10th Street such as Willem de Kooning and Jackson Pollock, in a seminal though all too brief era of creation.'

'That lot – I thought they were boozing and talking all the time? Didn't one of them say the club's function was oral waste disposal?'

'If anyone used that expression, I have not heard it,' Elliot said coldly.

'Anyway, it must have been an exciting period, while it lasted.'

'Indeed, the pressures of fame and wealth were soon to alter their lives, disrupt the circle of colleagues for ever, a fate that also was experienced in its turn by the members of the artists' colony of St Ives where Jix arrived in the 1950s, that fertile period when great art was being made in this remote corner of your great nation. And' – he stood up, in lecturing mode, pacing the small room – 'not only was he a member, during the short years of his painting career, inexplicably, so far, terminated while he was still a young man, of the art colony which flourished here when it was still a town of sons of the soil and sea, the fishermen's town, but as it happened his home is in the neighbourhood also and that gives rise to another aspect of great interest, to me and to the psychologists of creativity also, since while the art he created may be categorised as second rate, nevertheless he was a Cornishman by descent unlike all but one of the other denizens of the art colony – Lanyon was a local man rooted in this soil.'

The pedagogue's sentence reaching its full stop, I agreed that being a native might make a difference, and found I had unleashed another mini lecture.

'One cannot spend more than the briefest period of time studying this subject, still less researching it in this area without recognising the belief, I refrain from using any more definite term, since as an outsider I am ill equipped to determine the validity of the idea, that those of local stock and breeding have a different perception of their native environment from that of their colleagues who moved to settle in it as outsiders. This is frequently, not to say invariably, asserted in discussions of Peter Lanyon's work, during and after his life, as it is of the Newlyn school artist of the previous generation, Harold Harvey.' Suddenly he switched mode. "Oh, Auntie, fetch the family tree/have I Cornish blood in me?" he declaimed, and added more quietly, 'I quote.'

'And Jix – what was his real name?'

'Jon Hicks.'

'That certainly sounds Cornish.'

'As he was, both by descent and by marriage. Jonathan Hicks was in fact distantly related to his bride, Miss Lucia Polhearne of Polhearne.'

'Wait a minute, did he change his name? You don't mean Jix is Jon Polhearne?'

'That is the case, yes.'

'How strange, you mean he was a painter for – how long?'

'He may have gone on painting privately but as far as I know he never exhibited after the early 1950s.'

'And then quarter of a century later out comes that book, and it's under a different name. His juvenile pictures are forgotten. But what about the *City of Benares*? What's the connection?'

'He was one of the survivors of that tragic episode.'

'You don't say so! How could I not have realised?'

Everyone who does any research gets a kick when connections and titbits of relevant information turn up out of the blue. Of course I was interested, even if this detail would be no more than a footnote. This book was not about that shipwreck. I had to focus on the reason why children were evacuated, what they were escaping, where they were going, how they lived and when they came home again. The tragedy which ended the official programme of overseas evacuation needed to be described and discussed but not at great length, and I already had several vivid accounts from other survivors.

'The use of his wife's famous old name may have masked the historical fact, possibly intentionally, for this man has chosen privacy and secrecy. My research up until this point has of necessity been in libraries and archives, in my own country the United States of America, I have conducted interviews on the West Coast, and in Florida and New York, and also in yours, London, Edinburgh, Oxford, and I have serendipitously acquired material and discovered hints or pointers that lead me ever onwards.'

'It must be difficult to write about a living artist who won't cooperate, it's an awkward situation.' I didn't actually mean to imply that he was wrong to try, but he must have been asked before how he justified trespassing on other people's privacy because he answered the unspoken criticism.

'An artist, perhaps more accurately in this case I should say a former artist, who was at least for a time, or believed himself to be, touched by the gods, or should I say inspired by a muse of fire, and consequently he belongs to the world, not to himself.'

'D'you mind if I ask, have you written creatively or made art yourself?'

'No, in actual fact it is the case that I have not,' he said. 'But I understand where you are coming from in posing that question, since although you are undertaking a historical work I know that you are also the author of many novels. So I ask you the question, have you not surrendered the right to privacy by virtue of offering your works of imagination to the public?'

'I've always rather agreed with Mrs Gaskell —'

'The Victorian novelist.'

'She told a journalist that the public should have no more to do with her than to buy or reject the wares she offered.'

'In her case there may have been justification for that view, but I would give you this response, that if you have cooperated in interviews about your private life then you have thereby surrendered the right to claim protection from scrutiny for those other sections of your life which you chose not to discuss.'

'That's a hard doctrine,' I said, having been interviewed myself and also interviewed and written about other people.

'However, and please believe that I have no intention of insulting you or being in the least discourteous, I think it is the creation of great art which removes a man from the company of his peers and confers immortality upon him. I still take the view that with immortality goes responsibility and one of an artist's responsibilities is to allow light to be shed on the magical process which has created riches out of nothing.'

Rosenwald-speak made me long to press a fast forward button, but his ideas were a welcome distraction from this inexplicable, infuriating, frightening limbo.

I remembered reading about the famously reclusive J.D. Salinger's unofficial biographer who, in spite of recognising his subject's 'regal aspect', persisted in working on his life against his wishes and without his cooperation. The biographer said he felt a duty to puzzle out this wondrous personage. All the same he admitted that Salinger had the right to repel biographers, as though owning one's own identity and preserving one's secrets was just some kind of game. Wincing, I was reminded of my own eagerness to find out more about one of my favourite authors, Patrick O'Brian, a man who notoriously preserved his privacy. It was thrilling to be commissioned to write a profile of him, and exciting when he agreed to cooperate. He invited me to meet at his London club where he treated me with the infinite courtesy of his novels' eighteenth-century heroes. But the mortification that followed is also engraved on my memory, when an American researcher proved that most of what O'Brian had ever said about his life was a tissue of lies.

'I believe the story and personality of an artist are highly relevant since without such knowledge we fail to understand the art,' Elliot began, back in lecturer mode.

'But was this particular artist a great artist? Is he immortal?'

'I cannot make that claim, either for his small oeuvre as a painter or for his writing. However, the collateral fascination is derived —'

At that moment, two hours and five minutes since I had entered this room, the door opened. I stood up, expecting to be escorted to one of those bleak interview rooms that are shown so regularly on TV, with concealed observers behind the glass, a tape recorder whirring and a good cop and bad cop. Instead, a burly, fatherly man came in. He apologised profusely for keeping us waiting, mentioned but did not describe an urgent problem that had delayed our appointments and said coffee was on its way. I made the automatic, insincere reply.

'That's quite all right.'

Elliot announced that it was far from all right. 'This lady has been kept waiting here for an inordinate length of time.'

'As I said, sir, I regret that, but it was unavoidable.'

'What is all this about? Why are we here?'

They didn't interview us together so the answer was given to us separately. But from what Elliot later told me, our reactions and remarks could just as well have been in chorus. Shock, horror, sorrow, pity.

The body of an unidentified elderly woman had been found in a room at Gatwick's Ramada Hotel at ten fifteen on Wednesday. They didn't go into detail, but I discovered later that a wretched eighteen-year-old from Croatia, doing casual work as a chambermaid, had knocked, called out 'Room service' and found her pass key didn't work, so got the hotel detective to do the necessary; unfortunately, when he got the door open, she followed him into the room.

'Oh, the poor girl,' I exclaimed.

'Yes, it wasn't very nice,' he agreed, adding that the heating was full on and the victim had bled from a head wound.

At this point there was a pause.

I've read thousands of crime novels. I've spent most of my life inventing, imagining and then describing the details of violent death and its consequences. Shouldn't all that have desensitised me? Why was it different to be told about this violent death than to read or write about others? The explanation has to be the one that I give when asked why 'respectable ladies' like Dorothy L. Sayers and Agatha Christie (or myself) choose to write about crime. Among many possible reasons, including money, the first, I think, must be that we are trying to neutralise fear. If we imagine and write out our terrors they might, may, should or usually do evaporate.

Here was fear realised though I didn't even have to see the consequences or smell or touch the end result. This was only dismay and disgust in the head. But it was sickening to visualise a woman I knew and liked, whose voice and scent and soft hands I remembered so clearly, in the condition of characters I had only imagined. There's no need to describe myself turning into that televisual archetype, the weeping witness being offered sugary tea by a young policewoman. Best to draw a veil: eventually I was able to listen to more of the story.

They could see that the victim was a prosperous elderly woman. The rings, no longer on her fingers, had left pale indentations on the skin. Small diamond studs were still in her ears. Her clothes were not extravagant but not cheap either, Jaeger and Liberty. But the pockets were empty and there was no handbag or case. They couldn't identify her.

The room had been booked and paid for with a credit card by a Mr E. Johns. Nobody took much notice. Single men often booked double-bedded rooms at that hotel, nudge nudge.

'So how did you find out who she was?'

'Calls for that room were put through to the incident room.'

'Of course, that's how you got her name.'

'We'll need formal identification, of course.'

'I've got to ask – do you know what happened?'

I didn't get an answer at the time, which was probably just as well, but the police had already concluded exactly how, where, why, when and above all who had inveigled Connie Thorne to that room, where she was knocked out with a blow to the back of the head from a blunt instrument, probably a rock inside a nylon stocking. Then another nylon stocking was tied round her neck and made tighter and tighter by some bar or stick pushed into the loop and twisted round and round: a garotte. She had been strangled. Death is dreadful, but that is a dreadful death. Even now it's hard to think about the awful, ugly meeting of the lively, living person and her end in a violence which I might have visualised, with chilly professional accuracy, any time during my career.

Onwards. Connie's body was left on the bed. Her killer took anything that might identify her and went out of the room, leaving the 'Do not disturb' card on the door handle and a plug of superglue in the keyhole.

I didn't know those details that morning. But they did tell me why there had been the delay in seeing me. It was because Simon

Peter Kelly had been arrested. By the time I saw them, he had already been charged with the murder of Mrs Constance Thorne.

'Does he admit it?'

I got a non-answer, as did Elliot when he asked the same question. I had no idea if Spike had confessed or, if he had, why he would have done such a thing.

All we were told that day was that anyone who had seen the victim or the accused in the last few weeks was being asked to help with information. Had Mrs Thorne said anything about going abroad? Or could I think of any reason for her to be staying near the airport? Had I ever seen the deceased with Simon Kelly, also known as Spike? Did she talk about him? What did the nature of their relationship seem to be?

They probed perseveringly, but I didn't have very much to tell, I could only explain why Connie and I had first met and describe my visit to Goonzoyle.

As for Elliot, I had no idea at the time what information he had, and when we met or spoke again he always took care not to let me, another writer, know what he was really up to, for fear that I'd scoop his exclusive information before his magnum opus appeared. Because he was so reticent, I just assumed that he was taking an inordinate amount of trouble to collect and double check tiny details. All the same I didn't doubt his story, being quite familiar with the obsessions of scholars, however little relevance the sad fate of Connie's young brother and all the other lost child evacuees apparently had to Jix's biography. Presumably Elliot saw Jix as a man haunted by survivor's guilt – not an implausible idea, I thought, for that inchoate, undigested emotion might account for the emotional blankness I saw in his paintings.

In fact Elliot told the full story – no doubt in his usual slow, ponderous style – to the police. He had to get it off his chest. He still expected to make his scholarly name but all the same was bursting with regret and remorse. He believed it was all his fault.

I learnt much later what Elliot Rosenwald had said. He told the police, 'I feel shockingly, painfully responsible for this tragedy. I directed this young man's steps towards Cornwall and thereby he encountered Constance Thorne. I encouraged him to seek out the author of the book whose manuscript was in his unknown mother's possession. It was a dreadful mistake.'

Spike had no idea he was adopted until he was twenty-six and an unemployed arts graduate. His mother died while he was in Bali. He flew back to Edinburgh to find that Jean Kelly had died in as good order as she lived. Her husband, Simon's 'dad', was a long distance lorry driver who was killed on a French autoroute in Simon's first year at college. Jean had been a social worker, who on retiring the previous year left her office casework sorted and files weeded. Then she got rid of all the inessentials in her small house near the zoo. Simon returned to find that the cremation had already been conducted, as specified, the cupboards were tidy, her documents sorted in labelled filing boxes: tax, house, insurance. And there was a cardboard carton marked 'Simon, strictly private.'

Its contents were folded inside a cotton cloth printed with a faded Indian tree-of-life pattern. There was the canvas holdall with the carbon-copy typescript inside, a folder of Simon's inoculation and exam records, and an unmarked envelope containing a letter written on the day Jean was told her illness was incurable. It was addressed to Simon, and broke the news that she and Tam were not his real parents. They had always intended to tell him but the right moment never came and the years passed and it became more and more difficult to think of disrupting his security. She was sorry. But he had to understand that she had loved him as her own since he was five weeks old.

'Your birth mother left you with a neighbour and didn't come back. The police called Social Services and I was working in south London then so I was the care worker who came for you. I fed you and took you to a temporary foster home but in that short time I already realised how special you were. Then we heard that the poor girl had taken her own life, she was mentally ill at the time, and she fell to her death from a cliff top near a place in Cornwall called Trevena.

'You were put up for adoption, Simon, because nobody could find out who you really were, your birth was not even registered yet. Your poor mother called herself Jennifer Galloway but that was really someone else she had met in a commune in West Wales. While she was there they called your mother Moondust. People remembered that she was pretty and sensitive and kind. They thought she might have been a psychology student. One day she just left the commune without warning, and nobody knows where she was till she moved into her bedsit, and that was six months before your birth, and she was quite alone, never had visitors or invited the neighbours in. They said she always had a smile if they met on the stair and she kept the room clean and nice, with picture postcards stuck up. She was a great reader, always borrowing library books. She said she was a typist. Her neighbour said the tap tap tap sometimes drove her mad.

'Simon, I have written down every little thing I know about your mother, and I kept this bag and her Indian bedspread for you, but there were no letters or photos so all there was is in this box.

'Simon, I am sure your birth mother was not a sinful or bad woman, judge not lest you be judged, nobody can help having post-natal depression. You must try to remember her kindly, Simon, I do believe she was a loving, caring person.

'When your father and I moved to Scotland we took you as our son, but you should have been told this before, Simon. I am sorry. I want to explain when you come home but if you ever have to read this letter I hope you understand.'

Chapter Twenty

ROSINA HAD MANAGED pretty well since Matthew died. Other people saw her as one of those tough self-sufficient elderly widows who make good lives for themselves without putting on a show of mourning for an indecent length of time or alternatively, doing what her father would have called 'going to the bad'. Or, in Rosina's case, returning to it. There had been moments of admitting into her consciousness unacceptable fantasies in which she went back to Paris and found a toyboy, or advertised for love, or inserted a highbrow come-on into the lonely hearts column of an upmarket literary journal, as someone of her age had recently done and then written a confessional book about sexagenarian sex with strangers. 'I admire you so much for keeping your dignity,' an acquaintance of many years had said, and added, less convincingly, 'but then you never were one for wearing your heart on your sleeve.'

True. Rosina had wept and grieved, but she took no notice of the advice to wear black and keep herself to herself for at least year, Victorian style. She had cleared out Matthew's wardrobe within a week of his death, she knew exactly what bureaucratic hoops needed to be jumped through, what societies, clubs, former employers and colleagues needed to be informed. People told her she was wonderful.

The tears were shed in private. So only she knew that gradually there had been fewer of them, that the scar tissue was growing over the amputation site. But there were still some days when, alone in the house, she felt absolutely unequal to keeping herself going. The telephone didn't ring. The postman brought nothing but bills and circulars. The email in-box said, No new messages.

She had turned into useless baggage, not wanted on the voyage.

This was one of those days. Nat had gone out at dawn, Morwenna hadn't been in touch for ages, her closest friend and neighbour was in Italy on holiday. Out in the garden, on wet grass and stupidly near the cliff edge, Rosina's foot slipped. Simultaneously her mind was flooded with two instinctive and contradictory feelings. The dominant one, luckily, was to save herself, and she grabbed on to the fence, so abruptly and vigorously that her shoulder was still feeling the effects. But even before her body was still, her mind was full of the notion, what would it matter if I'd gone over the edge? So what?

As she was walking back to the house, the postman swerved into the drive, scattering gravel with his racing turn and skidding to a halt. He had brought the daily dose of junk mail, no interesting letters now that most people communicated by email – oh oh. An official letter. The logo on the brown envelope consisted of five letters of doom: DEFRA. The Plant Police were coming this very day. She stood up to get ready for them, and then sat down again. There wasn't really anything to do except wait.

Matthew's face looked out at her from the silver frame. He would have been philosophical about this, she would have taken strength from his calm strength.

'Stop it, Rosina,' she said aloud. Remember how you snapped at him for not caring enough, remember how you told him he was overcautious, too conventional, even boring. It had irritated Rosina that Matthew never even drove over the speed limit. Memories should be truthful. He wouldn't let her get away with equating her camellias and her children.

Yet, looking back, Rosina realised what a lot he had let her get away with, and suddenly wondered why, and then – a revolutionary thought – wished he hadn't. Morwenna's clear voice: 'Why d'you let Mum get away with it, Dad? You tell her.' She must have been about ten, already chippy and poised for adolescence. Sitting at the table in the bright white kitchen in London doing homework: drawing her family tree. 'You can't just tell me they were horrid and not say why. Aunt Lucia didn't think they were beastly.'

Nat: 'Bet they were nicer to her then.'

Morwenna: 'Dad doesn't care, he said so. Why can't we go?'

'You can, if you want,' Rosina had said. 'I'm not stopping you. If you're invited.' But an invitation did not come, or if it ever did, Morwenna had lost interest, or so it seemed. For all Rosina knew, she'd made her own arrangements, might actually have gone to Polhearne. Come to think of it (and why hadn't Rosina thought of it before?) Nat must have been over to see the place, it would be extraordinary if he hadn't. Less extraordinary though still surprising was that today, at last, she didn't seem to mind, at least as far as inspecting his inheritance went. Throughout her married life Rosina's mind had always, automatically, blanked out thoughts of him: Jon Hicks Polhearne. She had trained herself to forget him and when she was forced to hear him mentioned would find herself feeling peculiar. Once when Morwenna kept returning to the subject until Matthew lost patience and sent her to bed, Rosina found herself, without conscious thought, washing her hands at a running tap till the water came out cold. Morwenna wouldn't leave it alone. 'But he's famous, and he's my uncle! Why can't we talk about Aunt Lucia's husband? It's not fair.'

Had that, in fact, been the attraction? It would be psychologically primitive but could be true to say she had been paying her sister back – for what? Winning? Winner takes all. For not protecting her, for not seeing that she needed protection, for not being treated in the same way, if she wasn't – though that was something Rosina never knew. When Rosina turned into a black-clothed, kohl-eyed, chain-smoking, philosophising, argumentative Parisian she was in a set of people who all hated and repudiated their families. For a while she put hers out of mind.

Then Jon turned up. Somehow he insinuated himself into her society, made friends with friends of her friends, drank in her familiar bars, so unobtrusively that by the time she saw him, he was already accepted by the others. How did he manage to be unnoticeable to the point of invisibility? Soon he was there in the background and then he turned up at a reading in Shakespeare and Company. Soon he had slipped into the group, wearing its black clothes, sharing, belonging and speaking very little. He didn't know much about the ideas and books they discussed, he had apparently lost interest in art, but pretty soon he had blended in. You couldn't see the join. It was a polyglot set, where questions were not asked. Nobody cared where you came from or where you were going. Beatniks lived in the present. Soon Rosina's reflexive loathing seemed like just another part of her discarded past.

'There is nothing to hate in that man,' a Russian girl called Irina said. She was bonily thin, white-skinned with red spots on her cheeks, and given to portentous insights. 'He is hollow within.'

'He's married to my sister.'

'That excites you?'

She could not admit to inhibitions. In this world women had chucked their traditional roles as wives, mothers or spinsters but conformed to other stereotypes. Rosina could be a courtesan, whore and/or ball breaker. But she still had a personal sticking point. Jon had been the man who brought sex to life in Rosina. He was also the one who linked it with shame and pain.

One day she woke up, as so often, in a tangle of people and bodies, after the kind of session where you didn't know who you were touching or who was touching you or even if sensations were in your own skin and nerve endings or someone else's. Her eyes opened on limbs entwined with hers and looked up to see Jon's face. Rosina screamed, leapt up and ran naked out of the room. By the time the others had come to, or come round,

Rosina had gone. They found her in the Café Mabillon, having a farewell drink.

'Don't go.'

'It's him or me.'

They chose her and someone must have sent him home because Lucia's baby was born ten months later. Jon resumed his guise of country gentleman and Rosina her determination to have nothing to do with him.

Old history; now that it was decades too late, Rosina thought, Matthew should have made me face up to it early on. He should have made me move on.

Since he died Rosina had found that 'never speak ill of the dead' was a description, not an injunction, because one simply didn't want to. But it was a quite new idea, to realise that Matthew wasn't perfect. He'd been silly too, a surprising realisation because Matthew's image was Mr Sensible, reason personified.

Rosina knew what his reaction would be to the Plant Police: he'd say it was wise to take every precaution, officials should certainly have the right of entry to any private garden and the power to order the execution of plants and shrubs at will. The penalties for obstruction ought to be serious. So Matthew would be telling her, even though he'd mourn the destruction no less sincerely, if less demonstratively, than Rosina.

This is like waiting for the knock on the door in the small hours when the secret police come to take you away.

Giving herself a mental shake, Rosina told herself to keep a sense of proportion. More apt to remember Matthew's deep voice quoting Cavafy's poem called 'Waiting for the Barbarians' or even to think of waiting with a sick child in the old days, when doctors still made house calls.

She looked at the clock and said aloud, 'Anyway, it's far too early for civil servants.' She went upstairs, caught a deterrent glimpse of her reflection, and turned the bath and radio on. She lay in the hot, scented water for the duration of a ritually inconclusive bout between one of the more aggressive regular presenters and a government minister who had rehearsed his lines and repeated them unaltered at least four times before she stopped counting. After that Rosina applied several layers of expensive cosmetics and creams whose end result, she hoped, was to make it seem she was wearing none of them. Then she chose clothes from the old days, a Sonia Rykiel trousers and top. She was going to hate them for their associations with what happened today, and it occurred to her she could pass them on to Grace, but meanwhile they were the props to an image that said don't mess with me. She tied round her neck an antique silk scarf, a semi-abstract design of waves and a lighthouse. Nat had unexpectedly brought it home the night before. 'A present, Nat? It's not my birthday or anything.'

'We – I just thought you'd like it.'

'I do, very much.'

'It's local, there was a firm in St Ives in the 1930s doing silk prints.'

'Crysede, it was called, and I've always wanted one. Wherever did you find it?'

'In Truro, an antique and vintage clothes shop,'

'Well, thank you, it's really sweet of you,' Rosina said, refraining from adding that it must have been a first for Nat, who had never noticed what he or anyone else was wearing.

Going downstairs again she saw that she had managed to fill in three-quarters of an hour. It was going to be a long day. She made coffee, not her usual strong black espresso but a mugfull of sugar and full cream milk, and at the back of the cupboard found some sweet biscuits of a kind she did not normally like, and realised that she'd crammed three of them into her mouth almost without thought. She put her coffee on the kitchen table, and saw that glaring at her on the top of the messy pile of magazines and papers was, inevitably, the page containing the latest news story.

'Plants affected by "sudden oak death" in Cornwall are to be destroyed and parts of infected gardens cordoned off under new government measures. Nine British trees have been affected by the disease which has destroyed thousands of acres of woodland in the United States. Environment Minister Ben Bradshaw is introducing border controls to prevent a similar disaster in Britain. He fears it could become a worse problem than Dutch elm disease. "The evidence from California and the US is that it has ravaged 80% of their native oak and we don't want to see that happening here to our native beech, chestnut and other trees," he said. Three disease sites have been identified in Cornwall – and at each one it is thought the fungus has spread to trees from rhododendron bushes. At the Lost Gardens of Heligan, rhododendrons are being controversially burned under the orders of the Department for Environment, Food and Rural Affairs (DEFRA) because it says the plants showed signs of the disease. Mr Bradshaw defended the action, saying the host plants for the disease in this country were rhododendrons and other non-native, imported shrubs, which tended to be found in many historic gardens and nurseries. "That's where it has been found and it is important we take tough measures now to prevent the disease spreading outside those gardens and into our native woodland."'

It was a beautiful day, one it was a shame to waste staring at a screen but Rosina couldn't face the garden. She went to the computer and read the *Guardian* online, though she took in very little about planned cuts to the coastguard service, the epidemic of obesity, plans for more toll roads, the death of a murder suspect, or the state of the economy. Then she checked what the *Times* comment writers were on about today. She ordered a book for Morwenna's birthday from Amazon, flipped through the webcam pictures on Radio Cornwall's site, (good surf on the north coast, rain in Truro) and looked at some bookmarked sites. A gardeners' forum called for people to join in a magical action.

If enough of them summoned up their own inspiration and creativity, aimed and emitted in 'bursts' towards those groups/individuals who were seeking to understand the origins of Phytophthora ramorum, it would, she read, help them in their quest.

I can just see it, Rosina thought. She was to try to enter a dialogue with the spirit of the fungus and/or the oak tree. Staring at images of plants infected by the disease, the writer claimed, would help her to help the spirits to magically build up the oaks' immune system, and would emit a summons to the predator, whatever it might be. Through meditation she could come into contact with the 'Collective Spirit of Bacteria' which live in oak forest soil. These bacteria could then themselves mutate into predators of the fungus.

Matthew would have been amused, but in her present mood of unrelieved negativity Rosina was simply irritated. What is this nonsense? she asked herself, and scrolled down to the bottom of the page where she found a list of inspirations and mentors. The only name Rosina recognised was Jon Polhearne's. That figures, she thought and was about to click on a link to something called a 'Wiccan Web' when she heard a knock at the front door and a voice call, 'Mrs Reid?'

Two people were waiting outside. 'We knew you were in, we saw you through the window.' They held out official cards encased in plastic with mugshots. They were spies, of a kind, officials with powers and rights to enter, expropriate or destroy. There was no point in arguing, Rosina knew. For the last few months the principal topic of conversation amongst gardeners had been the depredations of the storm troopers from DEFRA. Now they had reached her property. They would walk from rare shrub to precious tree sentencing them to death. She couldn't bear to watch.

'Will you go out and get started on your own?'

'Perhaps that's best.' The woman wouldn't meet her eyes, but the man had adopted a kind of bedside manner.

'I'll leave you to it.' Rosina went back to the desk. The windows of this room faced on to the lawn and a rose bed. The two people walked on to the grass, each with a clipboard. Then the computer emitted a friendly little ping and the icon of an envelope popped up. It was a message from Grace Theobald.

'Rosina: my grandfather died Saturday (St Mary's Paddington). Delia heartbroken, now desperate to clear his name. Announced late news, media fuss inevitable so cremated pronto this a.m. Unknown solicitor produced unexpected will (n.b. no property to leave) specifying burial in Trevena where last saw "dear wife Sheila". No can do, vicar says churchyard full (prob. excuse) but we plan to scatter at Trevena as soon as newspack moves on to next story, cross fingers the delay outwits media and vicar. I'll let you know. Please come.'

Rosina turned back to the desktop icon called Newspapers and Magazines, and re-opened the *Guardian* website. Murder suspect dies, the headline she had read without taking in earlier, proved to be followed by an account of Stephen Mark's death in a London hospital, plus a reprise of the finding of the remains of his wife a few weeks previously and of his being charged, and then of the events of 1951 when she had disappeared.

Dead, not disappeared: her body was in the mineshaft.

I knew it.

What did I know? Rosina's thought flickered away like an acquaintance's name during a 'senior moment'.

I knew she was dead all along.

Did I really? How? All these years?

Seeing Goonzoyle again might make memory clear, like vision when the bandage was lifted after a cataract operation. I'll go down. Meet Delia. Pay my respects to her father.

The article described his difficult life, continually moving on from one job, home and town to the next when rumours started about his past as they always, inevitably, repeatedly did. There was the odd quote from other residents of the old people's home, those who remembered him as a shy and retiring old man, and those who evidently did not. Reporting had been restrained while he was alive, since although he was never going to stand trial he was technically 'the accused'. Now that he was safely dead, the media were free to publish the evidence that might have been given in court. A picture was painted of the caravan holiday for a young family in austere post-war Cornwall and the drama of that evening in 1951 when the search and rescue teams turned out to hunt for Sheila Mark. There was no further need to pull journalistic punches, so it was unequivocally asserted that right until the end of his very long life Stephen Mark had got away with murder.

Chapter Twenty-One

'A MAN AGED 27 was remanded in custody yesterday charged with murdering a pensioner. Simon Kelly, who gave his address as Goonzoyle House, Trevena, Cornwall, was accused of killing Mrs Constance Thorne of the same address, at the Ramada Hotel, Gatwick, Surrey. Kelly, who appeared dressed in a black T-shirt and jeans, spoke only to confirm his name and age during the 10 minute hearing. He was remanded until 23rd May when he will appear before a judge at Truro Crown Court. There was no application for bail. Yesterday neighbours spoke of their shock at what had happened. Godfrey Hosking, 53, of Churchtown Farm, Trevena, said, "It is a real tragedy. Connie Thorne was a very nice lady and always had a friendly smile. She often said she was thrilled to be back home again, having moved to live in the area recently after living overseas since the war. She'd often say that she was still 'proper Cornish' and quickly made herself part of the community. She'll be greatly missed.'

Our papers are delivered after breakfast and in theory I don't look at them till lunchtime, having got some work done first. In practice any interruption is usually welcome, though that is not quite the right word to use for this front page story.

On page 5, placed at a cautiously un-contemptuous-of-court distance from that news report, 'our west of England correspondent' had written a feature with the title, 'The Village of Death'. Trevena, it said, had a permanent population of no more than 200 people, swollen when the caravans and chalets were full of their holiday tenants to perhaps ten times as many, which still left it a little place, which had seen or been involved in a sinister and statistically extraordinary series of unnatural deaths, none as yet explained, all of women. In gloating and gory detail the series of murders was recited: the skeletons in the mineshaft followed decades later by the murder of Constance Thorne.

I had seen previous references to Sheila Mark's disappearance, because unsolved mysteries are revived every few years, and I'd read the recent headlines about Stephen Mark's arrest, but I am that perverse kind of crime writer who is not particularly interested in true life crime. So until seeing that list, I hadn't quite taken in how peculiar it actually was.

The journalist was vague, speculative and malicious about Stephen Mark's daughter and granddaughter – at the time I'd not yet met Delia or Grace Theobald. But he was not clear enough for me to make out what he was suggesting. Was it that there was a connection between the deaths? Or that there could not possibly be a connection, given the six and a half decades between the death of the unidentified remains and Connie Thorne.

I had to work. That morning the postman and and three of Royal Mail's rivals came in procession to the door bringing stacks of things to read. Three novels to review; another two entries for a literary prize for which I was on the judging panel, the bound typescript of five years' worth of letters home sent to me by a man who had been evacuated to South Africa. A retired journalist, who had stayed on in America at the end of the war, had published a memoir of his experiences as a 'war guest'. The girl who had been cast as a younger sister to Elizabeth Taylor in a propaganda movie sent on loan her scrapbook full of black and white photos and her mother's letters, poignant in their brave determination to keep her end up.

An offprint: a psychotherapist's conclusions on the lasting consequences of evacuation, namely that they had often been disastrous. Young children were parted from their parents, sent to live with strangers and, in the case of overseas evacuees, were apart for literally years. Many had arrived back in England not knowing who their families were, walking along a station platform asking unknown adults, 'Excuse me, are you my mother?' Mothers, perhaps even more poignantly, had asked, 'Excuse me, are you my son?' Obviously they were traumatised, a verdict which seemed incontrovertible, but an uncomfortable one for me to accept, having been one of those children, away from home between the ages of two and five, myself. However, with proper objectivity, and trying not to take it personally, I copied the statement that 'much neurological evidence now exists proving that a lack of parental love in early childhood can close down the part of the brain that controls the capacity to express feeling, causing children to become emotionally numb.'

I turned to a package containing Pendry Dilwyn's dissertation for a class called 'History 263b' which one of Yale's university librarians had finally forwarded with a note explaining the delay. The candidate had handed it in by the due date in the fall of 1981, but said he was on the track of some extra material which he wanted to be allowed to include as an addendum. Unfortunately he died a week later, falling from a high window in New York's Plaza Hotel; the autopsy showed traces of drugs in his bloodstream. So the thesis had never been assessed or filed in the usual way, and had therefore been difficult to trace, but here it was at last and she hoped it wasn't too late.

It was called 'The Evacuation of British Children to the United States during WW2: Class Consciousness and Social Class Mobility.' Dilwyn discussed British snobbery in a tone of disgusted fascination. He used quotations from interviews and correspondence with people who were dead by the time I started my research. One was referred to in the thesis as 'Gwyn'. A footnote said that although this informant had passed away since sending his response to Pendry Dilwyn's small ad, his request to remain unidentified would be honoured. Gwyn had avoided the trauma of evacuation, and more importantly saved his life, by getting himself sent home from Liverpool before his group embarked on the doomed *City of Benares*.

'After spending a few days waiting in Liverpool, it increasingly seemed to me that ratting on the old country was a coward's way out. I remember one boy there, he was from a very poor background in darkest Cornwall but we got quite pally and he even picked up a few ideas from me but he boarded that ship and four days later he was dead, so I had a lucky escape. But I never wanted to go in the first place. It seemed to me that the place of an Englishman was in this country fighting the enemy and it was the duty of people like us to set a good example to those less fortunate than ourselves.'

Another informant described as 'a peer of the realm' was taken away from Eton to go to America with his mother on the *City of Benares*. They had booked expensive cabins on an upper deck. The teenager noticed that the traditional class distinctions of transatlantic liners were maintained. He only caught sight of the government evacuees once or twice, the second time on that last fatal evening when he was in the lounge, wearing a dinner jacket and reading a book about Scott and the Antarctic and hoping his mother would go to bed soon so that he could join some younger passengers she thought unsuitable, and smoke a cigarette out of her sight.

'I'll never forget the last moments in that lounge, I was eyeing a pretty American girl in a flowered dress but I didn't dare talk to her. There was a chap called Hicks. I knew him because he was in his first year at my prep school when I was a prefect. He left the room at a run. Seasick. Then I spotted one of the government evacuees, a chap who had a nasty habit of snooping around. There had been a row the day before when he got in the kitchen and injured his hand on some machinery, so badly they had to amputate a finger. I had actually spoken with the lad during a lifeboat drill out on deck. I mistook him for young Hicks who was the same physical type and for some reason, probably because I told him off when he cheeked me about my title, we got into an exchange about heredity. He said by rights he should be a gentleman and rich but I was not prepared to have any socialist talk and shut him up quickly. I was getting up in order to come the heavy-handed school prefect and make him go down to the lower deck where he belonged when we heard the explosion.'

Pendry Dilwyn broke off just where it was getting interesting, presumably for want of sufficiently snobbish quotes about the peer of the realm's escape from drowning, until one offensive sentence: 'More passengers would have survived if the crew had not been predominantly Lascars who, of course, panicked.' Dilwyn quoted this as a lead in to his own thoughts about social mobility and British class distinctions. I tried to follow the pure sociological theory but was relieved to be interrupted.

'Phone. It's for you, Professor Rosenwald.'

He had stayed on in Cornwall, not I gathered so much to do research, as because he felt both responsible for what had happened to Connie and that he had some kind of duty to Spike.

I was less hospitable to him than I care to admit now. I felt contaminated by the whole episode. Anyway, it really had nothing to do with me. But I picked up the receiver, and listened to long, periphrastic apologies for disturbing me at home and another leisurely justification for still being in Cornwall. Elliot didn't feel that he could abandon the young man, however ghastly a crime he might have committed.

'I've got to get him a lawyer, an attorney.'

'He'll have talked to a duty solicitor,' I said.

'They say there's some sort of public defender, I don't know if it's pro bono.'

'We have legal aid, you know.'

'It's not good enough, he needs an expert.'

'I wouldn't have thought he's very well off, d'you think he can afford it?'

'This is on my tab. I owe it to this young man, to myself.'

'Does he actually want you to help him?'

'I believe he does, but no matter, either way this is on my conscience, I cannot walk away. However, I am at something of a loss here, I do not understand your system and I am a stranger in this area. So I want to ask you for some names, trial lawyers, if that is what you call them in this country. Do you know of the right person?'

'No, but I know a man who does.'

There are several lawyers in my family, though all of them specialise in civil law, so it was not difficult to get a recommendation, and that evening I called Elliot to give him a name.

Spike had been refused bail on the grounds that he might scarper. He was on remand in Exeter prison so the local branch of Wootton Hardman sent somebody described as 'one of our criminal specialists'. Her name was Marika Hardman, and it turned out that she was the great-granddaughter of the firm's founder, but even if nepotism had played its part in her appointment heredity also did its work since she turned out to be highly efficient, although she looked so young that she had to prove her identity with a series of phone calls and arguments before they would let her inside the jail. When Spike was brought in to see her he thought she was a social worker trainee. But she knew her job, which turned out to include briefing Elliot in exhaustive detail.

Much later, I saw Marika Hardman for myself: getting on for six feet tall, painfully thin, and so much in the habit of bending that her spine was already fixed in what would soon be a painful curve. She had drooping eyelids and hair. In sum, not at all what you'd expect a defence lawyer with the dogged instincts of a fox terrier to look like.

Spike had instructed her to tell Elliot everything. Elliot sent in a message asking if he could pass information on to me. Miss H, as Elliot referred to her, reported back that Spike didn't care if it was all published and said what about getting his story into a blog?

The murder charge was based on these facts.

The police had found that the Gatwick Ramada's Room 503 had been booked for four nights by a man who paid in full, in advance, in cash. The man was tall and thin, that much the receptionist remembered, and was wearing dark glasses, a peaked cap and a zipped jacket with a high collar that covered his chin. But she hadn't really taken much notice. The photo they showed her could have been the man, she supposed, but then again, maybe not.

Wasn't it unusual to pay cash? Yes, not many people did, but not so few that she remembered everything about the man who had done so.

Wasn't it peculiar to book four nights at an airport hotel? No, visitors to London often did, OK so it was under the flight path but their sound insulation was excellent and had the questioner seen the hotel's facilities? You'd have to go a long way to find anything better. The upshot of the interview was, they couldn't say for sure that the booking had been made by Spike but couldn't say it wasn't him either. Someone did remember Connie turning up. She'd arrived in a taxi and when a receptionist asked 'Can I help you?' had said no, she was meeting someone in his room, she knew the number. 'She was very nice, she had a sweet smile but I thought she looked very worried. In fact I wondered if I should escort her, but she said she was all right. How sorry it makes me that I let her go alone.'

Surely somebody must have seen the room's occupant at some point? What about the chambermaid? Didn't he have room service? But that drew a blank too. The cleaning of the hotel rooms was subcontracted out. Teams of young people were employed, most from Eastern Europe, nearly all speaking no English, and the turnover was so fast that the same person never came two weeks running. Two different students had cleaned

Room 503 that week and neither of them could remember anyone in it or anything about its condition – until, of course, the last morning when the body was found.

'It didn't seem to me that there was strong evidence against Spike,' Elliot told me later on, 'even though it turned out that he did go to London that week. But then I learned that he did have a good deal to gain.'

Connie had made a new will not long before she died. She'd left Spike everything she possessed. By any standards one had to agree he had incontrovertible motive.

Chapter Twenty-Two

IT WAS SUCH a long time since Rosina had driven the full length of the peninsula from East to West Cornwall that the volume of traffic took her by surprise. How dramatically it had increased in the last few years. And surely all these industrial estates along the main road were new? It was a windy day, blowing from the south-east with intermittent, vicious flurries of rain. It seemed to be taking twice as long to get down west as she had expected, not that it mattered, since she had left hours earlier than necessary. All the same, it was annoying, when she was nearing St Budy, to find herself in an almost stationary queue of traffic.

Almost without thinking about it Rosina swung the car into a narrow lane. Funny how the most trivial details stayed in the memory for decades: this was a short cut to Trevena but it would first lead her directly towards Polhearne.

Previously Rosina would have jammed on the brakes the moment she'd registered that thought, and rejoined the queue of traffic no matter how long it took to get through. Now to her own surprise she found herself actually feeling interested in the idea of seeing Polhearne again.

She remembered this road as an unmade country lane with overgrown hedges where she'd pick blackberries in September and at this time of year great bunches of bluebells and Ragged Robin. Now the street was lined with little houses hardly bigger than the shining cars parked beside them. Hadn't this been part of the Polhearne estate, a back drive leading to the farm buildings? Now there was a school, the 3P Primary School, built of glass and metal frames in primary colours with lots of tarmac and marked-out parking places.

Here we are. Rosina considered her own feelings: heart not beating fast, nor pulse racing, nor skin sweating, nor hand trembling. I'm not quite myself today, she realised.

The brown heritage markers had disappeared since her other visit, the wrought-iron gates were standing open and one of the gatepost eagles had disappeared. The drive had acquired pockmarks and potholes, almost back to the rough, unmade state of fifty years ago, and the grass on either side was long overdue for cutting. She stopped to read a notice, enveloped in clear plastic, that was stapled to a fencepost. A draft tree preservation order on the yew trees. She took a pen out of the glove box and wrote, 'Also known as Lucia and Rosina.' Driving on, she wondered at herself. What was that about? And where was the 3P Fellowship? The only place she had seen the three entwined letters was outside the primary school. Had they finished, died off, moved out, or what? She reached the car park which had been so organised and busy last time. Now there was no sign that the house was open to the public or serving any other function, and only two cars were parked up at the far end. Rosina stopped by the path to the house. The ground was wet but it wasn't raining at that moment. Getting out of the car she smelled woodsmoke, realised it was the wrong time of year for bonfires, and then that that she could hear the buzzing of a chainsaw. So the Plant Police had handed out death sentences here too, condemning Polhearne's ancient rhododendrons, direct descendants of seeds and cuttings brought back from the Far East by nineteenth-century plant hunters. Rosina looked towards the overgrown area they used to call The Shrubbery, where bushes and branches were tossing around in the erratic wind, and saw, in a blur without her driving glasses, three people talking. The authorities and another of their hapless, helpless victims: a man in a mac, a woman, and a tall man with bushy hair like Nat's. It tweaked up a momentary discomfort because Polhearne was

Nat's birthright, quickly followed by the familiar reassurance that he did not want and could not have it. The place would be sold. Good riddance.

She walked down towards the house, which showed little sign of life. The direction posts had gone, the windows in the long central wing were shuttered. Rosina had arrived with a mind almost blank, without intention or agenda and until this moment would have said that she didn't take any interest or have any personal concern about what went on at Polhearne. If somebody had told her that the house had been burnt down, she would not have minded. She might even be pleased. Seeing it empty and dejected provoked only curiosity. She walked across to the laundry where the visitor centre had been: locked. So was the studio.

Rosina stood by the granite mounting block. With shoulders back and head high she took out of the dusty recesses of her own mind the hidden set of experiences of which even Matthew had heard only a curt outline before she told him, 'I don't want to think about it again, ever.' Gradually the memories receded, though once he said, 'It's twenty-five years on and there's still a skeleton in your closet.' Meera, probing away with her psychologist's metal detector, had heard the ping of bricked-up secrets too. Right noise, wrong place: there were blank walls in Rosina's mind, but this wasn't one of them, it was more like a cupboard whose door she'd locked and hidden behind wallpaper so that nobody would suspect it was there. Once out of sight, it stayed out of mind.

Rosina imagined her hand reaching for the handle. It felt easy to open the secret door at last, and pull out the memory, still clear and bright though no longer complete. What her naughtiness had consisted of was gone. But no crime she committed could have fitted that punishment. And had anyone known? Lucia? Mother? Was it possible she'd still have said, 'You're a naughty girl, go to your father,' if she knew what happened next? Or was he doing it to Mother too?

His estate room, the door locked. Cigar stink, blaring operatic arias. She wouldn't cry, or scream, or say a word. He wanted her to. He laboured for it. Bitterly stubborn, she clenched herself in lip-biting, gut-wrenching silence. As she grew he laid it on harder, from hand to riding crop to walking stick. She wouldn't look at the red, sweating man, closed her ears to his heavy breaths and panted words. 'It's for your own good,' he'd say, or 'Spare the rod and spoil the child.' Afterwards he'd press and stroke the sore skin and then beside, and inside. The salt smell of his fingers wet and dry.

She never told. Even Matthew only knew her father was old-fashioned and believed in corporal punishment. Boys took getting 'six of the best' for granted in those days and that was what Matthew thought she meant: unsuitable, unkind, but not more. Not perverted. A flagellant.

The last time was out here, on this spot. At fourteen, which was late even then and unimaginably so by modern standards, she had just started her periods, a biological function that seemed utterly inadmissible and shameful. Nobody must ever know about the damp, stinking bulk of padding between her legs. She had an unfamiliar ache in her tummy and felt queasy. 'You won't tell Father,' she'd begged, and Mother said, 'Don't be disgusting, one doesn't speak of such things.'

It was the last day of the holidays. The last day of Polhearne, though she did not know it. She'd ridden in on her bike, feeling awful. More awful than a period should warrant; something had happened.

'Rosina!'

'No, Father, you mustn't, don't!' Running into the courtyard. He'd grabbed and dragged her, fingers so tight round the flesh of her arm that later on, the bruise was like a tattoo. He put his hand on her mouth, touching the skin which had been touched by a man's lips, that very day, and a dreadful tingle rippled down her body, a moment when, impossibly, she framed the thought, Yes, go on, before clamping her lips together and trying to jerk herself away as her mind shrieked NO!

Forced down, braced and cringing over the rough stone. The pain stinging, red hot, sharp. Liquid on her thighs, trickling out. I've wet my knickers.

Suddenly it stopped. He stopped. 'Are you bleeding? You disgusting little — Get out of my sight. Go to your mother.'

She'd gone towards the house. Someone was there. Cousin Jon. He'd come back. He was standing in the doorway, his mouth a little open, like a man ready to kiss...his arms beginning to move towards her. What he'd done, and not done – watched and not interfered. He could have made him stop.

She swerved out of his way, and their eyes met, but he didn't say anything and she ran past him and up to the nursery bathroom. The sanitary towel was saturated and blood had leaked on to her knickers and thighs.

She'd seen him. He'd seen her, he'd understood. Oh, the shame of it! He'd kissed her. And then watched. From that very doorway. Of all people. After what he'd done.

I won't forgive him. Ever. I'll never speak to him again so long as I live.

Chapter Twenty-Three

~

ELLIOT BROUGHT WINE, roses, plus chocolate when I finally asked him round to supper. He also brought information.

The DNA tests on material from the room where poor Connie's body was found matched Spike's sample. There was a complication of material, hotel rooms always have traces of previous occupants, hairs, nail clippings, a glass with traces of saliva or sweat, but the match had been found.

'I didn't think they could be so certain.'

Elliot launched into pedagogue mode. 'Every nucleated cell in the body contains a complete sample of deoxyribonucleic acid, or DNA, which is identical to the DNA in each of the body's other cells and which differentiates you from every other person on earth other than an identical twin. The suspect's DNA profile matches the DNA profile from the crime scene so Spike is "included" as a potential source of that evidence. However, to exclude other, possibly related, sources —'

I interrupted his flow. 'Elliot, don't forget that crime scenes are my stock in trade.'

'Yes indeed, so you will know that the strength of this inclusion depends on the number of DNA locations examined, and safe custody of the evidence, on which points we are dubious.'

The efficient Miss Hardman had bulldozed her way through obstacles and opposition. She had requisitioned from the prosecution autoradiographs, laboratory reports and proficiency testing results, and still wanted validation studies, population databases, and raw samples: those had been delivered to a private laboratory for analysis. It was going to cost Elliot a fortune, and more still to have a rush job done. He believed there was still room for doubt.'

'But if they are looking at samples from that room, there'd be Connie's, other hotel guests and the real killer if it wasn't Spike, and they'd be quite different. Surely only very close relations could be similar, a father or brother, and we know Spike hasn't got any.'

Elliot was writing something down in his notebook. I saw that the glint in his eye was that of neither a benefactor nor a rewarded researcher. Elliot had realised that his own story and point of view, as an unworldly academic caught up in unaccustomed drama with famous names in it, would rework into a book for the general reader and a six-figure advance. He didn't actually make notes but when he started fumbling in his pocket I knew he'd recorded our conversation. I told him not to quote me, I'd been off the record, and sitting down to smoked fish and salad added that we must talk about something else. Elliot had been sight seeing. St Michael's Mount, uniquely romantic, the Eden Project, strangely inventive, Truro Cathedral, most impressive, and today he'd finally decided the time was ripe for a visit to Polhearne.

'Did you snaffle the recluse at last?'

'That is not my desire.'

'But you're writing about him.'

'I prefer to remain uninhibited by personal acquaintanceship or doubts as to my own motivation. My objectivity must not be called into question. Seeing his home was enough. I found it most interesting.'

'Were the inmates dancing in forest glades with fairies? Did the cook ask the carrots for permission to eat them?'

'I do not follow your question.'

'People call them the local tree huggers.'

'I heard they had moved away and regretted the news, for I am an admirer of such projects, having paid a profitable visit to Findhorn and been greatly impressed by that enterprise. I think one should not mock any who commit themselves to the attempt to find the inner god within us all. But I was informed that the last inmates at Polhearne had left.'

He went on to tell me about the great old house being in a shocking condition, crumbling untended away. He'd got chatting to a young couple who were making a list of the dilapidation visible from outside, the rotten window frames, rusted gutters, missing roof slates and doors off hinges. 'They were probably from English Heritage,' I said.

While I hunted out and made him decaf Elliot inquired about my first meeting with Connie. I told him about tea at Brown's Hotel, agreed that it would be historically unsound to delete any unkind adjectives about her and suggested he took a look at the transcript of our conversation. He did so while I sat reading Spike's account.

WITNESS STATEMENT
SIMON PETER KELLY

1. I am Simon Peter Kelly, of no fixed abode, presently in HM Prison, Exeter.

2. I was born on 8th February 1976. My name was Simon Peter Galloway. I was adopted in infancy.

3. In 2002 I learnt that my birth mother went by the assumed name of Jennifer Galloway and she had died on 30th March 1976. This information was in a letter written before her death by my adoptive mother. She also left me the only property belonging to my biological mother, a sketchbook and a typescript which I believed was a draft of *Paint, Prophesy, Predict* by Jon Polhearne.

4. I took both these items to London and showed them to Professor Elliot Rosenwald. I knew he was an authority on the art of St Ives in the 1940s and 1950s. From his knowledge and experience he identified the sketchbook as containing work by the artist known as Jix, otherwise Jon Hicks Polhearne of

Polhearne House, St Budy, Cornwall. Although I did not know how these items came into Jennifer Galloway's possession, it was obvious that both the typescript and sketchbook would increase in value if properly authenticated by Mr Polhearne. After a contract was signed between me and Professor Rosenwald, we agreed that I should arrange to meet Mr Polhearne.

5. I emailed, wrote, and tried to telephone Jon Polhearne but received no reply. I consequently decided to visit him in Cornwall intending to purport to be an aspiring member of the 3P Fellowship. On arrival at Polhearne House I found only two remaining members in residence. They permitted me to stay at the community for a few days but Mr Polhearne remained unavailable throughout. I intended to discuss the next step with Professor Rosenwald, who was staying in St Ives at the time. I decided to walk there along the coastal footpath.

6. However while I was doing so I met Mrs Constance Thorne. Although I was a stranger she invited me to stay with her at Goonzoyle House, Trevena, Cornwall as her guest. I returned her hospitality by doing domestic and gardening work and also undertook research into Mrs Thorne's family history at the Cornwall County Record Office in Truro.

7. Mrs Thorne was very generous to me, giving me presents including clothes, and free use of her second car. Despite the difference in our ages I formed an intimate relationship with Mrs Thorne.

8. Before leaving London, I had previously commissioned a detective agency, Skillsearchers, Praed Street, London W2, to investigate the identity of my biological father. I had no birth certificate and consequently no knowledge of my birth mother's real name or of my father's but it had occurred to me that if Jon Polhearne had given his manuscript and sketches to my biological mother, he might have had an intimate relationship with her.

9. I received a letter on Saturday 5th April informing me that there was no evidence of any kind to suggest that Mr Polhearne had known Jennifer Galloway. I was also told that the agency had traced at the St George's Hospital, Tooting, London, a document dated the day before I was born, on which the line for the mother's next of kin had pencilled beside it 'the baby's' and the name Edward Johns, 107 Chester Terrace, London NW1. The detective agency had learnt that he moved to Ireland in 1976 but he had not so far been traced.

10. I read this letter aloud to Mrs Thorne who became violently agitated. I did not understand why, but was alarmed by her uncontrolled anger, directed not only at me but at a friend who telephoned while we were talking and mentioned a radio programme about the Second World War in which her brother was featured. Mrs Thorne slammed the receiver down, grew hysterical, and shouted at me to get out.

11. I was concerned that my presence seemed to be making things worse. So I left Goonzoyle and took the opportunity to call again at Polhearne House, but could find nobody in residence. I left a note for Mr Polhearne explaining that I was studying his work, and my credentials as a researcher into local and family history on behalf of Mrs Constance Thorne. As I left I met a neighbour who told me that Mr Polhearne had gone away for a few days as he was to be at an investiture on the following Wednesday to receive an OBE.

12. When I returned to Goonzoyle Mrs Thorne was calmer. She explained the reason for her reaction, namely that Edward Johns was the name of her late brother and she thought he might have survived after all and was afraid that I was her blood relation, in fact her nephew, and consequently that our relationship had been incestuous. However she had soon realised this could not be the case, since there was no doubt that her brother had died at the age of thirteen as one of the victims of a wartime disaster.

13. After some discussion we agreed that Edward Johns is not an uncommon name and coincidences do happen. Alternatively, the identity of the dead boy had been stolen. I had read about the epidemic of identity theft and fraud and knew that it is possible to acquire the birth certificate of a deceased person and use it to prove and construct a false identity.

14. Although Mrs Thorne had calmed down she still seemed distressed. I felt it would be better to give her a few days on her own so decided to go to London to discuss further lines of inquiry with Skillsearchers. There was no suggestion of my not returning and we arranged that I would get back by the end of the week. We parted on good terms. Mrs Thorne dropped me at Buriton station on Saturday 5th April. That was the last time that I saw Mrs Thorne.

15. In fact I left the train station once Mrs Thorne had driven away and hitched to London. I did not wish to mention to Mrs Thorne that I was short of ready money. I called at the Skillsearchers office. They advised that questions to my adoptive parents' friends and neighbours would come better from me. I made inquiries but found nobody who knew anything about my parentage. I returned to Cornwall where I found that Mrs Thorne was not at Goonzoyle. I had no idea where she had gone. I did not see her in London. I did not know she was in London. I do not know why she went to the hotel at Gatwick. I have never been to that or any other hotel at Gatwick. I do not know who would have wished to harm her. I know nothing whatever about her death except that I regret it very deeply.

⌒⌒

Up to this point the story Spike told Miss Hardman had been sanitised, his own voice disguised by the legalistic format. But the witness statement was followed by an unimproved transcript. The typist omitted Spike's ums and ers and lawyer's prompts and questions, but it sounded a good deal more like him, as he explained again how he had met Connie and went on – apparently answering a question – to describe the one thing connected with his birth mother that still survived, the canvas rucksack and the papers he had found in it.

'I told you already, I showed them to Elliot Rosenwald. What do you mean, why? It's obvious. I knew he was writing something about Jon Polhearne – no, not before, had to look him up, didn't I? What d'you think I am – course he'd have to pay, I knew who to go to if he didn't want it, but he was cool. We made a deal. There were still things he wanted to know for his book and I wanted to find out too, so it wasn't because of her I came, it wasn't anything to do with her dying in Cornwall, geddit? Visit her grave? No way, I just wanted to – say again? Did I what? Well, I walked the coastal footpath so I must have gone past the place but don't ask me where. What I came for was to see Jon Polhearne, there had to be a connection. Jon Polhearne. You know. What? I told you – she topped herself. Went over a cliff. Yeah, there'd have been things in the papers, 1976. It was somewhere near Trevena, I do know that much.'

If Spike had bothered to look up the inquest report he'd have known that the only witness to Jennifer's suicidal leap had actually been Jon Polhearne. Stop. Wait a minute, I was being very slow. Surely he'd said she was a complete stranger, at the inquest all those years ago? It would be on record, easily checked, but I felt certain he'd denied knowing her. If they had been in touch, even if they'd corresponded without ever setting eyes on one another, he'd still have had to recognise her name.

'Excuse me,' Elliot said.

'It looks like Spike's mother got the manuscript somewhere else, she can't have known Jon Polhearne after all,' I began, but for once he put his ponderous courtesy aside and talked over me.

'Constance Thorne knew who it was all along.'

'Sorry?' I said.

'Now that I have read your transcript it's obvious. The moment she was told what was known about the remains found in the mineshaft, the period when the unidentified female died and the fact that she had been expecting a child, it had to be obvious to her. There was no way Constance Thorne wouldn't have been cognisant of the individual's identity.'

Elliot held out a page from my first conversation with Connie that day in Brown's Hotel, pointing to one paragraph. 'Ted was that excited when I went to the station to say goodbye. He'd got on the list because of Dad being out of the way, and he couldn't stand our stepmother, specially once she was expecting, with poor Dad over there – I was that relieved when they said she'd gone off with her fancy man. But Ted was gone by then, went off by train, 8th September 1940. It was the last I ever saw of him.'

'Her name was Nancy,' I said.

'It is sad and shocking,' Elliot said.

'Yes, a tragic story.' Poor long-forgotten Nancy, not off with her fancy man after all. Though surely people couldn't just disappear, even in 1940, there was probably some record of inquiries. She had a boyfriend at least, perhaps family too, but they probably assumed she'd gone off with a man.

'I can't understand why Connie didn't say anything.'

'We should leave that mysterious reticence aside for the time being. The important fact is that we have pinpointed an actual connection between two of the deaths at Trevena.'

Although I write about amateur detectives who poke their noses into other people's business, that doesn't mean I have the least desire to do so myself. Nor, evidently, had Elliot.

'Were I a character in your fiction, I believe you would describe his sensations of elation at making this discovery.'

'But then he or she would probably not tell anyone and sally forth into some dangerous situation for the sake of a dramatic denouement.'

'Whereas I find myself dejected and even fearful of the responsibility that knowledge brings.'

'Cheer up, Elliot,' I told him. 'In real life we pass the information on and someone else decides what to do about it.'

Chapter Twenty-Four

ONLY A COUPLE of dozen homes stood in Trevena even now, although several were less than five years old, permitted as 'in-fill building' in a 'conservation area' officially classified as 'of outstanding natural beauty'. Trevena was a village, rather than a hamlet, because it had a church, pub and shop, though Mrs Tucker's stores had been converted into a timeshare holiday let, the pub was now a surf school, and pinned on to the church noticeboard was a typed page saying that owing to the diocesan surveyor's unsatisfactory report on the safety of the tower, until further notice all acts of worship would be held at St Piran's Church in St Budy. Most of the ancient trees had gone, killed by Dutch elm disease in the 1970s, but self-seeded ashes and some quick-growing conifers had taken their place. Yellow lines had been painted on either side of the road. Nearly all the houses were spruce because only people with money could afford to buy in seaside locations, the red telephone box had long since gone and nearly every thatched or slated roof had its television aerial or satellite dish. All the same, the feeling of the village seemed surprisingly unchanged. Anyone getting out of the car beside the church gate heard the age-old chatter of rooks overhead, saw identical bluebells and primroses still growing on the grassy banks, and that hole in the thatch of the disused chapel looked exactly like the one that had been there fifty years before. A woman in a grey trouser suit was standing by the lych gate when Rosina arrived.

'Delia?'

'Rosina.'

The two women looked cautiously at one another, two minds

with but a single thought: I'd never have recognised her, do I look as old as she does? This is going to be awkward.

'I expected it would look completely different by now.'

'I haven't been here myself since...' Rosina didn't finish her sentence. Since I left home.

Delia said, 'That house over there, surely that was a post office? Didn't it have a bench or seat outside it?'

'It was a general stores, run by a witch – really, that's what they called her, she had a reputation of casting spells. I had to pluck up my courage to go in for sweets.'

'Sherbert lemons. It was the first time I tasted them.'

'I'm not sure they existed during rationing.'

'My daughter Grace used to tease me about my deprived childhood.'

'Mrs Tucker, that was her name.'

'And now we're old enough to be witches ourselves.'

'Or wise women.'

'How hard that is to believe,' Delia said, holding her hands out palm downwards. 'Age spots, blue veins, knobbly joints, one doesn't ever quite believe one's going to get them too.'

Rosina said, 'I try to remember what George Sand told Flaubert, "The day I resolutely buried my youth I grew twenty years younger." What d'you think, maybe ten years younger if it's burying middle age?'

Delia had a shiny black holdall slung over her arm, presumably containing a polythene bag or screw-top jar or some sort of tasteful funerary urn. The very idea of human ashes, as horrible as the word 'cremains', made Rosina queasy. Matthew always said he would be like his old father who spent the last year of his life bedridden with a massive oak coffin at the ready under his bed and his funeral service planned out in every detail except for its date. It was another of the many plans aborted by pancreatic cancer. But he'd been buried in the ground, planted as his father called it. Suddenly the knowledge and image of what was happening to the once beloved flesh hit Rosina, alongside the thought of the skeletons that had brought her here, and the process that had turned Delia's stepmother from pretty, breathing, blushing flesh to something unthinkable.

'Are you all right?'

'Of course,' Rosina said. 'Tell me, did Grace bring you down?'

'She met me at the station and dropped me over here. She'll be back later.'

Rosina complimented Delia on her dynamic daughter.

Delia knew Rosina had one of each, she'd seen their names in Matthew's Who's Who entry.

Rosina believed Delia had been a librarian.

Delia had heard that Rosina was a wonderful gardener.

Then Rosina said, 'This is silly, we're circling round each other like suspicious cats.'

'You always were direct, I remember that. From the very first moment when you spoke to me down on the rocks.'

'Have you been over there yet?'

'Just did, it hasn't changed at all.'

'Though it's been a long time.'

'More than half a century.'

'Unbelievable, really.'

'I know, it feels like yesterday,' Delia said.

'Staying here? Really? But if you do remember it why d'you need me?'

'I didn't see anything.' Delia's protest came out in a kind of muted shriek. She went on more calmly, 'Sorry. But that's the whole point. I never knew what was happening at all, they kept me out of everything, the way kids always were then, I had to stay inside with a neighbour while the search was going on. They wouldn't let me look for Sheila myself. I kept thinking she might have been meeting a friend, because she'd met someone she knew in St Ives the day before. The trouble was that I didn't see who it was.'

'How come?'

'I had to go into the public toilet so she said she'd wait outside on the pier. It took ages because my penny got stuck in the slot, and while I was in there she met someone she knew, I heard her through the ventilator. She said, "Oh, it's you," and I remembered it ever since because she sounded so surprised and happy. I thought it was my father, but it wasn't, he'd not been anywhere near and nobody else was ever found who admitted knowing her, not even other people who had been in her class at the village school when she was an evacuee. Though she'd have changed a lot.'

'So would they. But you say she met someone she knew. Which means, if there was only one person she did know, it must have been —'

'My father. That's what the police thought too. But he really loved Sheila, you know, and so did I, which is why it's so important to discover what really did happen, even more so now he's gone, curiously enough. It's my only excuse for pestering you, I know this is probably the last thing in the whole world you'd choose to be doing.'

'Oh, that's quite all right,' Rosina murmured automatically.

'I just hope you'll help me out here. You see, we met here that day, not pre-planned but you were going back to school so I hoped you'd come and say goodbye. So I hung round by the slipway. But when you turned up you'd obviously forgotten about me. You weren't going to stop, but I thought you were and got in the way. You fell off and everything fell out of the bike basket. You were in such a tizzy! You kept saying you had to get home, you shovelled your things back all higgledy, and rushed straight off. I was left standing there with a bit of paper you'd missed, a painting torn out of a sketchbook. We came across it recently so Grace took it to a gallery down here and it turns out to be quite valuable. It's yours, of course.'

'No no, not after all these years.'

'It has been a long time.'

'I'm so sorry, I seem to have been very rude and hurtful. I do hope you weren't too upset,' Rosina said, recognising the falsity of her own tone.

'Actually I minded like anything, but that was all overtaken by what happened to Sheila. It's only recently I've realised you were going like a bat out of hell on that bike because you'd been frightened. You saw something. And that's where you were coming from.' Delia gestured inland. Beyond the chapel and the pub, up the brilliant emerald slope of the field above the village, over the bushy hedges on the skyline, loomed the grey shape of Goonzoyle.

'I forget,' Rosina muttered.

Delia had prepared for this moment; the sheaf of papers was in her jacket pocket. Rosina took it from her outstretched hand, put on her reading glasses and unfolded a newspaper cutting with the headline, 'Scientists Unlock the Secrets of Selective Amnesia'.

'We have shown how the human brain blocks an unwanted memory, that there is such a mechanism, and it has a biological basis. Our results seem to be counterintuitive. It's funny because from a psychological viewpoint most people are quite the opposite in life, because very unpleasant things keep intruding into their thinking. But our experiment shows that people are capable of repeatedly blocking thoughts of experiences they don't want to remember, until eventually they find that it is difficult to retrieve the memory even when they wish to.'

As Rosina was reading, Delia continued rapidly, 'Don't take this the wrong way, but Grace told me what you said and I couldn't help wondering – do you forget simply because you don't choose to remember?'

Chapter Twenty-Five

AS EACH GENERATION of oldies dies off, the art bought in their younger days reappears on the market and their diaries, photos and letters appear in sale rooms or archives departments. This normal, natural course of events sometimes throws up Koestler-style coincidences. It was happenstance that gave me a bad night, which meant that I got up at dawn and read, responded to and acted upon my messages before going out. More remarkably, one of them alerted me to a writer called Hal Macrae whose wartime reminiscences had just been deposited at the Australian War Memorial.

I found the material on its website. Googling Macrae showed he had emigrated to Melbourne in 1947 and been a teacher before becoming a full-time novelist. I had not heard of him before but realised I would have to read his books because they all seemed to be accounts of his own mental illness which had been caused by the childhood trauma of evacuation. At the age of thirteen he was dispatched ('like a parcel, with a label') overseas, shipwrecked, returned to Scotland and immediately put on board another ship. On reaching Canada he was selected ('like a prisoner in a slave market') by a foster family and taken off to their farm where he lived without love or comfort for four years ('like a cow in a cattle shed'). When he got back to England, he and his parents did not recognise each other and at home he found a younger brother born in his absence ensconced in his room. As a result, he had written, 'I became a loner, could never make lasting relationships or trust anyone, I lost the capacity to love.' That quote was on a 'twentieth-century writers' site. On the Australian War Memorial site I found a draft letter

Macrae wrote but apparently never sent to Ralph Barker when he was researching the book about the *City of Benares* disaster.

'I was sharing a cabin with three blokes. They were playing cards in another cabin and I was in my bunk when there was a sudden thudding noise, the sound of being hit, not like an explosion. I knew it was a torpedo, and could tell it was towards the stern of the ship. Straightaway all the alarms went off, sirens, bells, hooters, so I got the door open, and went into the alleyway, and then I came upon a heap of debris, it was very dark but there was a dim light, God knows where from, and then I was at the edge of a hole, a huge black hole in the middle of the ship with water filling it up as I watched. So I ran back and up the other stairs and I got to the muster station but there I found the lifeboat already had crowds of people in it. Somehow I forced my way in but while it was lowering down it swung from the davits and some people fell out into the sea. Then the boat hit the water, so rough, and when it was cast off the block and tackle dangled low and swung violently, and then some bloke pushed me out of his way and I got brained and catapulted into the sea, down, deep. I thought that was it. I was done for. But the life jacket bounced me up and then I heard, "Swim, Hal, swim." I think it must have been my own voice in my head. Well, swimming was the one thing I was good at, but I couldn't see which way to go. Then I felt something scrape against my head, it nearly knocked me out, but I saw it was a kind of flat raft so I grabbed hold of that. Other people were clutching on too, it was dark but sometimes there was a flash of light and you could see that people were sliding away, dying, their bodies floating around. I had to keep awake, because if I fell asleep my grip on the planks would go.'

'I kept seeing mirages, phantom ships to the rescue. But when it got light there was no other ship or boat or even raft in sight. There was me and two other boys, the only ones left. I thought they were brothers because they looked alike, but one of them spluttered out that his father was a colonel of a regiment and the other one was his batman's boy, and then the other said he was as good as anyone and as a matter of fact his real father was the colonel's own dad so he was the rightful heir and nobody else would be able to tell any difference, and if only one of them was going home to claim their inheritance it was going to be him. In any other circumstances it would have been funny. Or frightening, he sounded that set on it all. As it is, the memory's tragic, those boys arguing about their social status while they were facing death. I was only saved myself by a fluke. Or a miracle, depends how you see it. My hands were so swollen and painful I couldn't hold on, it was a peculiar moment sliding back from the raft and seeing the gap between it and me get wider and knowing that was it, I was a goner. But I was so tired and miserable I didn't care.

'But as I told you, I could swim so I kept myself afloat automatically, even when I could see I was all alone, with nobody for miles around. But there was. Ages later, hours probably, I bumped into something floating – it was a body, someone who died of cold or shock in a lifeboat, and the others had pushed it over the side. And so it was nearby, this isolated boat full of Lascars and an Englishwoman with seven kids she'd saved, and a steward or bosun from the *City of Benares*, and they pulled me in. The next morning we were spotted and picked up by HMS *Hurricane* and landed in Scotland at Greenock. A week later I was on board another ship and back on the Atlantic Ocean. But that's another story.'

Chapter Twenty-Six

~

THE TREE INSPECTOR arrived just as Nat got to Polhearne himself, and seemed stiffly on his dignity at the short-notice response to his long-standing demand for a meeting. But he turned out to be a nice enough chap. They walked round for a long time and eventually reached an agreement. When they started to go down the slope back to his car he asked with what sounded like genuine sympathy, 'Are you really going to take all this on? It's quite some challenge.'

'God knows I don't want to,' Nat replied. 'But I'll be prosecuted by your mates on the council soon for letting a listed building fall down.'

'Haven't you got tenants? I thought —'

'In theory. But apparently they've all scarpered.'

'Isn't the old man still here? I thought I saw him.'

'He is still here all right, but he's not technically the tenant and in any case he's past caring.'

They had reached the car park and Grace said, 'Isn't that him now?'

Tall, thin and stooping, dressed in tatters of tweed and leaning on a stick, the man was moving across the courtyard. Its stone surface was almost completely obscured by weeds.

'Here goes,' Nat muttered. He squared his shoulders and walked towards his uncle. Grace hung back watching as one tall man met another. She could see that Nat was slightly bent in a deferential pose, and quickly realised that the other man was either deaf, or perhaps simply did not want to hear. He seemed to be batting Nat away with his hands. Then she saw Nat step around to face him. The old man stopped and listened and then he moved his hand to his forehead and made a peculiar gesture, as though he were pulling a non-existent forelock. When Grace came closer, Nat had put his arm round the old man's shoulder and was trying to steer him in a direction he was resisting. Jon's expression was at once determined and baffled. He seemed stubbornly determined to make for Nat's car.

Nat murmured to Grace, 'I'd better stay with him. Can you go in and see if there's any sign of life? Look at the mail and bills, he can't really be living here alone.'

The official said, 'Would it help if I tell Social Services about him? It's always extra difficult with people who live in places like this, nobody quite likes to interfere.'

'It's OK, thanks, I'm on the case.'

'Rather you than me.' He edged politely past to his own car. Grace waved, made an encouraging face for Nat and went into a cold and very dirty room which smelt like the lair of some animal. She moved round realising that she was confronting the detritus of years if not decades, a far more depressing sight even than she had expected though Nat had described it in some detail, having paid many visits to this house over the last few years. He had never felt able to talk about the taboo subject with his mother.

When she and Nat first discussed Polhearne, Grace had been able to make several suggestions. She knew exactly which grant-giving public organisations it was worth applying to and which charities might be interested. More recently their conversations had a changed direction, with an unspoken agenda. If Nat and Grace were more than friends, if this wasn't a simple fling, fun today and forgotten tomorrow, then Polhearne would be part of her own future.

They had played the game together. What would one do with a derelict stately home? After a series of impractical ideas about centres for archaeology, forensic or otherwise, or high-tech research labs, Grace had a brainwave one day while she was driving from a jumble sale in a village hall, where she had bought some original Biba fabric, to an out-of-town sale at which one of the London auction houses was offering the contents of a time capsule draper's shop.

If the Tate could do it in St Ives, and the National Maritime Museum in Falmouth, why shouldn't the William and Mary also establish a national museum's out-of-town branch? The Costume Galleries of the West at Polhearne: a draw for tourists, a solution to storage problems in the main museum and a future for the house. Grace's vision was so complete that it had run ahead of itself. The house would be converted into a unique museum and she would be its curator. She even imagined herself living in the owner's flat, happily ever after.

Fantasies of that kind were not at all characteristic of Grace Theobald, nor part of her self-image.

The men's voices were moving away. Was that Nat saying 'Come back, not that way'?

Grace brought herself down to earth by beginning to do a bit of tidying, picking things up and putting them down in different places. Cups over there, dirty plates here, unopened bills there, circulars, invitations, junk mail heaped in a pile the size of a decent bonfire. Nothing had been opened. Grace half-heartedly picked up a few actual letters, wondering if they mattered, if she should act like a secretary, if that would be a) officious and b) pointless. A good many of these letters were addressed to people who must be former Fellowship members, Johann Wasserstein, Mr K. Blaine, an E. Johns, whose mail had already been forwarded from an address in County Cork to a post office box number in Plymouth. Here was a message in handwritten capitals on lined paper torn out of a reporter's notebook.

'TO JON POLHEARNE: ARE YOU NEVER HERE? I REALLY NEED TO SEE YOU ABOUT JENNIFER GALLOWAY'S MANUSCRIPT. I AM STAYING WITH MRS CONSTANCE THORNE, SHE'S KEEN TO TALK TO

YOU TOO, HOPES TO PICK YOUR BRAIN ABOUT GOONZOYLE. GET BACK TO ME SOONEST. SIMON KELLY'

It almost could have been a blackmail note. Simon Kelly, whoever he was, was going to be disappointed of what he wanted, whatever that was.

Still visible through the grimy window, Nat was following anxiously as the old man edged further away. Grace decided not to wait. She couldn't resist a quick glance at the rest of the famous house. She could just see if there was any point in pursuing the museum idea.

Outside Jon Polhearne's bestial den was a long stone-flagged passage, an inner hall, another hall, a gallery; and opening off them, room after room that might once have been gracious, elegant, pretty or cosy. They had all been left to decay. There were mouse droppings and cobwebs, mould and stains, peeling wallpaper and broken panes of glass. There was motheaten fabric and threadbare carpet, damp-spotted pictures and tattered lengths of faded fabric. The House of Horrors image was increased by the rows of balding, grinning animal faces, shooting trophies mounted on the walls. Each door opened on to an even more depressing sight. Up, along, down, up, through – the place was a maze. And nobody had tended any of these rooms for years. The nutters had dwindled, most left ages ago. 'They folded their tents and stole softly away,' the nearest neighbour had told Nat. The man was a script writer and hobby-farmer who had contacted Nat offering to rough-cut the grass for silage. That was a good two years back. He was the one who'd called Nat this morning at dawn to say the old man's last companion had collapsed in the local supermarket and been carted off in an ambulance. 'Someone's going to have to do something, he shouldn't stay there alone.'

Grace had come to a door marked 'Private' which led into a bedroom with a four-poster, good mahogany furniture, cushioned window seats, gilt-framed watercolours, an Aubusson carpet. It was the first properly furnished room so far seen, but festooned with cobwebs like Miss Havisham's in the film of Great Expectations. Grace's feet left prints in the thick dust on the floorboards at the edge of the room. The tables were veiled in it, and the silver-backed brushes and the fossilised jar of anemones. When Grace drew her finger across the dressing table the dust rose like powder in the still air. The mirror was darkened by it and so, when she pulled open the shutter, were the small panes of the sash window, but she could see Nat trying to stop Jon plonking himself firmly in the passenger seat.

This room led on to another smaller one that could only have been called a 'boudoir' but must have been Lucia Polhearne's retreat. Grace wiped her hand across the glass covering a kidney-shaped table and saw baby photos underneath staring up at her. Lucia's son, before she knew there was anything wrong. She opened one door in a row of built-in cupboards with dulled mirrors as doors. A faint, ghostly smell of gardenias wafted out. Rows of clothes were still hanging inside and for a moment Grace was distracted, ruffling her hand along the hangers to reveal labels. Nothing very posh, this was a St Michael and Viyella lady, though there was an early Paddy Campbell suit and a Hardy Amies dress that would be well worth – stop it, Grace told herself. She turned her attention to a shelf of box files, all labelled and amateurishly covered with flowered wallpaper. Bills, receipts, bank statements, Father, Mother, Rosina.

Nat might want to rescue that one. Grace pulled it out, sneezing vigorously.

'Grace!'

'Coming. Oh Nat, it must have been a glorious place but everything's in an unbelievable state, I've never seen such —'

'I know.'

'Where's the old man?'

'He got into the back of the car like a taxi, I told him we were going on to Trevena but he keeps saying he's coming too. I left him there in the hope he'll get bored. What have you found?'

'This. Do you think your mother might want it?'

'Dunno. Let's take it out in the fresh air, come on, and maybe I'll chuck few lighted matches around on the way. Burning the whole place down might be the only solution.'

'Got any matches?'

'No. Just as well, I suppose.'

They perched on a granite block in the courtyard and Nat opened the chintzy box. 'It's Mother's school reports, music certificates, all that stuff. Recorder, Grade 3. And this must be her diary.'

'Don't look, Nat,' Grace said quickly. 'Girls are so silly, I'd hate you – I mean, I'd hate anyone to see mine.'

'You might show me all the same, one of these days.' The tone of his voice was as eloquent as the words he refrained from adding. Then he said, 'I can't anyway, it's locked.'

'You could take it home with you.'

'I'll ask her.' Nat took out his cellphone, pressed two keys and then pointed at his battered car. Jon Polhearne had climbed into the back and was sitting upright and still, eyes forward, waiting to be driven away.

Chapter Twenty-Seven

IF YOU PAY enough for a really rush job, a DNA testing lab will get the results back to the customer very fast. They landed on Miss Hardman's desk, and as she started leafing through the pages she asked her secretary to get her Elliot.

His mobile phone provider had poor coverage in Cornwall so I told him to call her back on mine, which meant that I heard the whole conversation on the hands-free set. Even so there was interference and his voice crackled through the air.

'It's breaking up,' she snapped.

'The reception's bad here.'

'Where the hell are you?'

'We're on the way to meet Jon Polhearne, I'm with —'

She was not interested in his movements. I could hear her loud voice barking into the telephone. 'Listen, the cops have gone too far this time, I'm going for an acquittal, it's a miscarriage of – what? OK, I'll go through it.'

She skipped through the preamble: terms of the contract, including that the client was to note that routine testing for relationships was automatically performed and charged for. Evidence samples supplied, differential DNA extraction protocol, Chelex extraction method, PCR amplification, ABI 377 automated DNA sequencer; 'You don't need all that.'

On to actual facts: the specimens were derived from blood and other body fluids, hair roots, a teaspoon, paper tissues and a toothbrush.

Several samples had been received. Those from the crime scene were found to be: two female, identified by the police as attributable to two unrelated women, the victim herself and the cleaner; and two men. Specimens taken from the accused, S.P. Kelly, had been supplied for matching.

'Here it comes, Professor Rosenwald, are you still with me? Those bastards screwed up, the samples were contaminated.'

'Does the report say so?'

'No, but it's full of crap about probable relationships. It's unbelievable, they've found a match between the victim's DNA and Spike's, for a start, and then between Spike and the other male sample, and round in a circle with a link between that man and the victim. I've got to call —'

'Wait, doesn't that explode the evidence against Spike?'

'It might if it wasn't completely bonkers. As it is, this is just a joke. I told you, I'm going to —'

'No.'

'No? No what?'

'There was a relationship.' He paused. I decided not to help him out. Some time ago I had realised that he was keeping his cards very close to his chest, and I was longing to know what his secret was since it was obviously something about the paintings and the writings of Jon Hicks Polhearne. I didn't even take my eyes off the road, for I could imagine without seeing the reserved, awkward expression on his big, oblong face, his crewcut of grey hair and his small, light blue eyes gazing suspiciously through thick horn-rimmed glasses.

Her voice was squawking impatiently down the line. 'What d'you mean, relationship? Elliot? Professor Rosenwald? Speak to me!'

He cleared his throat thunderously. 'The fact is I have to begin at the beginning, otherwise it is impossible for you to understand my position, and the position of your client.'

'There's no time for that now, cut the cackle!'

'You can only understand this, if you understand that when Simon Kelly, Spike, produced that annotated carbon copy of a typescript, it was for me a moment analogous to stout Cortez gazing upon a peak in Darien. Looking at the words of the famous book, and the original language which had been changed to the final version, I realised that the handwriting was not that of the author, but that all the changes which were inserted on those pages appeared in the final publication. At first I did believe that the typescript was a carbon copy kept by Spike's mother who had presumably been its copy typist, presented with one of the author's discontinued sketchbooks, from the brief period when he intended to be an artist, possibly given to her as an expression of his gratitude.'

'Elliot, listen, I really don't have time to hear your thought processes.'

'You'll understand that my area of expertise is the analysis of textual notes and of linguistic style as well as the recognition of an artist's unique features, and it is the combination of these forms of evidence that enables a scholar —'

'Elliot!' Her voice was a shriek down this crackling airwave. 'Please, please, I implore, save that up for later and tell me what you concluded, for heaven's sake. What is this about?'

'If you don't know the nature of the evidence that led me to believe —'

'I really don't care about the evidence just now!'

'Very well.' He sounded huffy. 'If you want to take my process of reasoning for read I will tell you merely its result: that is, that the mother of Simon Kelly, known, although mistakenly, only as Jennifer Galloway, had been the mistress of John Hicks Polhearne, and that it was she who in point of fact was the actual progenitor, dreamer. In fact it was she who actually wrote *Paint, Prophesy, Predict*.'

'Who cares who wrote the book —'

Who cares? I thought. I care, and I haven't even read it! 'Are you saying she ghosted it?'

'Who's that? Elliot, who is there? This isn't a secure line.'

I replied before Elliot could. 'He is in my car, I'm giving him a lift.'

'Right, well, OK, but —'

'Elliot, do explain, did they do a deal?' I pressed him, and at the same time Miss Hardman snapped:

'The point is, was he the father?'

'From the evidence I have collected I infer that he did father Ms Galloway's child.'

'So if Spike's his son —'

'Miss Hardman, in 1940 Jonathan Hicks was an overseas evacuee,' I interrupted rather loudly. 'Miss Hardman, I think what I can contribute is relevant. Oh oh —' I was distracted and jammed my foot down on the brake, as we came round a bend to see a motionless procession of cars in both lanes.

She announced, 'I need to agree a course of action with Professor Rosenwald before —'

'I think you had better hear this,' Elliot said.

'Oh very well, go on,' she said grudgingly.

I did: 'On the same ship was a Cornish boy called Edward Johns.'

'The name on my client's birth certificate.'

'And his sister was Constance, later Mrs Thorne.' I heard breaths drawn to interrupt but kept my eyes on the road as we began to edge forwards, and carried on. 'The ship was torpedoed in September 1940, those two boys shared a life raft but only one was alive when an American fishing boat picked them up. He couldn't talk but his papers identified him as Jonathan Hicks. He must have gone to foster parents —'

'Kinsmen,' Elliot said. 'He was fostered by relations whose ancestors had been part of the Cornish diaspora of the nineteenth century, a Mr and Mrs Sturrock, the latter now a lady of a great age living in Florida where I was able to visit her towards the end of last year and discovered that she had far from affectionate memories of the boy.'

We came up to the bottleneck. A high-sided lorry had blown

over across two of the three lanes, and lay on its side, with traffic police organising the queues.

'Did she say anything useful?'

'To quote her, the lad was sly and ungrateful from the first moment even when still unable to speak and in hospital with blood poisoning from an infected wound where his finger had been amputated.'

'One of the evacuees hurt his hand quite badly. It was Edward Johns.'

'What? You're breaking up.' The phone went dead, and we seemed permanently stuck. I turned the radio on and heard a traffic report. The wind, already gale force, was predicted to increase to storm force 10 and police were advising motorists not to go out unless strictly necessary. The main road through Cornwall, the A30, was blocked in both directions east of Buriton because a tree had blown over, blocking both lanes. Delays of up to an hour were predicted. I turned off both radio and engine and hoped Elliot wasn't going to be the kind of passenger who complained about forces beyond the driver's control.

He undid his seatbelt, steepled his hands in a thoughtful pose and began to deliver a lecture. 'Let us postulate a resentful, envious child called Edward Johns who seizes his chance to take Jonathan Hicks's place. The Sturrocks accept him without question as their kinsman. He cherishes a burning desire for the life of wealth and privilege that was the inheritance of the boy whose place he has taken. John Sturrock is a competent minor artist of the mid-twentieth century, and as the boy grows to manhood he finds he has a talent for deception and can create acceptable mimicry of contemporary abstract art. However, when he returns to Britain in order to escape military service, he adopts a different role, marries an heiress, recreates himself in the simulacrum of a country gentleman; but also, perhaps to ensure a fail-safe escape route, he re-establishes himself in a distant city in his real name. He impregnates a young woman who is the possessor of remarkable talents and attributes, which she describes in a unique piece of writing. At an unknown stage he comes into possession of its final typescript. Does she come to confront him? Does he even know there is a child?'

'Jumping forward to the present day, does he actually know that his long-lost sister's back?'

'Spike was never able to make personal contact with him, so it is unlikely that he encountered Spike's hostess.'

'I'm pretty sure Connie never went to Polhearne,' I said.

'Nor he to Goonzoyle.'

'But Elliot, when you sent Spike here, you didn't know any of this, did you? What were you expecting to happen? In fact, what are you expecting him to say today?'

The car, though low and usually stable at speed, was rocking uncomfortably in the fierce gusts. It should have felt cosy inside, but didn't. 'At this moment in time I shall confront him with my knowledge. However, at that earlier stage Spike was not apprised in detail of my suspicions. He knew only that the sketchbook contained work by Jix and that in an unexplained manner his mother had possession of the typescript of his book and had made or at least suggested fundamental changes, some but not all of which appeared in the published version. However, my conclusion arose from textual deconstruction confirmed by my colleague's computer analysis. The childbirth section alone —'

'The what? I told you I haven't read the book.'

'Short, admittedly, and capable of additional interpretations, but after careful and experienced scrutiny we had not the slightest doubt that the words were composed by a woman. Since then both fortuitously and fortunately the conclusion has been ratified by a communication received in a long-delayed response to a query made many moons back. As our journey is interrupted and I have realised that you are to be trusted with the information this is perhaps a convenient moment for you to have sight of it.'

'Dear Professor Rosenwald, thank you for your letter. I am indeed the Jennifer Galloway you have been seeking. I have to say that as a primary school headmistress, retired, the mother of three and grandmother of five, it seems incredible – even to me – that I was ever a hippy called Dawn. Even more unthinkable to remember the life of our commune in Cardiganshire! However your interest is not in me but in the girl who stole my identity. I wish I could tell you and her son more about her, but she never said a word about her background or experience. One of our few rules was that we took people as we found them without asking questions. So I only knew her as Moondust, and had no idea where she came from. I do remember that she was pretty and soft-voiced and scatty. You understand that forbidden substances were in general use, so it seemed quite normal for people to go round in a dream. But Moondust was also a very driven person who was obsessed with her dream life – having, interpreting, understanding, acting on the message of the dreams. I see now that she must have learnt conventional Jungian theory at some stage, and added on a kind of mystic, magic system of interpretation. In the end I suppose it boiled down to a kind of fortune telling. She used to keep a dream notebook and she once said they should be published. I remember she was terribly hurt when one of the boys said nobody was interested in her dreams and told her to shut up about them.

'You asked if she was a painter which reminded me that she did take up art at about the time she started going off to meet her boyfriend. She said very extravagant things about him, he was her soulmate, her heavenly twin, she had seen him in her dreams and she even read aloud from her notebook to prove it. She'd say they met in the parallel universe of her dream life when he was at home with his wife.

'Then one day she came back saying he'd stood her up. And the same thing happened again. And then she had to recognise that she was pregnant, and the father had left her in the lurch. Then one morning she was gone and never came back. Neither did my driving licence and chequebook though I never missed them till weeks later. I assumed she had an abortion as we had discussed. So when I found out what happened it was all a surprise, with my name attached to a suicide. But by then I was at teacher training college in Sheffield and myself as Dawn, or my friend Moondust, already seemed like characters from fiction. I am sorry not to be more helpful but that period of my life is old history, and I remember very little about it. Yours sincerely, Jenny West.'

'So you see,' Elliot said, 'Jon Polhearne was not The Artologist. Whether she was a ghost writer, as you suggested, or whether it was copyright theft, or expropriation of intellectual property, I cannot tell, but nevertheless I shall, so to speak, put my cat among the Polhearne pigeons.'

I felt a sudden wave of frustration, and said, 'I must stretch my legs.' As I pushed my door open against the battering wind, I added, 'You already did that. And Polhearne's long-lost sister died.'

Chapter Twenty-Eight

THE MOMENT THE lid was lifted the wind took all that was left of Stephen Mark, a cloud of dust and ashes which almost instantaneously became an inherent part of the earth on which he had last seen his wife. Delia had decided to scatter her father's remains in the churchyard illicitly. It would be a good place to remember him in, lonely and peaceful, with the sound of rooks in wind-blown trees, and waves breaking on the rocks.

When the two Theobalds turned away, Rosina saw that both daughter and granddaughter looked lighter and brighter. The tiny ceremony had done what folk wisdom promised in its unavoidable clichés, they had 'drawn a line' and 'achieved closure'.

Grace was eye-catching in asymmetrical layers of fabric in many shades of grey, her face and stance girlish rather than, as before, commanding. She must have met someone – and just as Rosina was noticing it, Grace said in a betraying tone, 'Nat's waiting outside.'

So that was it. Very good, Rosina thought. She met Delia's complicitous glance and walked beside her down the gravel path, past the coffin stand and out through the lych gate into the village street where Nat, obviously agitated, was staring at the road beyond the ex-shop and shuttered pub, to a tall, thin figure moving up the hill in a rapid but uncoordinated lurch. For the first of the few times she had seen him in fifty-two years, Rosina recognised her cousin without revulsion.

'I couldn't stop him coming in the car,' Nat said.

'Who is it? Is he all right?' Delia asked.

'That's Jon Polhearne, and there's nothing wrong with him

except egomania, laziness and selfishness,' Nat said crossly. 'My car reeks of unwashed clothes.'

'Actually,' Rosina remarked, 'by rights you should say it's Jonathan Hicks and you've brought him to his ancestral home. The family owned all this before the war.'

'Where's he going?' Grace said and Rosina was caught by an unfamiliar memory, compelled by an impulse that was virtually involuntary to say:

'He's going up to Goonzoyle. It's where he left her.'

~

April 1951

She pedalled out of the stable yard aching all over, bruised and marked by the punishment her father had the right to administer. She needed to believe she deserved it. She had to endure. Nuns offered flagellation up to God. She'd read it in books. In stories of the old days at sea accounts of floggings occurred in every chapter. Even in the antique children's books up in the nursery, good parents beat the wickedness out of their children, or schoolmasters did, and then made them kiss the rod and thank them. Everyone goes through it, she used to tell herself. But she was bigger now, and she had a tummy ache and a headache and her bosoms ached. And there was the horrible feeling of damp padding 'down there' and wet clots oozing out of her and scratchy hooks where the sanitary towel was attached. Mother said young girls couldn't use Tampax. Rosina thought it was possible that she might mean shouldn't, but didn't dare go into a chemist and ask for it aloud. Maybe Aunt Muriel would say it was all right and buy her a box. But Rosina didn't see how she could mention it to Aunt Muriel either. It was another of the subjects one couldn't talk about, only put into written words, anger, misery and pain in code and in tiny handwriting poured on to the page of a five-year diary with a clasp and key.

Otherwise there simply wasn't a way to broach such private subjects, there weren't the words or anyone to say them to. Implicit in being Father's daughter was the impossibility of complaining or of talking about or hinting at what it involved. Rosina didn't even know if Lucia had ever gone through it. But she doubted it: not demure, obedient Lucia.

It's something about me, I've done something that makes him be like that, I bring it on myself even if I'm not sure how. All my own fault. At least school began tomorrow, though the moment she got on the sleeper train tonight she'd be dreading the end of term and coming back home. In her mind the house was mapped by its hidey-holes where he wouldn't look for her because if she was out of sight she might be out of mind. A corner of one of the attics, behind a bin in the wine cellar, huddled inside the nursery window seat. Nanny's voice, inaudible, and then his. 'By God, woman, my father beat the living daylights out of me, his father beat him and his grandfather before him, he that loveth, chastiseth.'

Another murmur and then he shouted, 'That family!'

Oh dear. Nanny had mentioned her first employers again, Mother's cousins, now remembered in a rosy light – but not by Father. 'If someone had given old Edward Hicks enough good hidings he might have learnt some self-control and young Jonathan wouldn't have bastard spitting images getting above their station in every cottage in Trevena.'

Nanny's next remark was just audible. Girls were different, she told him, he should be ashamed.

'You forget yourself, Nurse O'Connor,' he said in a terrifying voice, and the next week Nanny moved into the old people's home and pretended she was quite pleased to be back in Goonzoyle in a bed in the corner of what had once been the Madam's own bedroom. Rosina couldn't imagine the rooms as they must have been before the war, because nowadays the house was just like a hospital with visiting times and lino and the smell of disinfectant. Nanny would be glad to see her and hug her gently, seeming to sense where she was tender and raw; she would say, 'Bear up, that's my good, brave girl.' But riding along the bridle path, her bike bucking like a pony on the unmade surface, Rosina thought she should really be going in the other direction, not towards the barrier of the sea but east along a road out of Cornwall. Why don't I run away from home? Because I don't dare. Anyway, I can bear it just so long as nobody knows. If anyone found out, if anyone actually saw, I'd die. I'd kill myself.

When she reached the back drive to Goonzoyle, Rosina stopped to wipe her eyes and blow her nose. It wasn't quite visiting time yet and Matron was strict about it so Rosina left her bike near the house and walked a little way up the path. It was nice here, quiet and out of sight, with the honeyed smell of gorse and young bracken, and if she got herself up on the overgrown wall, using the gate as a stepping stone, she could look down at the village below, the dunes beyond and then the sea. Below her the field was brilliantly green and soft. She climbed down and sat with her back to the wall, not touching because the contact would hurt. The hedge was full of wild flowers and high in the pale sky a lark was singing. I could make a den and move in, they'd never find me. I could stay here for keeps.

She heard the growl of a car, and Cousin Jon's Oldsmobile edged along the narrow drive. He's come to the rescue, she thought, he'll take me in his arms and kiss me, and this time I won't be surprised and it'll feel nicer, he'll hold me with his arms, all strong and warm, and then we'll get into the car... She had nearly reached the gate to go through and meet him when she heard someone coming along the lane, humming. Rosina knew the tune's words. 'There'll be blue birds over/the white cliffs of Dover.' She peeked cautiously over the wall, her face masked by the grass and brambles, and saw Delia's stepmother, all smart with scarlet lipstick and her hair up in an Edwardian, with a high roll above her forehead and the wind blowing an escaped curl, and wearing a red dress, carrying a little handbag and with a green knitted cardie draped on her shoulders.

Jon had got out of the car. Mrs Mark was smiling brilliantly. 'Here I am,' she called. 'Teddy Johns, alive and safe after all – I'm so happy, you can't imagine!'

Cousin Jon didn't look very happy. Unsmiling, he said, 'They call me Jon these days.'

'I couldn't believe my eyes yesterday, it didn't seem possible, not after your name was in that list, those poor drowned children. I cried about you for weeks. But here you really are!'

'Yes.'

'And this place! But your cottage has disappeared, where was it?'

'Down the lane but nothing's left of it.'

D'you remember the day you showed me your secret den with all your treasures? We had a picnic.'

'It was over there,' he said, jerking his chin.

'Can I look?'

She walked towards the bank of bright yellow gorse, her pleated skirt swinging against her calves. She had nylons on, already laddered, and Cuban-heeled shoes. 'Through here?' she said gaily. 'You see, I haven't forgotten anything.' She went through, taking no notice when her cardigan caught on a thorn, fell from her shoulders and stayed hanging on the bush.

He followed her, bending under the branches of an elder tree. Rosina could still hear Mrs Mark's merry chattering voice. Then a sudden gasp, an exclamation – 'What are you – don't – no —' and after that a scream, a loud, fading shriek, and a crashing of undergrowth and a faint final thud.

Rosina couldn't move. In fact she could hardly breathe. What had happened? She saw Jon emerge alone between the gorse bushes. He picked up the green cardigan, carefully removed a scrap of wool from the bush and wound it round one of the buttons, moved towards his car, opened the boot, put the green cardigan in, shut the lid very quietly, got in, released the handbrake and let the car roll silently down the slope towards the road. Rosina found herself falling and sliding down against the wall. She waited, trembling and gasping, staring after it. Suddenly it seemed to be stopping. Had he seen her in the wing mirror? Rosina rushed at the gate, and ran, urgently, without thought, to her bike, and pedalled desperately, past the front of Goonzoyle, across the gravel, along the smooth front drive, out on to the public road, down the hill, speeding through the village to get away.

'Where he left whom? Rosina, what did you just say?'

Rosina was shaken back into the twenty-first century. That was Delia's voice. Delia, whose stepmother's death Rosina had witnessed but never mentioned, which she had forced or allowed herself to forget during the decades. Whose killer was one of Rosina's closest relations, her sister's husband, her nephew's father. Whom she had allowed to get away with murder.

'She called him Teddy Johns,' she whispered. That distant moment was revived as clear as yesterday, freshly unwrapped, untarnished by use during the intervening years.

'Teddy – that's Edward. She called him Johns?' Nat's voice was sharp.

Grace said, 'All those forwarded letters I found at Polhearne, they were addressed to Edward Johns. I thought it was one of the Fellowship people.'

'Mother? Are you all right?'

Rosina moved back inside the church gate and sat down heavily on the granite coffin stand. 'I knew it all along, why didn't I take it in? I let myself think I'd heard wrong, the man called him Jon, not Johns, the address in Regent's Park was his own. He used that name. He had another life. And I just closed my eyes to it all.'

'Mum, what's wrong? I don't get it.'

'He really was Edward Johns, don't you see?'

'Do you mean he set up a false identity?' Grace asked.

'Oh come on, Mum, you're not suggesting he's a bigamist or something?' Nat was humouring her.

'Not then, it was long before. He took Jonathan's place.'

'Why on earth – honestly, Mum, that's a bit far-fetched, isn't it?'

'Ted Johns was a working-class boy with no prospects. The Hickses were —'

'I get it. Posh and rich.'

Rosina painfully squeezed out the words. 'Two boys adrift at sea. One of them dies. They're taken to a foreign country. When the survivor says the identity papers are his, why should anyone question it?'

'By the time he comes home nobody's left to tell the difference,' Nat said.

Delia said, 'Except for my stepmother.'

'Sheila must have remembered him from that term she spent here as an evacuee,' Grace said.

'If they happened to meet and – oh no – oh my God – Gracie, that's what I heard that day! He was the person she met in St Ives! I told you, Rosina, I heard her, she sounded so happy. He got her to meet him up there, at Goonzoyle. Where they found her.'

Nat sounded embarrassed, as he asked, 'Are you suggesting that he, my uncle, killed her? Just to preserve his secret?'

Rosina spoke steadily. 'It's come back to me, clear as day, clearer. I didn't understand at the time. Was there a missing jersey involved?'

'That was a clue, the police found it in a cave,' Delia said. 'I had to identify it, my father wouldn't have known about her clothes.'

'He put it there to confuse them.'

The old man's shambling figure was nearly at the top of the hill. In the village street below, the four people stared after him and strangers in passing traffic stared at them. Nobody else was on foot. Trevena had become a village of two-car, two-job families and was virtually deserted in the middle of a working day.

Rosina was surprised to find herself feeling happy. Then she realised it wasn't happiness she was feeling so much as a deep sense of personal vindication. At last she knew her loathing for Jon was justified, and always had been.

Delia was simply relieved, though Grace was distressed. She didn't know Nat well enough to be sure how he'd take this.

In fact he didn't give a damn either way. What Nat was worried about was Grace being put off him.

Nobody suggested it or said anything, but they all began to walk, a posse of unlikely vigilantes, following their target back to the scene of the crime.

Chapter Twenty-Nine

~

THE OLD MAN moved remarkably fast. By the time his pursuers reached the junction between Goonzoyle's lane and the public highway, he was out of sight. Rosina had turned round and gone back for the car. Driving up away from the village she saw in the rear-view mirror someone parking in the space she had just left, a female driver and a large square-headed man passenger: myself, and Elliot Rosenwald, who wasn't going to be put off by finding Polhearne deserted when, at very long last, we reached it. I said that there didn't seem to be anyone round to ask so we might as well give up and carry on to Goonzoyle as planned. No, Elliot was set on his predetermined programme, so while I sat taking in the details of the long, low, ancient house, horrified at its state of dereliction and the thought of what it would take to put it right, Elliot went to find the man he had noticed on the way in. He turned out to be a local government officer, who was examining two ancient yew trees which seemed mysteriously to be labelled with girls' names. He said Mr Polhearne had driven off with his landlord who had mentioned a funeral in Trevena.

There was no sign of hearses or mourners when we reached the village church though one car was parked there and another was driving off as we arrived. The wind was coming straight off the sea. I could hardly open the car door. When I did I felt my skin being scoured, as though with sandpaper. Elliot went carefully round the interior of the church and looked at the tombs outside, making a note of every Hicks. By the time had seen enough I had completed a mild and a fiendish Sudoku, and by the time I pulled up on the gravel outside Goonzoyle's front door, parking beside the car that had been moving away from the church just as we got there, nobody else was in sight. I began to describe to Elliot my first visit to Goonzoyle, and Connie's quest for the original furniture and fittings. I had really taken a fancy to the doughty old woman and idiotic tears came to my eyes again, as they had when I first heard of her fate. Elliot took the packet of tissues from his door pocket and handed me one.

Rosina also found her eyes were watering, as she tried to shield her face from the dust coming off the ploughed earth now the windbreaks, in the form of Cornish hedges or dry stone walls, had been removed, leaving one big field instead of the three awkwardly shaped enclosures she remembered.

This was the place. She'd been here when Sheila appeared, and disappeared.

Nat shouted, 'Look out!'

Jon Polhearne came hurtling out of the bushes at the same moment that Rosina heard Grace scream.

Rosina rushed towards the sound. 'Nat, are you all right? Nat!'

She came through the undergrowth and on to an area of flattened bracken and brambles beside the lip of a hole in the ground. A picture flashed into her mind: the bottom of the mineshaft and her son lying still. Then she saw Grace kneeling at the edge, her hand held towards Nat. He pulled himself up on the ground.

'No worries, Mum, all the scaffolding's still there.'

'What happened?'

'He lashed out with that stick of his, that's all, but I'm fine.'

'No thanks to the old man.' Grace sounded as shaky as Rosina suddenly felt.

'He's lost it, completely out of it,' Nat said. 'Why get rid of me when all the rest of you are still around? Mum, are you OK?'

'I'll be fine when that...that...' Rosina could not think of adequate swear words or curses. 'When that man's been stopped. Where's he gone?'

Delia, panting, her hand pressed on her chest, pointed and Rosina turned to go. Grace and Nat spoke in chorus.

'Rosina, wait!'

'Don't, Mum, not till we've called the police. He's dangerous.'

'Yes,' Rosina agreed. 'I think he always was.'

Delia had pointed along the footpath that took walkers across a neck to a headland and, if they could face a steep climb, down to the western end of the beach and the Sheep's Pool where generations of local children had learnt to swim. There was usually a swathe of fine sand, though the winters' tides might sweep it away, leaving shingle and exposed rock platforms. There was a deep cave, where half a century earlier Sheila Mark's knitted cardigan had been found.

Nat pulled Delia back from the cliff. 'Careful.'

'Where can he be?' Rosina fretted.

'He could have cut across the fields.'

'But we'd have seen.'

'He can move at quite a lick.'

'Listen, what's that?' A police helicopter hovered and descended, hovered again, unsteady in the buffeting wind, and then it rose into the sky and flew off southwards, very low over Elliot and me as we approached on a lower path.

Grace had lain down flat to see, but not be blown, over the cliff edge. 'There he is, by that rock pool.'

'Right,' Nat said. 'You stay here.'

'Wait till the police turn up,' Delia said.

'Oh really – one old man —'

'But Nat, he tried to kill you!' Grace said.

'Listen, he got lucky with that stick, but only because I wasn't looking. You lot wait here, OK?'

'As if!' Grace hissed and closely followed Nat and Rosina

while Delia lagged behind to dial 999 again. Rough steps were cut into the cliff and shored up with planks, treacherously slippery. The rope hand-hold had frayed apart. At the bottom they stumbled in procession across the shifting, ankle-turning shingle.

He was hunkered down on a flat rock, head on knees, with his blue-veined, brown-spotted hands dangling and trembling. Rosina came up to him. She stared at her lifelong bogeyman in silence. She thought, If he's dropped all his disguises is anybody left? Then, assuming an ancestral authority and accent, she said:

'You, Edward Johns, Ted. Stand up. Now. At once. Look at me.'

Nat tried to get between his mother and the old man. Rosina watched calmly as he pushed himself upwards. Then he put his hand to his forehead to clasp a wisp of wild white hair, pulled his forelock and replied, 'Yes, ma'am.'

For a moment they all froze, staring at him; and he was momentarily blank, his whole face and body waiting to assume some chosen persona. Then he made an inarticulate sound, a wounded, angry groan, and ran away, his long, uncoordinated legs lurching and stumbling across the rocky platform. Its surface was rough with mussels and limpets, slimy with bladderwrack, wet with salt spray. The gusting forceful wind had to be fought against and the encroaching waves broke menacingly on to the slippery shore.

I had reached the cliff top above and was watching from a vantage point by a red noticeboard, with a lifebelt attached and a local authority notice painted in large white letters: 'DANGER: KEEP WELL BACK FROM ROUGH BREAKERS.' Pinned below was a card inside a see-through plastic envelope, with a handwritten message: 'Number of fatalities in the last 12 months: 2.'

The lanky, bent, awkward figure was going much too near the water's edge. 'Get back,' I shrieked, in a pointless, automatic reaction. Even Elliot, standing close beside and holding my arm, could not make my words out against the roaring wind and water. Like the upper circle audience of a performance by mime artists, we watched the drama's final scene unfold below.

Three dark shapes hovered hesitating behind the old man. More than sixty years before, his feet had trodden firm and sure on this beach. He stumbled, recovered himself, half turned to look over his shoulder and plunged onwards, close to the foaming breakers.

Then a wave like a mini tsunami roared into the shore and poured its white water further in than any had yet reached, and engulfed the fugitive. Instantaneously, from one moment to the next he had disappeared. I saw the younger man shrug off his anorak, the lifesaver's preliminary gesture. The tall woman put her hands on his chest, shaking her head, and one of the others grabbed his arm and pulled him back. He stood hesitating. From the cliffs above, and on the shore, nothing could be seen but a sheet of unstable froth. The old man's body had been swallowed up, his debt paid at last to the patient sea.

Chapter Thirty

ONCE YOU START to wonder whether deaths are natural you realise how many might not be, since the perfect murder is the one that seems like natural death. In the end nobody can be sure how many people were killed by the man who was known as Jon Hicks Polhearne, though the question is endlessly discussed. When my book, *Out of Harm's Way*, is published, the connection with real-life crime attracts attention so I am invited to lunch clubs, book festivals, conferences and broadcasts, ostensibly to talk about the wartime evacuation of children overseas. Audiences show gratifying interest. They also ask a lot of questions about Jon Polhearne, most frequently whether I believe he pushed his stepmother into the mineshaft. I don't actually know any more than you, I say, though I can certainly imagine it.

I see a skinny boy trying to dodge as Nancy bars his way. She won't let him leave. He's got to get away, nothing will stop him. Does she slip as he shoves past, or does he actually lash out? It is as impossible to be sure of that, as to assert as fact that he pushed Jonathan Hicks' face into the water when he caught sight of the trawler and stole his documents and his identity. Yet it is so likely that I can believe it, and even, if only for a moment, sympathise with the loveless child as he wonders why the other boy should have all the luck. It wasn't fair. In that desperate situation, came the desperate thought. Who would know the difference between them? As for Pendry Dilwyn, did he jump to his death in the hotel where Jon was staying or was he pushed? We can all guess, but nobody will ever know.

'It wasn't his fault,' a war artist suggests. We are in a studio at Broadcasting House, recording a radio discussion programme.

She is doing PR for an exhibition about children in Iraq called Images of a Lost Battle. I am talking about overseas evacuees.

'Why was it not his fault?' the presenter asks. The artist speaks directly to me in reply.

'That deprived childhood, the lack of love, the trauma of leaving home —'

'Do you think that's a justification?' I ask. 'Don't forget, he may well have killed his own stepmother even before he left. He was desperate to get away, he didn't want to be working class all his life. In fact,' I add a little flippantly, 'you could just as easily blame his behaviour on the British class system.'

'I think you're wilfully underestimating the effect of overseas evacuation on a child. How could anyone ever feel secure again? Or believe that they are loved?'

I say, 'Childhood experiences shouldn't be excuses, only explanations, though I agree, they do help to understand how Ted Johns became so calculating so young, and desperate too. It was a desperate act to kill another boy, if he did, or even to steal his identity papers. Later I'm sure he became a total fantasist, he had to believe he actually was Jonathan Polhearne, living in that house by right, and that he'd written every word of *Paint, Prophesy, Predict*.'

'A Walter Mitty character,' the presenter inserts.

'Except,' I add, 'he must have known what he was doing when he went back to using Edward Johns's identity, leading a double life.'

The war artist persists. 'You still can't blame him, he was so damaged. I think getting one's kids out of the way like that should count as a war crime. Tell me, how old were you when you were sent away yourself?'

'I was evacuated to Canada when I was two, and came back three years later.' I replied. 'But I don't remember anything about it.'

'Not even your parents' faces?'

'I can see you've read my book,' I reply lightly. But she persists.

'It must have been the most dreadful trauma, quite enough to do terrible, lasting harm. It made Jon Polhearne into a criminal and turned you into —'

'A crime writer,' the presenter interrupts and neatly leads the programme on to the artist's own motives for venturing into war zones.

After the programme I re-read the summing-up section of my own book. Some former evacuees claim the experience made them independent and adventurous, others that its legacy was lifelong insecurity and inability to commit. A few said they had a deep need for one thing: to put down roots. Which is exactly what Jon Polhearne had done. As indeed did I, by marrying an aboriginal Cornishman. Whether I grew deep roots in his home ground or got stuck in its mud is a question whose answer varies along with the weather and my temper, but the need for security is the one thing I admit to having in common with Jon Polhearne. I may have a criminal imagination, but whether there could be a real murderer in me is not a thought to confront head on. All the same, I feel an affinity with my contemporaries who were harmed by the well-meaning decision to send them out of harm's way. There, but for some lucky chance, would I be too: mad, miserable (or perhaps I should say, more mad and permanently miserable) and with criminal impulses that escape the confinement of the printed page. As it is, my image is as misleadingly prim and proper as Rosina Reid's.

Our first meeting was so peculiar and dramatic that I think we would have kept our distance afterwards if it had not been for email. Through that impersonal but intimate medium, Rosina eventually told me how she had scrutinised her own past and gradually began to see it in a new light. She found old evidence. Excavation of the paper archives still surviving from the early days of the National Health Service produced a slim cardboard wallet of notes. Rosina Valentine Polhearne had seen the local doctor very rarely; the record was handwritten, full of abbreviations, in a tiny convoluted scrawl. It listed vaccinations, measles, a polio scare and a broken wrist. Then, in 1951, came a single entry in a different handwriting, regular cursive and obviously feminine. 'Observation: underweight, poor colour and stance, extremely nervous, query paternal abuse? Action: keep eye on patient plus family pro tem. Report suspicions?'

Rosina was baffled by her own secret code invented for the long-forgotten schoolgirl diary, but eventually she sent me a triumphant message, the single word, 'Deciphered'. Set down there was information that memory had edited out: plans to run away, or to appeal for help; arguments with herself about writing – to whom? The King? The Prime Minister? The Bishop? Her headmistress? In the end she wrote to the vicar, dithered but eventually dared to deliver it, and waited. And waited. He never replied or even acknowledged her complaint. Then there were descriptions of Mother's angry scars glimpsed through a crack in the door; the daughter had been horrified but also gleeful. Serves her right. She should look after me better. Another spied-on moment when Mother cowered away, forearm protecting her face, from her husband. Once there was a plan to concoct a poison. Lucia refused to join in having given up the struggle, defeated by their abusive father. But Rosina was a survivor. She defeated him.

And finally: did Jon, alias Ted, ever prophesy or predict? Or did he only, always, pretend? In another kind of book I would invent the missing answers but true stories are stranger than fiction, and their endings are never neat.

LIMERICK
COUNTY LIBRARY